SKIN
Shed My

All my love,

Maddox Masters

ISBN: 9798430557690

Edited by:
Cover Art: Nola Marie, Daria Loshlin
Photographs: Volodymyr, Canva
Library of Congress Control Number:
Printed in the United States

NOTE OF THANKS

Special thanks to Sionna Trenz, who has been my figurative wall since the inception of Maddox Masters. Even if it was just to virtually dry my tears, she has been an indelible component in this process, and I couldn't have done it without her.

Also, special thank you to Daria M. Loshlin for not only writing Hayes Davenport but creating a character that fits perfectly within my fictional universe in a way that few will understand. For now. It was so much fun adding this little snippet, and for anyone that has not grabbed it, *My Soul To Break* is available on Kindle Unlimited.

CONTENTS

DEDICATION

This book is dedicated to Maddox Masters. You started me on a path that I never saw coming. I thought you were a small blip in a story, but this journey was always your story. We've reached the beginning of the end, and I can say it has been a hell of a ride. I hope I did you proud

EPIGRAPH

The fragile cannot endure

The wrecked and the jade

A place so impure

The static of this cruel world

Cause some birds to fly long before they've seen their day

—Alter Bridge (Blackbird)

TERMS

Cher (Sha) — darling, dear, or sweetheart

Bahbin — pouting facial expression

Beb — babe, sweetheart, darling

Coullion (Coo-yon) — dumb, ignorant, or stupid person; asshole

Stronzo — asshole

Fratello — brother

Che cazzo — what the fuck

Laissez les bon temp rouler – let the good times roll

Ça c'est bon — That's good, tasty

Bienvenu — Welcome

INTRO

Let th ewind carry you home

Ronnie Van Zandt once sang, "if I leave here tomorrow, would you still remember me?" It's an ironic song, considering years later it would be memorialized as prophetic. Van Zandt and several other members of Lynyrd Skynyrd died in a plane crash on their way to Louisiana just a few years later. Van Zandt often said he wouldn't live to see thirty, and he was correct. He was just a few months away from that milestone.

I often wonder what he thought about in his final moments. What does anyone really think about as they look death in the eye?

I've heard it said that people see the light at the end of a tunnel, blindingly bright that leads them to wherever.

I've heard others who have lived to tell the tale say that their life flashed before their eyes. Moments that were forever burned into the recesses of their mind played like a movie on the screen. Moments they wished they could change and moments they wanted to return to would fill their vision on repeat. Moments they knew they would never have again.

Different religions have their thoughts as well. Some believe there is an eternal home waiting for us with streets of gold to walk on where we stand before God in thanksgiving. Others think that we are born again to try to reach enlightenment. Then some believe when our consciousness dies, we cease to exist.

In my time of dying, I don't see a blinding light, and my life doesn't play on highspeed repeat. I see each moment clearly, almost in slow motion. The moments that have made me who I am and remind me why I am here. The moments that make me hope we cease to exist because I know I won't make it to any type of paradise, and the thought of repeating this life sounds worse than hell.

I am Maddox Masters.

Welcome to my death.

PROLOGUE

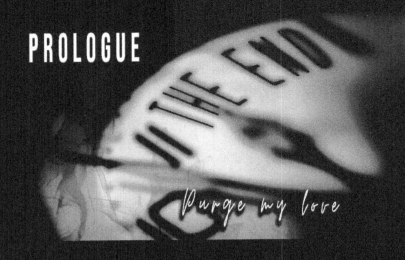

Present day

The wind whips around us as we stand out on the balcony lifting her golden curls like a whirlwind. It's fitting, considering I feel like that's what we've been. Barely knew each other three months, but it only took a second for her to get under my skin. That's been the hardest thing to accept and understand.

I drag a shaking hand down my face. My stomach turns, threatening to spill its contents. My heart races uncontrollably, and sweat begins to coat my body. "You're what?" I ask, hoping against hope that I heard her wrong. Or maybe it's a terrible joke.

"I'm pregnant, Maddox," she tells me nervously, but there's no denying she's happy about the fact.

I shake my head, denial on my tongue. "Not possible," I hiss. "You said it wasn't possible."

"I said it was nearly impossible. There was always a chance."

I shake my head again. Everything around me begins to spin. My knees start to shake.

I can't be a father. How could anyone expect me to be a dad? I'm barely holding it together.

A child shouldn't be dealt this kind of hand. He's doomed to inherit every fucked up thing about me. No one should be subjected to this misery.

And she shouldn't be cursed to watch a child suffer. Tortured, knowing there's nothing she can do to stop it. Nothing she can do to help.

"Maddox, you'll be a great dad," she tells me as she wraps herself around me.

She's happy now. She thinks her dreams are coming true. But what happens when she realizes she's signed up for hell?

She will hate me for this. Hate me for cursing her child with my genes. Hate me for infecting her life.

Absolute terror and rage flow through me. This? This can't happen. I won't allow it. I won't let her go through anymore. Damn sure, not because of me or my evil seed.

"Get rid of it," I growl through clenched teeth.

I feel every muscle in her body go rigid. She begins to shake her head, refusing to accept my words.

I untangle her arms from me, pushing her away. I squat until we're at eye level with my hands cupping her face. "Get. Rid. Of. It."

Her eyes fill with tears. My heart breaks knowing I put them there with my words, but better a little break now than to see her life ruined. "I mean it. Get rid of it. It will be easier than when you lose it. Or worse, when you don't, and you have to raise the spawn I've created." I grab my hair by the roots, tugging. Everything around me starts to spin.

"Maddox, I've never wanted anything more than this. Yes, there is a good chance I'll miscarry, but I want to take that risk." She drops her hands to her flat stomach. "This baby is a piece of you and me. You'll be a wonderful dad. You'll see."

"I won't see. I don't want anything to do with that—that thing."

"You don't mean that," she croaks as the tears spill from her long lashes. "You don't mean it."

9

"I've never meant anything more in my life."

The look in her eyes nearly levels me. And I hate what I know I have to do. Because she's not going to let go otherwise.

"What did you think? You would come out here and tell me this, and we'd ride off into the sunset? That you'd make this huge announcement, and we'd become a happy little family? You've been kidding yourself. I told you that this was not going to last." My heart splinters and shatters with every lie I tell. "Did you think I was only going to fuck you for the rest of my life? I was never going to fuck only you. I've been fucking whoever I want since I started fucking you."

I hate myself. I hate every lie I tell her. I hate the way her shoulders hunch forward, and she wraps her arms around herself like she's holding herself together.

"You're lying," she whispers. "You wouldn't do that to me. Not after everything."

"I'm not. Ask your friends. They can tell you."

"Why are you doing this? I thought you loved me. I don't understand."

I take a deep breath, closing my eyes and digging deep to find my resolve. When I open them, I push down everything but the need to make sure she does what I told her. To make sure she hates me. "I was never going to love you. You were just easy and convenient. I can't love you when I will always love Zoey."

Shock and pain register on her face, but she'll get over it. She'll move on quickly enough. In the end, she'll thank me.

She turns on her heels, running back inside. The moment she's out of sight, I collapse into the chair and let my head fall into my hands, knowing I've broken the most important thing in my life.

CHAPTER ONE

I've lost myself

Present day

I lean back in the chair on the balcony overlooking the river as I exhale, watching the smoke swirl around me. I'm antsy, irritable, and just tired. Everyone inside is enjoying themselves while I sit out here alone. They don't need me and my dark shadows ruining another night for them. And it will be destroyed. I do not doubt that.

My phone rings, distracting me from my dark thoughts. I squeeze my eyes tight at the name that illuminates the screen. The only person in the world I cannot bullshit when I say *I'm fine.*

"Hello," I answer as if it's any other call on any other day. Like I haven't been avoiding for weeks.

"'Bout fuckin' time, asshole," my best friend calls out through the line. "Was wondering when you were going to stop avoiding me, mate."

Precisely as I said, he knows me too well. It's exactly why I've been avoiding most of his calls, but tonight I need to hear his voice. Selfish on my part because I already know this conversation won't end with his mind being

"Is that what you're doing, Madsy? Because I don't think you'd be avoiding me if you were. How are you handling it?"

What a loaded question. If I say I'm okay, he'll know I'm lying. If I admit I'm anything but, he'll worry. Although I suppose he'll do that either way.

Instead, I do what I've always done. I deflect. "How are you, Ry?"

"Not gonna lie, mate. This shit is hard as fuck. Thought it would be easier by now."

"It never gets easier, Ry. You just have to remember why you're doing it."

We've both been through hell the last few weeks. As literal as you can get. Going through detox and withdrawals is a bitch. You'd think it would be enough to stop someone from ever picking up a bottle or looking at a line ever again, but it's seldom the case. I am the prime example of that.

"I'm proud of you, Ry," I tell him honestly with a catch in my voice. "So fucking proud. You've manned up for your girl and your kid. Can't do better than that."

"Mads, you're not doing well, are you?"

My eyes snap shut. I wish he didn't know me so well. As well as anyone can know me considering I've got more secrets than the Pentagon. "I—no, I'm not, Ry. Got a lot of shit on my mind. Too much, too fast, too loud. Don't think this is going to take."

"You've done it before, Maddox. You can do it again."

"I don't think so, Ry. Still not sure I want to. Only reason I've gone along with it this long is that... I just—I need to breathe, Ry. I can't do that when I feel like a boulder is sitting on my chest."

"Maybe you should see a therapist, Mads. I know you don't like them, but—"

"Bastian's had me seeing one for a few weeks now," I tell him through gritted teeth.

"They don't help if you don't talk about it. I get it. You know I get it, but when I finally started talking about it, it finally started feeling like I could deal with it."

"Fuck that," I hiss, getting agitated. "I will never talk to another psychiatrist." If I've learned anything over the years, I know those bastards are the lowest of low.

"They're not all assholes, Mads."

"Yeah, well, this one wants me to write everything down in a journal to help me remember shit I've been trying to forget for years." Like I need help remembering my life. I never forget anything. Not a face, a date, a smell. Everything stays with me just as fresh and vivid as the day it happened. Doesn't matter if it was twenty years ago or—last night.

My eyes betray me, drifting to gaze through the balcony's glass that overlooks the main living area of the loft. Long, blond, curly hair a couple of shades lighter than my sister-in-law's—fuck, that's still weird to think of Verity as my sister-in-law—and the same whiskey-colored eyes meet mine. Red and glassy from crying, making me feel worse than I already do. The disappointment and sadness I see in them feel like a knife to my gut. I wish I could tell her I didn't mean what I said, but I can't.

"Where'd ya go, mate?"

"What?" I ask, realizing he's been talking.

"I was asking about the journal bit, but now I really want to know where your head went."

"I—uh—I did something, Ry. Probably the stupidest thing I've ever done."

"Well, in a long list of stupid things we've done, what could have made it to the top?"

I consider what to tell him. How much to tell him. "I hurt someone I care about."

Silence greets me until he realizes I'm not going to just continue on my own. "That's all you're going to give me? Who'd you hurt? And how? Maddox, you don't go around hurting people. That's my thing."

"I had to, Ry. She doesn't understand."

"Are you talking about Zoey?" he asks, suspicion lining his voice.

"No. Not Zoey. It's—um—you know what? It doesn't matter. I did what I had to do."

"Fuck that, Maddox. You're telling me you've met a girl you care something about, and you've chased her off? Why would you do that? You haven't given two shits about a girl and her feelings in over a decade. Why would you do that?"

"You've asked the same question twice in a single breath," I mock, trying to deflect the tension.

"And I'll ask it again if I need to."

"Just trust me, Ry. It's for the best."

"Maddox, were you falling for this girl? Because you sure as fuck don't sound like you're talking about a random piece of ass."

A low growl slips from me at his comment. He doesn't mean anything by it. It's just his way, but the remark rubs wrong, regardless.

"Holy shit. You *are* falling for her. Maddox, so help me, if you fuck this up, I will personally kick your ass like you've never had done."

"Just drop it, Ry. It doesn't matter now. I did what I needed to."

"Goddammit, Maddox," he grunts, and I can already see him gripping his hair in frustration. "Why—"

"I'm glad you called, Ry," I cut him off because I can't tell him. Not this. He would probably hate me as much as she does right now. So I change the subject. "I need to tell you that I'm not mad at you. For calling Bastian? I was never mad at you. I know why you did it, and I'm sorry for the worry I've caused. I don't want you to worry about me, Ryder."

"I'm always going to worry about you. You're my best friend."

"Promise me, Ry. Promise me that you'll stop. That you'll focus on Heaven and Tyler and music and the guys. I don't want you to worry about me anymore. Or blame yourself. Or make yourself crazy. I need you to promise me."

"I can't do that, Maddox. You know I can't. Why would you even ask that?"

14

"I need you to try, Ryder. I need you to focus on your family and yourself, okay? Always remember that I love you, but it's time you put them first."

"What the fuck? Why does it sound like you're trying to tell me goodbye or something?"

"I've got to go, Ry."

"Maddox, don't hang up on me. Not until you tell me what's going on with you."

"I'm tired, Ryder. That's all. Just tired. I've got to go."

"Maddox, don't you—"

I end the call and turn my phone off. I know he'll be calling back. He's not going to give up that easily. I give him an hour or two before he starts calling Bastian, but I'm not worried.

Like I said, selfishly, I needed to hear his voice. I needed to let him know that I was not angry and loved him.

Because he was right.

It was goodbye.

CHAPTER TWO

Present Day

I quietly open the balcony door, taking care that no one hears me. The less they notice me, the better. It's become a frustrating challenge. There was a time when I could easily slip away, utterly unnoticed by anyone. Now I can't take a fucking piss without everyone knowing. And it has nothing to do with being the front man for Sons of Sin and everything to do with everyone wanting to control my life. Well-intentioned or not, it's been unwanted from the beginning, and I've become more and more irritable with each passing day.

I'm thankful for the layout of Bastian's loft.

Loft? What a joke. The guy turned an old sugarcane warehouse into a twenty-four thousand square foot "loft" with a fucking garage nearly the same size to house one of his addictions. Cars.

But as it happens, the layout works for me right now. There are two doors to the balcony, although "balcony" is a bit of a stretch as well. One leads to his and Verity's bedroom that you couldn't pay me to go into. The other leads to a small conservatory-type room instead of directly into the central part of the house. He has it designed so that you don't have to go through the main living area to get back downstairs.

I hit the bottom stair when voices filter through the space, coming from the very hallway I need to go down. I nearly turn around, prepared to wait them out back on the balcony until I realize who's talking.

"Goddammit, Zoey, I am so fucking tired of this shit," Jax growls. "Maddox is not your fucking problem."

"What do you want me to do, Jay?" she sniffs, and my spine becomes rigid. I fight every instinct to go to her. "I can't shut off how I feel."

"I'm not going to keep watching you do this to yourself. You're not eating or sleeping because you're worried about *him*."

"I'm sorry. I can't help it. He's not okay, and no one will listen to me. Is it wrong of me to care?"

"No, Angel, it's not. I know you love him."

"Not like I love you, Jax. I swear it's not the same."

"You think I don't know that, Zoey? You think I'd still be here if I thought otherwise? It's not about that. I accepted that you have a bond with him a long damn time ago. This is about watching you stress out every fucking day over something you can't control. This is about watching you withdraw because you feel helpless. I almost lost you because of him once before."

"Jax, where are you going?" she calls out, sounding desperate.

"I'm leaving before I put my fist in his face again."

"It's not his fault," she says, sounding like she's moved farther down the hallway.

A loud bang sounds through the space. "Are you fucking kidding me now? It's exactly his fault, Zoey. He doesn't *want* to get better."

I take a chance and peek around the corner when it gets quiet. They're still there. His large, tattooed arms are wrapped around her tiny frame. I pray she doesn't look this way because my resolve for what I need to do will fall to pieces once those icy orbs meet mine.

I need to keep my resolve. I won't keep doing this to her or Ryder. What other choice do I have when they will never let me go on their own? The quicker I remove myself from their orbit, the better they will be. They can place their energy and focus on their families.

17

After another minute, I watch Jax scoop her up as if she were nothing more than a child. Against his six-and-a-half-foot stature, that's exactly how her five-foot frame appears. He carries her into the bathroom without another word.

Soon as the door clicks, I make my way down the hallway, grabbing a set of keys out of a bowl on a table near one of the exits. I open the door that leads to another set of stairs that goes to the garage. I've heard that Bastian once had these stairs sealed off but realized that having the only interior access to his garage wasn't such a great idea when the elevator was out of commission for a few weeks. Turns out, even Sebastian Delrie can't snap his fingers and produce an engineer to fix an elevator out of the forties.

Taking the steps two at a time, I reach the garage quickly. Now I need to figure out which one of the damn vehicles the mystery keys belong to. Knowing Bastian, I will also need to disable the tracking system.

I look at the keys in my hand and find myself grinning. I don't hate Bastian. I never did, and probably never will, but taking his prized fifty-nine BelAir gives me a satisfaction I wasn't expecting to feel.

I walk to the car, dragging a finger over the polished hood with a sad smirk on my face. One more thing, I'll fuck up for someone because, after tonight, Sebastian won't look at his precious cars the same.

"Going somewhere?" a deep, dark voice calls out behind me.

I don't flinch or even turn towards the lurker. "Took you long enough to say something," I mutter. "I thought boogeymen were better at hiding in the shadows."

"You knew I was there," he tells me as I finally turn around to face him. I expected to be met with anger but see only... sadness. Not something I thought he was capable of. "You gonna answer me, *fratello?*"

"What are you going to do if I don't? Kick my ass? I think we've established I'm not the little bitch y'all thought I was. Choosing not to fight back is not the same as not being able to."

"Why are you so damned determined to fight everyone *now*? When all anyone wants to do is help you?"

"Why are you so damned determined to fix me, Bastain? I can't be fixed," I yell, throwing my hands in the air in frustration.

"I know what it is to run, Maddox. To shove down the demons. To feel guilt and blame where there should be none. It doesn't get better until you face them."

"Then you also know that sometimes those demons are too dark. Sometimes you just can't win. Especially when the biggest one is yourself."

His head tilts to the side as his eyes search mine. Brows lower into a deep V, arms cross his broad chest as he contemplates my words. "That what you think? That you're a demon? *Non sei un demone. Sono un demone.* You're just a man, Maddox. A man that's been through more than his fair share of shit, but a man nonetheless."

You're not a demon. I'm a demon. I shake my head. He doesn't understand. He has no idea the things I've done. Moreover, he doesn't have an inkling of the things in my head. The constant noise that never seems to go away. Too much, too often, and unrelenting, my mind is chaos and commotion nearly every waking minute and often in my sleep as well. That is when I sleep at all. Sleep and I haven't been on a first-name basis in over a decade.

"It's what I know, Bastian. You think you know me because you've watched me all these years, but you have no idea who I am. No one does."

"That's because you won't let them know. I get it. I do, Maddox. But you have people who want to be there for you. You have a girl in there that wants to be there for you."

I raise a brow. "That's nothing." I lie.

"I want to know what you did. She has been a mess all day. Is this about Zoey?" My jaw clenches at the remark, but I remain silent. "Is this because you still want her? Or because you're afraid you'll come in second place again? That she'll go back to her husband?"

"Fuck you," I hiss as my fists clench at my side, itching to slam into his face. He has no idea—not the slightest inkling of the disaster I've caused.

"That what you are, Maddox? A coward? Too afraid to face your shit. Too afraid to let people in."

"From what I hear, it's a family trait," I hiss. "You're not exactly open with everyone, Bastian."

19

"No, but I do let the ones close to me in. I share myself with them. You don't even do that. For all your posturing about Zoey and your little fuck buddy—"

"Ryder isn't my *fuck buddy*." I grit my teeth at his minimization of our relationship.

"I don't care what you are to each other. That's not my point. My point is that the two people you are closest to don't get to know you either. Not really. You pick and choose what to show people. What to tell them."

"They know me enough. I'm sorry if I don't sit around the campfire singing *Kumbaya*."

"Do they know you're a fucking asshole? Or a hypocrite?"

"Go to hell, Bastian."

"I don't need to go there, Maddox. Hell is my kingdom. One where you never belonged, and we *all* fought to keep you out."

I let out a mirthless chuckle because that's a lesson in futility I don't think they've learned even to this day. "I'm reasonably certain you all failed." I didn't look for hell, but it found me anyway. Sought me out like prey, tearing me apart until there's nothing left but pieces to feed on. And it keeps feeding on those pieces even now.

"Give me the keys and get inside," he orders with an outstretched hand demanding the keys.

"Or what? We fight again? Our faces still look like shit from the other day."

He gives me a smirk as he rubs the corner of his bruised eye. "I beat your ass. You beat mine. The cycle is vicious. *Corretto?* Thought I'd just bypass the exertion and get to the point where you do what I say."

I watch as he reaches behind him, already knowing what he's doing. He pulls the .45 from behind him, where it was tucked in the waistband of his jeans. He scratches the side of his head as his grin turns cunning, and his eyes show the intensity that intimidates nearly everyone whose path he crosses. "You either hand me the keys and get inside or—"

"Or what?" I cut him off with a challenging smirk of my own. "You'll kill me?"

20

"Nah. You're my brother, and I kind of like you. Besides, I get the impression that's what you want. But I'll shoot your goddamn kneecaps, *fratello*."

I grit my teeth as I slap the keys into his hand. "Fine. You fucking win. But you can't keep me prisoner forever."

"Not forever. Just until I know you're okay."

He turns to the side, gesturing for me to go ahead of him. "Whatever you say," I mutter. I slip my hands into my pockets as I walk back to the stairs that lead into his home, my fingers grazing over the second set of keys I grabbed. The set Bastian knows nothing about and won't until it's too late.

CHAPTER THREE

THE END

There's no going back

Present Day

The wind whips around my face as I make my way down the Bonnet Carré Spillway. Unlike most people, I love these spillways and causeways. Something about knowing there is nothing on both sides but water—no salvation of any sort should the structure collapse—has always been an odd comfort for me. And at these speeds, it feels like I'm being transported to my deliverance.

Bastian's Ducati won't go unmissed for long but slipping away in the dead of night while he "handles business" was easier than I expected it to be. However, I do feel bad for sneaking out on Christian and Drew. At the very least, I have a couple of hours' head start before they set out to find me.

Honestly, I don't know why Bastian continues on this path of—whatever it is he's trying to accomplish. Over the years, he and I have become friends of sorts. It struck me as strange at first, given that I was the big, bad guy that hurt Zoey, and his loyalty was always to Jax and Rory, his cousins, and therefore, also to Zane and Zoey.

One night he just appeared at the club I was at back in New York. I was just out of rehab and struggling desperately not to take that drink. I sat at the bar, drink in hand, staring at it. I'd had a shit day for no other reason hadn't returned from England, and I was alone to deal with the aftermath of my expulsion the year before.

I was forced to apologize to the one person on this earth I knew without a doubt deserved to rot in hell. To the person I would have killed that day had the staff not stopped me—the promise I made to make him pay. I can still see the smugness in his eyes the last time I saw him. Those memories will haunt me until my dying breath.

I was just about to bring the drink to my lips when a hand reached over, grabbing my drink, turning it up to his lips. Then he took me somewhere else. Somewhere that led me into a world of sex kinks and fetishes that allowed me to find release and relief. For a time.

His interest in me perplexed, but over time, I almost welcomed his unexpected appearances in my life. Especially when he helped me return to River City for Zoey's graduation so I could apologize for my sins.

Now that I know we share DNA, it all makes sense, though that revelation has been tough to swallow. Sebastian isn't a caring man. He's a man that revels in doling out his own warped form of justice and only cares about his *la Famiglia*. The family. I suppose it's one more thing that makes us more alike than not.

But his determination to make me "better" has been annoying.

It's that determination that tells me he will look for me, but by the time he realizes I'm gone, finding me will be much easier said than done. He'll have to do it the old-fashioned way. Louisiana may not be huge, but I figure it will take at least a day or two before he finds me. Or finds his bike anyway.

It seems like no time has passed when I find myself on interstate forty-nine heading north. My mind has been rushing as quickly as this bike. It's a constant I have struggled with for a long time, even as a child, but it has become worse in the last several years. I'm intelligent enough to realize the drugs don't help. They only exacerbate the issues I have in the long run, but the temporary relief they provide is the only time the world doesn't feel so loud, and everything slows down. The only time I don't feel like I'm drowning in regret and guilt and anger and turmoil. That's why I'm dumb enough to continue down the path I'm on.

The long stretch of road before me is dark and endless. It's an ironic state of events considering that's the way I've felt for so long.

I find myself thinking about what brought me here to this moment. Literally, it was the day I overdosed back in Craryville. I knew when I looked in Ryder's eyes that he would do *anything* to save me, even if that meant calling the one person I hated most at that moment in my life. The one person I thought had betrayed me the worst. He called Sebastian, knowing there was a chance, at least in his mind, that I would never forgive him. The fuckin idiot doesn't seem to understand that I couldn't hate him if I wanted to. He's been my saving grace for a long damn time. No matter how pissed I may be, I will never turn my back on him. Not in this life. Not in the next life either. Although, I hope there's not a next one.

Bastian didn't play fair either. He had no intention of it, laying me out cold with one hit. I can still feel the sting of those brass knuckles connecting with my jaw even now. Son of a bitch is lucky he didn't break my damn jaw, although I doubt he would've cared.

And when I woke up on the plane a little while later, I was the epitome of an ass.

Three months ago

I look around groggily, trying to figure out where the hell I'm at. It doesn't take long to realize I'm on a plane. Not just any plane. A private one. My jaw tightens as I recall the events earlier in the day.

When my best fucking friend stabbed me right in the back. I still can't believe he called Sebastian. I am so pissed with him I can't see straight, but I understand why he did it. Desperation is a funny thing, and Ryder was desperate.

I turn to look across the aisle to see Bastian sitting, legs stretched out long and relaxed with his hands behind his head, wearing sunglasses. I don't need to see his eyes to know he's watching me. It's just another day for him. Just another hit.

I look down to see I'm handcuffed to the seat. I roll my eyes, wondering what it is he thinks I can do at twenty thousand feet.

Actually, the handcuffs are probably a good idea because I want to beat Bastian's ass.

"Where the fuck are you taking me?" I bark out loudly.

"Already told you, *fratello*, I'm taking you home."

"I told you, I'm not your fucking brother. You think because I know now that suddenly means something to me? Twenty-nine years you've been nothing to me. You're going to stay that way."

"I'm taking you back to River City to dry out. End of story."

I laugh at that. At the sheer lunacy that he thinks he can force me to do anything. Like I'm one of his little minions. "What makes you think it will stick? What makes anyone think I want to dry out?"

"Doesn't matter what you want. It's happening."

"Don't you know a person has to want it for it to work? You get me clean, and the minute I leave, I go get a fix. Plain and simple."

"What the hell is wrong with you? Don't you know you almost died?"

I did almost die. The moment my veins filled, warming my body, I knew I would be taking my last breath.

I welcomed the freedom.

When I awoke in the hospital, I was instantly filled with sorrow. Sorrow that I had to wade through the muck and mire of my head. Through pain and guilt and remorse that I felt every day.

When Ryder walked into that room, the guilt compounded. He was wrecked. He tried to hide it, but I knew. I know him better than anyone ever could.

Regret filled every cell of my body. I wanted to take back those moments before I stuck the needle in my arm. Maybe I would've adjusted the amount.

The problem is, even now, I'm not sure what I would do, given a chance to go back. Use a little less to ensure that near-death experience never happened. Or a little more to make sure the job was done right.

"Maddox, I've tried to be there as much as I can for you. You know that."

"Don't make me laugh, Bastian. Sending your spies to keep tabs on me isn't being there for me. I don't want you there anyway. You know, I thought over the last few years we were at least friends. What a joke, right? You've been there for me. How long exactly have you known we were brothers again?"

He leans back with a loud huff. "A while."

"Say it, Bastian. Tell me again, exactly. You've watched out for me all these years because of some bond of blood. Tell me when you knew." I'm yelling. My jaw is clenched, and my fists are gripping the armrests of the seat.

"Since you were seventeen," he growls. "I've known since you were seventeen. We've been through this."

"So, when Jax and Zane were running me out of town—when you were standing there watching them do it, you knew." It's not a question. It's a statement of fact.

At the time, I thought it was what I deserved. I still do. I just want to hurt him. "You claim to have watched out for me all these years. You're dragging me back somewhere I don't want to be in the name of brotherhood, but you stood there and watched them send me out of town with threats not to return."

"If I hadn't done that, Jax would have killed you."

"You ever think maybe that's what I wanted?" I sneered. "I'm not afraid of Jax, Bastian. Never have been. Ever wonder why I didn't fight back every time he sucker-punched me? I promise you it wasn't because I was afraid of him."

"*Fottuto idiota*." Fucking idiot, he mutters. "If you weren't so strung out all the time, maybe you'd stop feeling sorry for yourself once in a while."

"Don't pretend to know me," I scoff.

He has no idea what I feel. What I've been through. He doesn't know how the weight of guilt and pain and sorrow and horror floods me every fucking second of the day. He doesn't understand what it's like to feel this heavy, heavy burden of grief and agony. Of knowing how many people you've let down and how many people you will continue to let down. Because fighting the voices and the addiction and the feelings I can't control have made it too hard to hold on anymore. I'm exhausted trying to keep it all together, so no one sees that I am anything but perfect.

The drugs? The drugs quiet the thoughts and the noise, even if only for a minute. They are the only time I'm not overwhelmed by these emotions. They help me forget the memories that terrorize every second of my life—cripple me—double me over in agony until I'm gasping for air and praying for death—praying for it all to just stop.

The only time I can think straight is when I'm high. It's the only time that my thoughts and feelings are bearable. The only time the nightmares aren't part of my waking state.

But drugs, alcohol, and sex are no longer working as they once did. The demons that have chased me for most of my life no longer hide in the shadows when foreign substances or endorphins are altering my brain chemistry.

I'm tired.

"It's all I could do, Maddox. Pops and your dad said I couldn't tell you or anyone else. They're the ones that worked out that deal, so Jax didn't kill you. All I could do was make sure you got out in one piece."

I release a low, dark chuckle. "I was never afraid of them. I was worried about Zoey. I was doing what my dad told me I didn't have a choice but to do, but I needed to see her."

"And do what, Maddox? What would you have done?"

The truth is, I've never been angry about being run out of town. I was broken, even back then. So utterly damaged by the choices I made. Choices I kept making, including one that made me hurt the most important person in my life. I didn't deserve to stay, or receive her forgiveness. Knowing all these years later that she gave it anyway has been a lot to handle.

But I want Bastian to feel a fraction of the guilt I do. If he's able to feel at all. I'm not always convinced he has actual emotions or feelings for anyone outside of his wife.

"I would've gone to her," I tell him, projecting as much anger into my voice as I can. It isn't that hard given the circumstances. I have been pissed off at him for days. This entire charade is the icing on the cake. "I would've told her I was sorry. I would have told her I shouldn't have done any of it. That I shouldn't have panicked after I did. We could've tried—

"Tried what, Maddox? Zoey was always Jax's. They were always going to end up together. They were written in the stars and all that lovey, dovey bullshit. She loves Jax."

Zoey does love Jax. That's something I've known from the very beginning. Even when we were dumb kids, I knew she loved him all those years ago. Her connection to him was unshakable.

But I also know how she felt about me. How she still feels about me. And that's the most brutal blow of them all. Knowing your soulmate's bond with someone else is even stronger.

"You were never going to win that fight, Maddox. Why don't you let it go? Move the fuck on."

"Why don't you?" I mutter. "Just forget I exist. You're under no obligation to me. You have never been. Let me live—and die—on my fucking terms. We both know you don't give a shit about me."

"Not happening. No matter what you may believe, I do care. I am not going to watch you kill yourself."

"Then. Don't. Fucking. Watch."

"You act as if you care about everyone, but you just really don't give a shit, do you? The only person you think about is yourself. You don't care what it would do to Zoey if anything ever happened to you."

"According to you, I don't matter to her anyway." I grit out, the lie tasting bitter on my tongue, but the need to push his buttons is strong. I'm not going to roll over and play nice. Not with him.

Bastian's betrayal has been the final blow for me. I can't take any more.

"Whatever, Maddox." He shakes his head with a chuckle. "That's not what I said, but for argument's sake, we'll say you're right. But what about your friends? What about Ryder? He doesn't seem like he'd handle it very well."

"Great friend, he is, huh? I know he's the one that called you, isn't he?"

"He's scared of losing you, Maddox."

"Right. So, he calls the one person he knew would piss me off the most. Great job he did." The sarcasm in my tone oozes like an infection. I don't even mean the shit that's coming out of my mouth, but I can't seem to make it stop. Anger and frustration pour out of me like a petulant child throwing a tantrum. I want to push Bastian's buttons, but even I know I sound like a bratty little shit. It's like I'm possessed by something.

"Stop acting like a little bitch. Stop feeling sorry for yourself. Bottom line is you're going home. You're going to get clean. You're going to get your shit together once and for all, or so help me God, I will make your life hell."

Apparently, he missed the memo.

My life is already hell.

CHAPTER FOUR

Unfurl your black wings

Present Day

I want to hate Bastian for dragging me here. It should be easy. Especially considering the physical hell of withdrawals I've gone through. I told him it wouldn't stick. I promised him I would go back the first chance I got.

It wasn't a threat. I wasn't being petulant. Okay, maybe a little, but I need it. But they don't understand. Even after all these weeks, I still feel it. The headaches and the nausea are constant. The dizziness never really goes away.

Not to mention they quiet the turmoil in my head. I can never explain it, not in any way that makes sense to anyone. Although, I suppose what they see and what I try to explain are often a contradiction.

On the outside, it probably seems I am comfortable around people. I can carry on conversation and smile in any room. I've worked off and on at Lucky's, a bar back in Brooklyn, since I was eighteen. I've played the role of playboy heir to the Masters' fortune, with the media hounding my every step. I've mixed and mingled among society's elite. Since I was seven, I've been in front of crowds performing my music.

Because on the inside, I'm a mess. The smile is so fake, it may as well be plastic. My ease and relaxed appearance is nothing more than years of perfecting my art—to never let anyone see just how fragile I am. After fifteen minutes in a crowded room, my heart begins to beat an erratic rhythm. Twenty minutes, I begin to sweat. Half an hour, my head starts to spin and pound, rendering me unable to concentrate on anything but the noise around me because by then, the voices become garbled, and I can't understand what anyone is trying to say. I come off as rude and uncaring when I'm actually struggling just to breathe.

On the inside, my thoughts and feelings are precipitously changing. Rarely do I have a complete thought. An idea comes, only to abruptly shift into another before the last comes to full fruition. Along with the changing thoughts come the changing moods.

God, I don't know how the hell I have fooled people for so long.

But these weeks without *any* relief from the madness has made the insanity worse. And yes, I acknowledge I must be insane. Kind of crazy in itself, considering they say the insane don't know that they are. It's probably an issue of my own making. Of refusing to deal with my shit. Of self-medicating to ease the crazy. But it's how things are now. Maybe how they've always been.

After driving an hour on the interstate, I decide to exit for a minute. The need to stretch my legs is fierce. The need to take a fucking piss, fiercer.

I walk into the truck stop with my hoodie pulled up over my head and my sunglasses on. I try to conceal my identity as much as possible. Not so much from fans, because it's unlikely I run into more than one or two here, if any at all. But I don't want the surveillance cameras to catch me. Maybe it's just paranoia, but I'm positive Christian could pull footage to identify me. It's also why I stayed out of the main parking lot with the bike.

After I finish in the bathroom, I walk to the counter, keeping my head low. I know I'm probably making the cashier nervous as fuck, but it can't be helped. I buy a pack of smokes and another lighter, paying in cash because it can't be traced by the psychopath I've somehow inherited.

"Your change," the guy behind the counter calls as I turn for the door.

31

"You keep it." I wave him off, not worried about whatever leftover money he's trying to hand me.

"Dude, this is like eighty bucks."

I look over my shoulder to see the kid, probably twenty if not younger, standing there with his hand still outstretched and a gaping mouth. I look him over curiously, then decide to take my chances. "Know where I can find smack or blow?"

He looks at me like I've lost my mind. Not unusual when you toss out words like that to someone who doesn't know. But something still tells me he can help me out, so I break it down a little more. "Look, kid, I'm looking for speedball. Coke? Heroin? Know who could get me some of that?"

His eyes grow wide, full of suspicion. "You a cop?"

I can't stop the laugh that burst from my chest. "Of all the cliché shit to say," I shake my head, dumbfounded that people are that stupid. "Kid, if I were a cop, I'd lie and say I wasn't. I'm in a hurry. Either you know someone, or you don't. It's obvious you don't have any."

He gnaws the lip ring sitting in the corner of his mouth, still looking suspicious, but finally nods. "I might know someone who can hook you up. If you have the cash."

"Let me worry about the money, kid. If they want to make some money, tell them to meet me out back in fifteen minutes."

"I don't know if they can get here that fast."

"I'll make it worth their while."

"You—man, you look like the singer from Sons of Sin," the kid chokes out in disbelief.

"Yeah, I get that a lot." I nod to the phone in his shaking hand. "Make the call, so I know if I'm waiting or not."

Ten minutes later, I'm leaning against Bastian's bike, puffing on a cigarette, when a blue truck pulls up beside me. A guy closer to my age steps out. He takes in the Ducati with a low whistle. "You the one looking to buy?" I nod without moving from my position. "You a cop? Nobody around here could afford a bike like that."

I laugh for the second time at the pure idiocy. "You think a cop could? They work for nothing. I'm sure there are plenty of people who *could* afford the bike. They just choose not to. Do you want to make some money or continue saying stupid shit?"

His cocky smirk falls into a scowl. He moves to stand directly in my face in some pathetic attempt to intimidate me. I lost the ability to be intimidated a long fucking time ago. "How about I just kick your ass and take your money, pretty boy?"

He seems to get more frustrated when I don't flinch or acknowledge he even spoke but instead expel the smoke from my lungs into his face with a smirk. "You can try, but I wouldn't advise it."

He does one of those douchebag moves, trying once more to get me to flinch. When he fails, he steps back, rubbing his hand over his face.

With my smirk growing, I toss the cigarette to the ground. Gripping him by his shirt, I force him back until he hits the side of his truck. "This is what you're going to do," I hiss through my teeth. "You're going to show me what you have. If it's what I'm looking for, you're going to give it to me. I will pay you with this watch on my wrist that's worth five grand. More than enough to cover. Then you will forget that bike and forget me." When he doesn't acknowledge what I've said, I pull my fist back, planting it into his gut. "Are we clear?" I ask as he hisses and wheezes.

He nods jerkily. Still scowling as I let him go, he turns to his truck, reaching in for something. I suppose it would've been smarter for me to reach myself. For all I know, he's not getting me what I want, but a weapon instead.

He turns around with the drugs in his hand, and I nearly salivate at the sight. The itch, the desire to get my hands on the object of my affection, strong and powerful, but I withhold from reaching. "I need to make sure it's good," I demand.

"It's good, man." His insistence doesn't reassure me.

"Yeah. I'm not taking the word of some dealer I don't know. Don't mistake me for a fool. Now, if you want to make the deal, show me it's good."

A little while later, I'm back on the road with my stash calling me from the bag at my side. But I still need more distance between River City and me. I can hold out for a few more hours. I can handle the noise for a little longer. I can hold the memories at bay for a while longer.

Who the fuck am I kidding? My memory is what gives me the most grief. My inability to forget is what causes the most torment. I remember everything. Every sin and every crime, the details are always vivid and bold.

I find myself pulling over. My breath quickens, and my heart races. Panic grips me just as it did the very day it happened. My greatest offense, my darkest transgression—the one thing I've tried so hard to run from has the bile and acid of my stomach on the ground by my feet.

I climb back on the bike, leaning forward to rest my arms and head on the handles. Trying desperately to push the memories aside, I reach for something happier. I grasp for the bit of goodness. There hasn't been much, but I have a few moments I can hold on to for a bit.

Searching, searching for something to push away the darkness. Ryder. Zoey. I think of them as I close my eyes, knowing full well how completely insane I probably seem to the passers-by. That air I've worked so hard the last several agonizing seconds to grasp leaves me when the vision behind my eyes isn't any of my friends. I don't see moments with Ryder or Zoey. My mother's face doesn't dance before me.

Instead, it's honey-blond hair and whiskey eyes that chase the shadows away.

Three months ago

"You're staying here tonight," Bastian tells me as he drags me out of the car, shoving a duffel bag into my chest. "Tomorrow, I'm taking you to the basement. I already know how the first few days of cold turkey looks. I don't want that around Verity."

"Do you know what the next few months of cold turkey looks like?" I snap.

"You're an addict, Maddox. It won't ever be easy." He tells me as he walks to the elevators of his warehouse home.

He doesn't have a clue, but I do. I've done this before. Last time I'd been using off and on for two or three years, the headaches and nausea lasted weeks. This time, it's been all day, every day for the last five years. I didn't ease into it. It wasn't a weekend party thing. I just needed everything to be quiet for a minute. I needed not to feel.

"When we get in there, you put on that act you're so good at performing. *Capisce*? Do not upset my wife or our guest."

Ordinarily, I would never think of upsetting Verity. She's a sweet girl that's been doled out far too much shit. She was trapped in a gilded cage, only let out and placed in a cell far worse. One where she was abused for many years. But if I upset her, maybe it will get Bastian to leave me alone.

Or he might shoot me.

Then I finally realize the second part of what he said. "What guest? I don't want to see anyone. I don't even want to see you."

"It's Verity's cousin. She's been staying with us for a couple of months. Since she left her bastard husband."

"What is it with you and the damsels in distress?" I grunt as I follow him into the antique elevator. "And I thought Verity's family cut her off."

"I cut them off. But she did have an aunt and a cousin she was close to. Verity contacted them once she was no longer afraid of someone finding her. She's stayed in touch, so when her cousin showed up a few weeks ago in tears, Verity offered her to stay with us."

"Bet you loved that," I chuckle, knowing Bastian does not like strangers in his city, much less his house.

"Yep. Been a blast." His jaws clenches as he speaks. "The girl—well, she's had a rough few months. Don't make it worse on her by acting like an asshole."

"Or what?" I taunt just to get under his skin.

He rolls his neck a few times, and I swear I see him counting. "You're not an asshole, Maddox. Stop trying to be."

"You have no idea how much of an asshole I can be," I warn.

"If you make either one of them upset, I swear I will break both of your hands. Can't play music without those."

"Fine," I relent because if he's not going to kill me, I don't want him taking one of the few things that helps me escape from my mental hell.

Before the gate slides open on the elevators, he shoves something in my hand. My brows furrow as I stare at the baggy of white power. "What's this?"

"It's been less than six hours, and you're already fidgeting and edgy. Told you, I'm not having you lose your shit around Verity."

"Dude, this won't even take the edge off," I scoff. I don't even know how many of these I do in a day, I realize. It's constant, though. As soon as I start coming down, I'm chasing the next high.

"I'll take care of it if I think you need it. You've been this long, though. I think you can make it through the night."

"If I didn't already hate you, I would now," I growl. "What I do isn't your fucking business."

"Good thing I don't care if you hate me, *stronzo*. I only care if you're breathing. You don't need to like me to do that."

"*Vaffanculo, bastardo*," I grit between my tightly clenched teeth.

And he is an asshole because he just grins. "*Bravo, bambino*." If he were more condescending, he could be president.

He raises the gate, and we step inside his home. In all the years I've known him, I've never once set foot in this place. I can't say I'm surprised by what I see, though. It's very Bastian with its concrete walls and steel beams. It's wide, open, and spacious, with ductwork and plumbing showing from the ceiling. A very recycle, reuse feeling to it.

Before we make it more than a few feet into the expansive place, Verity appears in front of us, and she looks a lot different than she did last time I saw her, which was—well, now that I think about it, it's been since before we went to Europe. I'm wracking my brain trying to remember how long ago that was. Six months? Two years? I can't even remember what today is. I don't forget anything ever. Except time.

It has definitely been a few months, though, because she wasn't pregnant when I saw her last.

"*Principessa*," Bastain says, pulling her into his arms.

"I missed you," she tells him softly with a kiss on his cheek.

When they release each other, she turns to me with a soft, shy smile. Verity is such a quiet, reserved girl, but she is all warmth and brightness despite everything she endured growing up. She's a fucking warrior as far as I'm concerned. "Maddox, I'm so glad you're here."

"I wish I could say the same, Verity," I whisper into her hair. "But I'm glad to see you under any circumstances. You get sexier every time I see you." I say that last part for Bastian's benefit. I get my desired result when he growls low, glaring daggers at me.

Verity shakes her head, her cheeks splotching red. She still can't take a compliment.

She grabs my hand, earning another growl from Bastian, and pulls me toward the kitchen. "I want you to meet my cousin. Quinn, this is our fr—I mean Bastian's brother, Maddox."

"You had it right the first time, Goldilocks," I tell her a little more sharply than I intend, but I'm antsy and irritated. Another blush rises, this time from embarrassment. I wrap my arm around her. "I'm sorry. I didn't mean that to be so harsh." I kiss the side of her head as she bobs her head in acceptance.

The girl turns around to face us, and I'm stunned by how much she looks like Verity. There are differences too, but they're subtle. Like her hair is a shade or so lighter, her nose a little less upturned, her cheekbones a smidge higher. The most significant difference is that Verity has always made me think of Goldilocks and Shirley Temple, and this girl makes me think of Hannah van der Westhuysen, who I've secretly had a thing for since Dane and I accidentally watched a show we thought was for Lyra. Turns out it wasn't Lyra appropriate, but he and I binged the entire show then vowed never to tell a soul.

My eyes trace every bit of her, from those loose curls falling to her waist down to sexy legs covered by tight leggings. Her petite frame makes her look childlike and innocent, though I know she has to be over eighteen. Bastian did say something about a husband, after all.

37

It's been a long time since I felt an instant attraction to anyone. But what I feel when I see her slams me like hurricane-force winds.

Good thing she's Verity's cousin. And apparently married as well. It will save us both in the end.

"Maddox, this is my cousin, Quinn Toussaint."

She looks at me with surprised, wide eyes the color of whiskey. Her cheeks turn an adorable shade of red as she bites the inside of her cheek. "Nice to meet you."

If my jeans weren't getting tight just at the sight of her tight body and the face of an angel before, they damn sure are now. Her voice is low, sultry, with a slight rasp. It sounds like pure, unadulterated sex, and my dick is pressing my zipper, praising the heavens.

"Very nice to meet you, Quinn," I tell her with a wink.

Her flushed cheeks spread to her hairline, and her eyes drop to the floor. Her discomfort slides over me, digging deep into my spirit. Her sadness is a palpable thing, and I wonder how similar hers and Verity's situation may have been.

Her eyes depict a defeated sadness that speaks to me. I understand that look, and I want to take it away. No one should have that look.

"I'm going to wash up," she tells Verity without looking up. Then, without another word, she rushes down one of the house's hallways.

"She okay?" I ask, watching as she disappears from sight.

"She will be," Verity says softly. "It's hard getting over a broken heart."

I nod with understanding, but more than that, I want to heal her broken heart. The question is, how do you heal someone else's broken heart when yours has never recovered.

CHAPTER FIVE

Present Day

My head, still leaning on the bike's handlebars, begins to pound as more memories pour in. It was never supposed to be like that. I wanted to help her, not cause her more pain. But it's my MO. I break and destroy all the good around me. I'm a wrecking ball, shattering everything I touch.

Even though she's the last person I wanted to hurt.

Finally, I can't take another second of the noise in my head. I can't stop the spinning of my mind. I can't handle the taunting coming from my backpack. It's not my method of choice, but out in the open for the world to see, I sort lines of the smack and blow on the seat of the bike then inhale each of them. Finally, clarity comes. Or my version of it.

Another hour passes in a blink. I'm pushing the bike and my luck beyond what's advisable, but the sun will be coming up soon. Once it's up, the bike will be too conspicuous to drive with the plates more than visible for tracking. I wouldn't be surprised if Bastian and Rory didn't have satellites in the sky tracking everything, but I have no doubt they have law enforcement in their back pockets. Knowing them, they have their own version of an APB

I lost time at that gas station. Then even more while I was parked on the side of the highway having a panic attack. Listening to the damn noise that screeches in my head with its nonsensical ramblings.

I spot a rundown hotel as I exit another small town. Realizing that I might not see another for a while, I decide to stop. It's a single-level building with a few rooms in front and back. The white paint is faded and peeling. The canopy over the entrance looks like it could collapse at any second. Potholes riddle practically every inch of the nearly vacant parking lot.

I walk into the dingy lobby, hood pulled up, glasses on, and ring the bell. A stringy-haired, pudgy man comes to the desk looking three sheets to the wind. I can sympathize.

"I need a room," I tell him, not bothering with pleasantries.

He scratches the scruff on his face while he looks me over. "Need a credit card and ID."

"Nah. None of that. I got cash."

He spits to the floor with a scowl. "Look, kid, I got rules to follow. No ID, no room."

I grab my wallet out of my pocket, removing a few hundred. "I need a room for a few days. I know this place can't cost that much. You take whatever the cost is out of that and keep the rest."

He eyes the money suspiciously. "You in trouble or something?" he asks as he picks up the money and starts counting.

"Or something."

He looks at me again after he finishes counting. The suspicion has been replaced with surprise and greed. "All right, kid," he agrees. "I gotta have a name, though."

"Bryan. Bryan Michaels," I tell him, knowing my old friend won't mind.

"Room in the back."

"Yeah. I can do that." He spends a couple of minutes gathering a key and towels. "I'm assumin' you don't want housekeepin' comin' around."

"You assume correct," I nod, taking the items from him.

"This should hold ya for a few days then."

I give a short nod then head to the bike. I feel pretty stupid with a pile of towels in my lap, but it's not like I have an audience. It's not like I should care.

I park in front of the room, carrying in the towels and my bag, then walk the bike inside. The room is shit. Dingy wallpaper that has to be from before I was born peels on the walls. The ugly carpet might have been red or something at some point, but now it's matted and brown. A table sits off in the corner with avocado green vinyl chairs around it and an ashtray on top. At best, the room is unremarkable, but I didn't come here for comfort. I came here because no one would suspect Maddox Masters of being in a shit hole like this.

Now that I'm here, I don't know what to do. The noise in my head is starting to buzz again. The swirling in my gut and pounding in my chest begins to resurface as it always does. There's a war in my head between memories I want to forget, music that demands to be heard, and words I can't get out.

The words. I have to find the words. That's why I'm really here. The psychiatrist told me to write down my memories. I think she thought it would help me purge my soul. But you can't purge evil, and that is what I truly am. I am the putrid, vile thing that slithers on the ground seeking to destroy. It's the way it has always been.

I have a plan. It's been coming to me in bits and pieces a little more every day. I've fought against it for years, but the battle is over. The war is lost. There was never any chance of winning anyway.

But how do I put to words what I feel when I don't know? How do I explain the shit in my head when I've never understood it. Do I tell them about the buzzing? Do I explain that I hear things that aren't there? Do I tell them I see things that aren't real? I suppose the only reason I've lasted this long is that I'm aware that it's in my head.

It's always been there. When I was a kid, people thought I had imaginary friends. An overactive imagination is what my mom once called it. She just didn't understand that, to me, they were as real as she was. And they told me to do things—things I knew I shouldn't but did it anyway. Like the time I broke my arm jumping from the treehouse because I thought I could fly. According to the doctors, it was a normal thing for a four-year-old to believe.

41

Then there was the time I was convinced I could breathe underwater. I tied bricks to my feet and jumped into the twelve-foot-deep pool. No one knows how long I was under, but it was long enough to lose consciousness. Long enough that my stunt resulted in a two-week stay in the hospital with damage to my pre-frontal cortex and aspirated pneumonia, along with no recollection of what happened.

I clench my fists and walk to the phone sitting on the nightstand. Picking it up, I dial the number of the only person I know that will help me without telling anyone about it. It rings and rings with no answer. I slam the receiver back onto its base with a frustrated growl.

My head drops into my hand, gripping my hair by the roots. I can't think without the drugs. I need to write, but the words are all mixed up.

The ringing phone has me jerking up. I look at the object with wariness. Paranoia runs thick in my veins as I wonder if this is a trap. When it stops ringing, my heart begins to race at a quicker speed. Sweat beads on my neck, and my hands start to shake.

Then the phone rings again. My vision begins to blur as I reach for the object. I pick up the receiver, my hand shaking so badly I nearly drop it. "H-hello." My voice cracks with fear, although I'm not sure what I'm afraid of.

"Mads." I breathe out a sigh of relief, my eyes closing shut at the sound of Bryan's voice on the other end of the lie. "That you?"

"Yeah, it's me. Why didn't you answer when I called?"

I lean back on the uncomfortable bed, rubbing at my temples. The pounding is relentless and getting worse. I hope he can get here fast.

"I was in the bathroom," he tells me.

I hear the sound of keys jangling in the background. "You on your way?" I ask anxiously. "I need it bad, Bry."

"I got you, Mads. I don't know why the assholes want to do this to you."

"They're not assholes," I growl. "They're worried about me."

"Not that damn worried. Not if they can watch you suffer."

Irritation fills me. Bryan is my oldest friend. We've known each other since we were small children. He knows all my secrets. Not because I trust him more than Ryder or anyone else. That could never be it.

I never wanted Ryder or anyone else to know the things I've done. I don't know if they'd be able to look at me the same if they knew. I couldn't take a chance that they would hate me. I definitely couldn't handle the inevitable looks of disappointment.

Bryan doesn't care about any of that. And he's been my accomplice for quite a few of my crimes. Hell, a couple had been his idea. So I don't worry that I'll let him down.

But he doesn't understand my relationship with my friends—my brothers. He's never understood my relationship with Ryder, trying to get me to cut ties with him on many occasions. I couldn't do it. Ryder needed me, and I needed him.

Sometimes I think that Bryan may be jealous of my friends. That I have people in my life that care about me. That I care about. Not saying I don't care about Bryan. I do. But our relationship is different. He's not a fair-weather friend. He's the devil on my shoulder. He instigates and encourages bad decisions. Probably a sign I should have cut ties with *him* long ago. It's not that easy to say goodbye to someone you've known most of your life. Besides, until recently, he would vanish for months at a time without a word.

"They're willing to watch me suffer a little now to save my life. That's how they see it anyway."

"They're killing you. They just want you out of their hair. You know that."

"Shut up!" I hate when he does this—always trying to convince me that my friends don't care. It's his jealousy. I know this, and it's why I put up with his crap. "Just get here."

"I'll be there in five minutes."

I hear a car start in the background. "You're that close?"

"I've been following you since you left Sebastian Delrie's house."

I sit up quickly, trying to remember anyone following me. There couldn't have been. No one would've been able to keep up at those speeds.

I suppose he had to have been there, but what does that say about me? That I've been so lost in the noise that I didn't notice. Does that mean that Bastian could be close behind?

He could be here any minute. Then he'll drag me back to River City where I'll continue to disappoint them all. Where I'll have to see *her*. I can't handle the pain I put in her eyes. More than that, I can't handle the pain I've put in my heart.

A knock at the door makes me jump. I sit on the bed, staring at the door like a bomb is sitting on the other side.

"Maddox, open the damn door," Bryan calls out.

I drop my head, frustrated with myself. My paranoia is escalating for no damn reason. I'm not afraid of Bastian. I'm not even afraid of going back to River City. I just don't want to.

I open the door to a scowling face. "What's wrong with you?" he hisses. "I told you I'd be here in five minutes."

I run my hand through my hair, shaking my head. "The usual," I admit. "Worse than usual, I think."

"I got just what you need to remedy that." He taps the pocket of his leather jacket.

"I need it." I do. The hit from earlier wore off much quicker than it usually does. It wasn't the greatest stuff, but it did the job for a minute.

He nods, pulling the package out of his pocket. He hands it to me tauntingly. "What's in it for me if I give this to you?"

"I won't beat your ass," I tell him with gritted teeth. "Like I did when we were kids." I gesture to his crooked nose, the reminder that I'm not playing games.

He tosses the package to me with a scowl. I swipe it out of the air and quickly move to the table. I pull out the drugs and all the equipment I need to get my fix.

"Need help with that?" I look up from the table to see him sprawled on my bed, arms tucked behind his head, watching me.

44

I raise a brow. He knows how I feel about shoes on the bed. I bite my tongue to stop from saying something. He catches the glare with a roll of his eyes. "You're such a damn spaz. Are you ever going to stop with the crazy shit?"

"Why is it crazy that I don't want your dirty boots on the bed?"

"Whatever." He sits up and removes his boots. I twitch to see them scattered across the floor but let it go.

He watches me intently with a wicked smirk while I do my thing. Five minutes later, I can breathe. "Better?" He grins, showing all his crooked teeth.

"Much," I nod as I lean back in the chair. Finally, the noise starts to settle, and I can think.

"So, what's the plan now that you've ditched the losers?"

"I've told you before not to call them that. Don't make me tell you again." Warning him is a regular part of our interactions. I don't know why I waste my breath. He's never going to stop, and aside from the occasional bloody nose, I'm not going to do anything.

"Whatever, Maddox. Are you at least going to tell me what plan that big brain of yours has come up with?"

"To get as far away from them as possible. They don't need me anymore."

"They never needed you, Mads. You're a fucking train wreck."

He's not wrong. They never needed me, but I still felt like it was my job to take care of them. To make sure they were all okay. Now they've all found success and love and happiness. Now I know they'll be okay.

Truthfully, I've caused them more worry than anything, but I've tried. I've tried to take care of them. If I haven't done anything right, I've made good business choices for the band. They'll all be taken care of long after the music dies.

"I can't leave them without an explanation." Now that the noise isn't so loud, I know I need to tell them something. I can't leave them hanging like that. Ryder would never get over it, and he's been through enough. And Dane, ever the big brother, would wonder if he could have done more.

Angel and Jake, I'm not sure they'd keep with the band, wondering how they missed the signs.

Then there's my River City family. What a fucking rocky start that was. What started as just Zoey has evolved over the years. I don't want Zoey blaming herself. Hell, I don't even want Jax to blame himself, though I doubt he would. And I need Bastian to know I don't really hate him.

I'm repeating myself a lot. Even in my head. It's like a broken record.

"I don't know where to start," I admit to Bryan. "I don't know who to start with."

"Why do you need to tell them anything at all? Let's just blow."

"I won't do that to the people I love. That love me. I need them to understand me."

"They won't give a fuck, man. How many times do I got to tell you, they don't care about you? They just want you for your talent and money."

I laugh at that. He's always thought that. Which is so damn stupid. Not one of them needs my money. Jake didn't grow up wealthy, but the rest did. And my talent? Honestly, I get tired of hearing how great I am when the others are just as talented. They don't need me. Not my money or my so-called talent.

"What made you so jaded, Bry? I've known you my entire life, but you've never told me." I think about it and realize I don't even think I've met his parents. I've known him since I was four, but he was always at my house. I never went to his house, but then again, I never went to anyone's house after my grandfather died.

"I'm not jaded, Mads. I'm real. The most real motherfucker you've ever known."

CHAPTER SIX

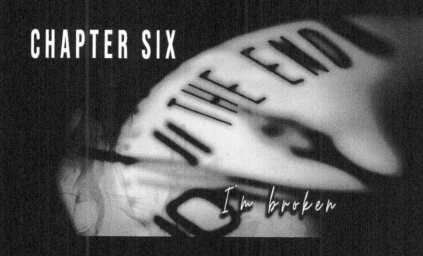

Present Day

Thump. Thump.

The sound of a ball bouncing on the wall grates my nerves. My current fix has done little to stop my mind from running back to that curly-haired angel whose heart I broke. The look of devastation in her eyes from two nights ago will haunt me forever.

I wish I didn't have to do it. I wanted nothing more than to mend her broken heart. Of course, I didn't intend for her to fall in love with me. I damn sure didn't expect to fall in love with her. I never believed I'd find that person that was completely meant for me. I thought I'd spend my life never knowing how to love anyone but Ryder and Zoey.

Whiskey eyes and lullabies.

That's what she was. Those eyes floored me the minute they connected with mine in Bastian's kitchen. They carried depth and beauty and so much soul with a single glance. I could see her pain, feel her hurt, but more than all of that was the hope that shined through. Beyond the insecurities and the painful shyness was always hope even though she had no reason to believe it.

Three months ago

I walk into the living room my first night back at Bastian's after ten days in the basement of Diamond Industries going through hell. My body still aches, but the most aggressive part of withdrawals is behind me. For now.

My steps falter when I notice a figure curled into the corner of the black leather sofa. A halo of golden curls practically glows in the moonlight. I ignore the noise buzzing in my ears when I see her shoulders shake slightly as she softly sobs into the throw pillow she's clutching.

Logic says I should go back to my room, but I can't. I can't leave someone who's very obviously hurting. Especially not when it's like her spirit is calling mine. Maybe that's what brought me from my room in the first place since I suddenly can't remember why I came out.

I keep my steps light as I move closer to where she's sitting, then clear my throat, so she knows I'm there. She looks up at me, her eyes shining with tears while stains of the fallen trail down her face. Her cheeks and nose are red and blotchy from crying.

And holy fuck, she's the most beautiful thing I've ever seen. I mean, I noticed the other day when I met her, but sweet Jesus, I didn't notice just how beautiful. She's almost painful to look at.

I've never been struck like this before. Not even—I blow out a breath at the thought that just crossed my mind.

"Are you okay?" I ask her, wanting desperately to hug her, hold her, tell her everything will be all right.

I have no business trying to convince anyone that anything will ever be okay. But this girl—something about her makes me want to hope. I want everything to be okay for her.

She shakes her head, looking embarrassed. "I didn't know anyone else was in here. I'm sorry."

That voice. I can't get over it. It's smooth and warm with a hint of smoke, like my favorite whiskey. It ignites my insides in a way I haven't felt in a long time.

I don't want her to apologize for crying. I don't want her to apologize for anything. Ever. "I just needed to get—" I shake my head. Having no idea what to say, I decide on the truth. "I honestly don't know why I came in here, but don't apologize for how you feel. I don't know what happened, but you have a right to your feelings."

"Do I?" she scoffs. Her eyes close shut as she inhales. I don't want her eyes closed. I want her eyes open. And on me.

I move a little closer to her. I don't want to overstep or scare her. But I need to be in her space.   Close as she will allow.

I really don't know what the fuck has come over me. I've only had this reaction to two other people, and it wasn't this potent even with them. This powerful.

I sit on the coffee table across from her, taking care not to touch her. She seems like she might bolt if I do. "Everyone has a right to their feelings," I tell her, keeping my voice soft and soothing. "Even if those feelings are shitty. It's the one thing that no one can take from us."

Her blond head tilts to the side, causing the curls to fall on her face. Her eyes meet mine—I mean really meet mine—for the first time. "You're not what I expected."

I release a quiet chuckle. "You had expectations?"

A smile lights her face for the first time. Not a big one, but a smile, nonetheless. "You're Maddox Masters. Everyone has expectations."

I don't let the smile on my face fall, though my gut clenches tightly because she's right. Everyone does have expectations of me. The difference in meeting those expectations always depends on the person.

I wonder where I fall for her. Did she expect the worst from me like the media did? The bad boy heir turned rockstar who had been on the fast track to destruction? They expected me to OD. They always expect me to fuck up. Sometimes, I actually liked them the best. If I let them down, it meant I'd done well. If I didn't—well, that just meant I'd lived up to their expectations, didn't it?

Is she a fan? If so, on what side of the spectrum did she fall? Is she one of the ones that cried and sent emails and letters telling me they hoped I got better? Or is she one of the ones that were stupid enough to think that a drug problem and overdosing made me a badass?

No. She wouldn't think it was cool.

Maybe she's part of that group of people that's disappointed in me. The part that holds me to a higher standard because of my name or celebrity.

I scratch at some phantom itch. I mentally argue about whether I want to know what her expectations were.

No one said I'd let them down. Bastian came close, but he never flat out called me a disappointment. A selfish bastard once or twice, sure, but he never said I disappointed anyone. Unfortunately for me, knowing they're worried is just as bad.

"Just so you know, you've kind of exceeded my expectations," she says as she watches me scratch at nothing, which pisses me off that she's watching me struggle. Then I realize what she said.

"How the fuck have I exceeded your expectations?" I snap then wince when she does. "I'm sorry. I didn't mean for it to come out like that."

"It's fine," she says, looking at her hands. "I just meant that you seem like a regular guy, that's all."

I laugh out loud at that. "I don't think anyone has ever called me a regular guy, but I am. I'm just a regular guy."

"You also seem really thoughtful. I'm not the best judge of character, though." She says that last part with furrowed brows and a frown.

"I'm sure that's not true." I don't know her, but she doesn't strike me as the type to misjudge people. She does strike me as the type to wear her heart on her sleeve.

She smiles again at me as she stands. "I didn't mean to interrupt whatever you were coming out here to do. I'm just going to go back to my room."

Or maybe she doesn't.

"You didn't interrupt me. I think I interrupted you." I nod at her spot on the sofa. "You were here first, after all. If you want me to go..."

"No. I really should go to bed. Try to sleep a little anyway."

50

I want to ask her to stay. Ask her to keep talking. I want to know why she was crying. But I don't say anything. I just smile and watch her walk away.

It's for the best anyway. I have no business getting in her business.

When she's out of the room, I walk upstairs to the conservatory, then out to the balcony. I pull the cigarettes out of my pocket and light up. I stare at the river, watching the barges push through with their horns bellowing in the air.

I lean back into the chair I'm sitting in, blowing the smoke from my lungs. I guess I should feel fortunate that Bastian didn't make me give up the nicotine too. Although it does absolutely nothing to offset my cravings for what I really want, I am not stupid enough to go after it. Not yet anyway.

I have missed River City. Homesickness has kept me in knots for years. Being here has me in knots too. This place is full of memories and regrets. I suppose it's better I'm here at Bastian's. There are no memories here. Not that I need the help, but there is nothing to pull my mind into the past.

Another barge comes through with its horn blasting. This one sends pain through my head and causes me to break out into a sweat. It's like the damn thing won't stop.

Finally, I can't take the noise anymore. It's put me on edge. Pretty sure Bastian doesn't want me losing my shit the first night back. So I go back inside.

I'm surprised when I see Quinn again. And she looks just as surprised to see me.

"Thought you were going back to bed?" I say I walk to the kitchen for a bottle of water.

She gives me a funny look. Her mouth opens and closes before she shakes her head, looking confused. "Have you been out there all this time?"

All this time? I turn back towards the window, and my gut clenches. I've lost time again. It's happened off and on my entire life, but lately, it's been more and more frequent.

I plaster on a fake smile and look back at her. "I guess time slipped away from me. Still trying to sort this shit out," I tap the side of my head.

51

"Is it hard getting off? Of drugs, I mean?" Her face turns the color of cherries as her gaze drops to the floor. "I'm sorry. I shouldn't have asked that. Verity just told me—"

"It's fine. The world knows what happened. To answer your question. Yes, it's hard, and it's painful. I hate to leave you in here alone, but I've got a headache. Think I'm going to try to get a couple hours sleep."

She gives me a nod, still looking embarrassed. "Verity will be awake soon."

"I'm sure she will, darlin'. And don't feel bad for asking what everyone wants to know. You can always ask me anything."

That earns me a smile that I carry with me to bed. And into my dreams.

CHAPTER SEVEN

Left the past unspoken

Present Day

The thing about being me? I lose track of time and perception, but I'm also aware I'm doing it for the most part. For years, I've been great at realizing everything I see and hear isn't necessarily there. I look for clues and tiny nuances that let me know if it is real or in my head.

It's kind of frustrating when you *know* you hear and see things that could potentially land your ass in a straitjacket. Like right now. That thumping hasn't stopped, and it won't stop until the delusion goes away.

"He still there?" Bryan asks, referring to the boy bouncing a ball in the middle of the table I'm sitting at. Bryan is the only one that knows I hallucinate.

"Man, why don't we just leave? If we go, maybe it will go away."

I blow out a heavy sigh. He doesn't understand, but he also doesn't judge. More importantly, he doesn't tell anyone. "He would just be playing with it on the bike," I tell him with a shake of my head.

Why a boy bouncing a ball? I don't fucking know. I don't know why I see half the shit I do. The other half? In my opinion, the other half is my demons

"I can't keep sitting here, Maddox. You said you needed to tell those assholes something before we leave, but you haven't even started."

"I don't know where to start," I confess. The bouncing stops. I look up to the boy staring at me "I don't know what to say or who to tell."

"Then just write one big cover all apology and be done with it, so we can go."

"Because they deserve more than an apology. They deserve to know the truth."

"Why should you give them anything? They've never done anything for you. The reason why you haven't told them anything is that you know they'll crucify you if they did."

"They should," I whisper. "I would if I were them."

"I'll never understand you. I don't get the guilt."

"It's called a conscience asshole. Wanting to be a good person."

"If being a good person does that..." He gestures to me with a scowl. "I'll keep right on with my asshole ways. I'd rather be happy than a good person. No regrets, baby." I don't even acknowledge him. When he says things like this, it makes me wonder how we've been friends for so long. I guess it's because he's always been there. No matter what or when or even where I'm at, when I've needed him, he's been right there. "Fine," he huffs when he realizes I'm not going to say anything. "You want to tell them all your dirty little secrets, Mads? Then start at the beginning."

I swallow hard.

I have always said I remember everything. That's not entirely true. I don't remember a lot after my trip in the pool. I lost a bit. No one really thought much of it. Doctors told my parents that most kids don't remember much of that time in their lives as adults anyway, so they shouldn't worry about long-term effects. But everything from shortly after is clear as the day it happened.

God, I don't want to do this. I've spent my life avoiding. Refusing to deal with the shit I have done and the chaos I have caused. I do everything I can to keep those memories from surfacing because they make it hard to breathe.

Logically, I know I'm probably just overdramatic. Everyone has bad shit happen to them, right? It's part of life. It's *supposed* to be how we handle it that makes us who we are. That's probably accurate because I am the guy that hears and sees things that aren't there, lies to his friends, and hides everything.

Maybe telling them everything serves no purpose at all. It could be that I'm just attention-seeking right now, I guess. I mean, I've gone this long. What difference would it make now?

No. I need to tell them, so they understand what's coming has nothing to do with them. They loved me enough. They were there for me as much as I allowed. I don't want them to spend their lives wondering if they could've done anything differently.

All of this? It's on me. It was never their job to take care of me. It was my job to take care of all of them, and I've fucked that up too.

But I'm done failing them. I'm done burdening them with worry and fear. It's time for a clean break from me and the damage I inflict.

"The beginning," I sigh. "That's a lot."

"If you're going to finally tell them what a colossal fuck up you are, then you may as well start there."

"How are we friends?" I grunt at him.

"Because I'm the only person that will tell you the truth. You, Maddox, are a complete screw-up that lets everyone down and leaves destruction in your wake. But I'll never abandon you for it. I'm always along for the ride."

"Looks like this is going to be a long night," I tell him as he hands me the notebook and pen.

I start to set it on the table but freeze. I look up to see the boy, no longer bouncing the ball, but staring at me with a smirk. I rough my hands through my hair, shutting my eyes and wishing the kid away.

"Dude, he's not real," Bryan laughs. "Maybe if you hadn't baked your brain so hard for so long, you wouldn't have these problems."

He's probably right. Except the noise has always been there. That could just be my mind always running at lightspeed.

"I know he's not real." My teeth grind that I even have to say it. My fists clench because even though I know the kid isn't real, I cannot physically make myself put the notebook on the table as long as he's there.

"Fuck this." I push away from the table, taking the notebook and pen with me. "You go sit over there," I bark out.

"Come on, man," he taps the spot beside him. "I won't bite much."

"Move, Bryan."

He chortles as he gets off the bed. "Man, thought you liked it both ways. I'm feeling a little insulted here."

I roll my eyes as I throw myself on the bed. I lean back against the headboard, crossing my feet at the ankles as I open the notebook. I look up to Bryan, who's sitting at the table now, and the damn kid that won't go away. "You're not my type," I tell him as I pull the cap off the pen.

"Damn, that's cold. Here I thought I was everyone's type."

"No one is everyone's type." I look down at the blank pages of the notebook. My hands shake as I put the pen to paper, ready to tell all the people I love my story.

My life has been a series of tragedies. Heartbreak and loss have followed me—stalked me like a predator. But it's always come by my own hand. I've disappointed the people who mean the most to me at every turn.

The irony of it all is that the only thing I want to do is to make everyone happy. I want to shelter and protect them from anything that would cause them pain and disappointment.

Once again, irony of ironies, that pain and disappointment are usually caused by me.

Journal entry #1

February 2001

"Mr. Masters," my teacher began with a sigh. I ducked my head low as tears fell down my face. Momma rubbed my back soothingly, but it made me feel worse. I might not have meant to hurt that girl, but I did. It was an accident, but it was still my fault. "Maddox pushed Madelyn, causing her to fall into the table. It knocked out her front tooth and split her lip badly enough to need stitches. Now, I know he didn't mean to hurt her, but this is just one in a long line of issues we've had with him."

"What do you mean 'issues'?" My dad practically snarled.

"Maddox is a—a sweet boy, but he lacks self-control. Throughout the day, I constantly have to remind him to be quiet or sit down. Sometimes he wanders around the classroom, and he will ignore me when I ask him to sit down. He's disruptive and often distracts the other children. Also, he seldom completes his work. More often, he stops before he's half-finished."

"I see." My dad looked over to me in that obdurate way he always did, but his tone was controlled in a way only he could manage. "What would you suggest we do?"

He wasn't going to do what she said. I knew that. He was patronizing the woman. I didn't understand how she didn't realize that when, at seven years old, I did.

The woman sat up straighter, the hubris plain in her eyes. "I am only a teacher." She mocked humility. "I don't have the training to tell you what he needs, but he may require special classes to better serve him. I cannot spend my entire class trying to corral him. It's not fair to the other students. Quite frankly, I'm not certain he will pass the end of the year testing. His grades and work quality are not indicative that he will."

She'd already called me dumb once or twice in class. Yelled out that I was stupid too. So, I knew exactly what she was saying to my dad, except she was trying to sound like a professional.

The thing was, I didn't mean to disrupt the class. I tried to do the work and listen to what she said. No matter how hard I tried to focus, I couldn't. I'd get the first questions of a worksheet done then an uncontrollable urge would come over me to start something else. I'd have this irrational need to get out of my chair and walk around the room.

"Perhaps it's time to take him to a professional, Trey," my momma said with a hand over his.

"He doesn't need a professional, Amanda. He needs discipline and structure. You've been too lenient with him."

I listened to them argue the entire way home. Over me. My knees bounced, and fingers tapped on my thighs as I sat in the backseat of their car. It seemed like they only fought over me.

"He's only seven, Trey. He's a little boy with a lot of energy and nothing that holds his interest."

"Just like Jewel was," Dad muttered. "Fine. Let's find something that will hold his attention."

They tried. Peewee football, soccer, tee-ball, even Tai Quan Do and karate. Everything was tried, and nothing held my interest. My dad was ready to hold me back until my test scores came in at the end of the year. I passed first grade with flying colors.

My restlessness was still an issue, but momma was determined to find something that interested me for more than five minutes.

She found it one Saturday morning. I awoke to noise coming from downstairs and voices I didn't recognize. When I walked into the family room, two men moved a piano into place.

The shining black wood captivated me. Its massive size intimidated me. But it was a beacon, calling to me, drawing me in with every step I took.

"What do you think, Madsy?" Momma asked with a wide, hopeful smile spread across her beautiful face. My eyes shifted to my father, who watched me with a mixture of hope and worry.

"This is so cool," I breathed as I ran a hand over the smooth, slick surface. "Can I play sometime?" I asked while I bounced in place.

Momma nodded her head furiously, her grin grew impossibly wider until all her teeth showed. "Absolutely. In fact, Daddy and I thought you might like to learn."

My eyes widened with excitement. "Can I try now?"

"Go ahead," Dad told me as he gestured to the bench.

I sat, then tentatively pressed an ivory key. Its sound exploded through the room like a bright burst of colors and shapes before me. That single note reverberated through me and filled the space with a beautiful cadence that ricocheted through my soul.

I felt it in my bones.

That moment was when I discovered my first love. I knew in that single, precious moment of time that music was as much a part of me as breathing. It felt like the missing piece.

Slowly, I moved my fingers over each key, listening to the full-bodied sounds as they bounced against the walls and the colors exploded before my eyes. I committed each one to memory.

Before my fingers knew what to do—before I knew what chords were, understood the crescendo could make a heart race, or the legato could soothe a soul—I was hooked.

After a few passes over the keys, an idea struck me. I had no idea what I was doing, but my fingers began to move, one note at a time, until a simple song was formed. It was rudimentary and unrefined, but the look on my parents' faces made me feel like I was Dimitris Sgouros when he debuted at Carnegie Hall.

Later that afternoon, my instructor was the first to toss around the word prodigy. It was a word I didn't know but decided I would learn because whatever it meant, it made my parents happy.

Unfortunately, as proud as they were about the newfound talent, the excitement was short-lived because the music didn't just have my interest. It was all I wanted to do. I didn't think about anything else. I'd spend hours at that piano without moving.

It became a new source of consternation for my parents when I began to withdraw. My behavior at school plummeted because all I wanted to do was vanish into my world of sounds and chords. I stopped interacting with the other students. I became even more unruly and defiant. My dad tried to use it as a source of punishment, but that only triggered tantrums.

"He's spoiled, Amanda," I heard my father yell one afternoon when I was nine. They didn't know I was sitting on the bottom step listening. "He throws fits to get his way. When that doesn't work, he shuts down and ignores everything. It's got to end."

My shoulders slumped as I listened to them fight over me. Again. I hated it. Just like I hated that I was letting them down.

"I've had enough. Next year he is going to a school where he will be disciplined."

"Trey, no. I won't allow it. You're not sending my baby away." Momma sounded panicked and breathless.

"I don't see any of choice. You say he's just a boy, but boys grow into men. And he's a Masters. He has got to learn control."

"I told you a long time ago that he needs a professional. His mind doesn't work the same way ours do. Ignoring that is the problem. That's exactly what happened to Jewel."

"Jewel was spoiled too. That's why he needs this school. They'll prepare him for the day he takes over Masters Corp."

"Goddammit, Trey!" Momma yelled. I jumped at the sound. Momma never yelled, and she never said bad words. "That damn company is all you ever think about. If I hear that one more time. You are raising a human being, your son. Not the next CEO. Do you even care about him?"

"That's exactly what I'm doing, Amanda. I'm raising the next CEO. He will represent the company and this family one day. But none of that means I do not love him. It's because I love him that I want this for him. If I didn't love him, I wouldn't have taken him. Don't ever question that again."

"Then act like it, Trey. Do you realize most days you can't even look at him?"

"You know why."

My entire body went rigid when I heard my thoughts vocalized, and the first of my tears began to fall.

I didn't hear anything else beyond that. I'd always felt this disconnect between my dad and me but hearing it out loud broke a piece of me.

60

CHAPTER EIGHT

Justified to waste away

Present Day

"Why did you start there?" Bryan asks, standing over me, reading my words.

My head snaps up as I glare at him. I don't like people reading over my shoulder. "You said to start from the beginning."

"They already know that stuff. I meant, start from the beginning with the stuff they don't know. Some fucking genius you are."

A low growl rumbles in my chest. I hate when anyone calls me that. I'm not a genius. A genius doesn't do the shit I do. "I don't know how else to tell the story. I can't tell it any other way. It has to be in order."

"You're such a damn fucking freak," he grumbles.

Another growl slips as I jump off the bed. My hand rips through my hair, gripping the roots tightly. "It has to be in order," I yell as I begin to pace across the room to the door as the buzzing in my ears gets louder. "If it's not in order, then I can't write it."

"Fine." He throws his hands up as he takes in my borderline panic. "Then write it all. Keep us here that much longer."

He doesn't understand. They might know the short version, but they don't understand it. I have to write it from the beginning. The noise gets louder, and I slap my hands over my ears, trying to drown it out.

"For fucks sake, Maddox, take another hit. You're freaking out. Or just drink this." He passes me a bottle of Jack. I try to remember if he had it earlier. I don't recall it. Did he leave while I was writing?

I pour a few fingers into a glass he's produced, turning up the contents, slugging it back in one go. I enjoy the burn as it slithers its way down my throat, but it doesn't do anything to calm the sudden panic I feel—the panic from wondering if I'm telling the story wrong. From second-guessing if I should tell the story at all.

My mind drifts back to Quinn. Her bright smile and beautiful eyes had me hooked nearly instantly. Even when she was sad, she still exuded so much warmth that I found myself drawn to wherever she was.

Since I was seventeen, I have been adamant that I would never move on from Zoey. If I'm honest, I never tried. It felt like it would be a betrayal after I so royally fucked everything the way I did. But Quinn got under my skin.

I snatch the notebook off the bed, ripping out everything I just wrote. Maybe none of that does matter. I am so fucking damaged. Something inside of me is irrevocably broken.

That's what Quinn didn't understand. She accepted the mood swings as part of my recovery. She had no clue that it really was just me. I hated every time I hurt her, but I hated every time she forgave me even more.

I hate it every time anyone forgives me for my fuck ups. They should hate me for the shit I've put them all through. I wish they would, just once, tell me what I already know. Why they continue to accept me, I'll never understand. I refuse to drag anyone else down with me any longer.

"Fine," I relent to Bryan's constant demands. "Let's go."

"Seriously?" he jumps up, shocked that I'm finally agreeing. Though, he doesn't give me a chance to respond before he's shoving my bags into my hands.

"Yeah," I tell him as I take the bag from his hands. My eyes narrow as I feel something wet hit the back of my neck. I look up to see water veining on the ceiling. "What the hell?" I mutter, walking to the window.

I pull back the curtain to see a downpour going on outside. "When the hell did it start raining?"

Bryan looks at me as if I've lost it. "Dude, it's not raining."

I shut the curtain and go to the door. I swing it open so he can see the hurricane-force rains and winds. I spread my arm wide toward the storm. "What do you call that?"

"If I were a fisherman, I'd call it a bluebird day." He tilts his head to the side with a raised brow. "Seeing things now, buddy?" The condescension in his voice is thick.

"Bryan, it's fucking pouring," I insist. "I am not driving this bike when it's storming."

"Are you joking? Maddox, it is not raining. You can't get wet from your imagination."

I drag a hand down my face, wondering if he's right. Have my delusions escalated?

Fuck.

It doesn't matter. The fact is, real or not, I cannot go out there. I can't leave this tiny room.

I fall onto the bed with my head pounding. The buzzing in my ears gets louder. I wish I'd brought my guitar. My eyes get heavy, and I let the effects of the rain and heroin drag me under.

Two months ago

I walk from the gym of Bastian's apartment into the kitchen. It's what I've done all day for the last five days since he won't let me out. He's got his guard dogs at all the exits just waiting on me to try to escape.

It's pissing me off. I'm on the verge of climbing the walls.

I walk to the fridge to grab a bottle of water. As I lean against the counter, I stare across his massive home at nothing. Walls. Walls. More walls.

63

My eyes begin to blur. The noise starts to buzz. My fingers tighten around the bottle until the contents spill out as I listen to the thundering in my ears. The walls begin to close in around me.

I slam my eyes shut, knowing it's not real. No matter how it seems, it is not real.

I focus on my breathing. I may hate psychiatrists and psychologists but one thing I know for sure helps is to focus on my breathing. In and out, I listen to the sound of my breaths. I concentrate on the rise and fall of my chest.

My chest squeezes tight as my heart pounds against my ribs, threatening to burst through the skin.

Breathe, fucker, breathe.

It's not working.

Fuck. Fuck. Fuck.

Sweat starts to trickle down my back. My shaking knees give out, causing me to slide to the floor.

I fucking hate this shit.

Then a voice comes through, and with it, a bright burst of color. I rock back and forth on the floor but I focus my hearing on the voice. I focus past the buzzing sound to the sexy, full-bodied sound that is coming this way. I haven't heard that song she's singing since I was a kid. It was one of my mom's favorites.

Her rich cadence lingers in the air as she sings the tribute to Elvis with every bit of soul as Alannah Myles once did. She doesn't have quite the rasp, but there's still a hint there.

Her voice is silk and smoke and like nothing I've ever heard.

Whiskey eyes and lullabies.

When she enters the kitchen, her eyes go wide at the sight of me on the floor, and her cheeks stain red. "I didn't know anyone else was here."

Now that's not true. I haven't left this place since Bastian brought me back from the basement. For fifteen days, I've seen nothing but walls and more walls.

Though, I suppose she doesn't mean in the loft. She probably means in the kitchen.

"Don't stop singing," It comes out a bit harsh. A demand instead of a request, but it drowns out the sounds in my head.

She shakes her head, her blond curly hair flying around her face. Those sexy eyes refuse to meet mine. "I—uh—I don't sing in front of people."

"Then pretend I'm not here. I want to hear more."

She opens the refrigerator, grabs what it was she came for, then turns away from me. "No. I'm sorry. I can't."

By some miracle, I'm back on shaking legs. The bile that had risen in my throat has receded though my stomach still flips. "Wait." I barely recognize the sound of my voice. It sounds garbled and distorted to me. I pant like I've just run five miles. Which I have, but it's been long enough that it wouldn't affect me any longer.

No. This is the result of giving in to the panic. Panic I'm afraid will return with vengeance if I can't get her to sing again. Panic that hasn't fully receded.

"Sing. Please," I practically beg, feeling more than a little pathetic. Also, aware that I'm probably freaking her out.

I know I am when I look into those amber eyes that are laser-focused on my hand that is gripping her arm.

"I need it."

"Maddox, let her go," Bastian bellows from the elevator gate. His eyes flame with anger at what he assumes I'm asking from her. "She can't get you shit."

"He was just ask—"

"What do you expect, Bastian?" I cut her off. He wants to make assumptions; I don't want him corrected.

"I expect you to have more respect for my guest." His weird multicolored eyes shoot daggers at me. Or maybe, in his case, they're actually bullets.

"Go to hell, Bastian. You wanted me here. Now deal with all that involves."

He crosses the room in a few long strides until we're face to face. "You want to send me there?"

"Sounds tempting." I give him a derisive smirk as I continue to antagonize.

It gets under Bastian's skin when people don't automatically concede to his demands. He is the boss of his world. Well, co-boss anyway. When he says something, he expects it to be done. If it doesn't, then he has no problem doling out punishment.

I'm not relenting to his demands or playing nice. He inserted himself in this crusade, but he had no idea that I don't follow orders. I did that once a very long time ago and swore I would never do it again.

"Give it your best shot, *stronzo*," he sneers, his Italian accent overpowering his Cajun one. (Yes, hearing that crazy accent is a mind fuck.)

My fists clench at my side. We've brawled more than a few times in the last couple of weeks, especially when the physical agony of withdrawals was at its worst, but I'm itching to go again. I want to provoke and incite him until he gives up this fucking crusade he's on.

The tension in the air is thick. The irritation and anger waving around the room are a heady mixture that is doing a decent job of giving me that temporary high. Now the pounding of my heart is the adrenaline rushing through my veins, begging me to swing. Ready to feel the ache of flesh on flesh against my knuckles. Ready to take a few blows myself in hopes the physical pain will help refocus my addled mind.

I take a step back, ready to launch the first blow when a halo of gold comes into view. "Don't!" she yells, putting herself in the space between Bastian and me. Her hands up, facing me, hoping to prevent the bloodshed from happening.

A strong sense of déjà vu washes over me. A scene similar to this once long ago, except it was me on the receiving end of the incoming punch. Just like Bastian now, I didn't flinch.

I also didn't fight back.

"Don't worry about me, *riccia*," Bastian says with a smirk. "He wants to play, then we will play."

She doesn't acknowledge him. Her eyes solely focused on mine, some silent message she's pleading for me to receive passes between us. And somehow, I know what the message is.

I drop my hands while taking another step back. I give her a curt nod through clenched teeth and make my way back to my room.

I stay in my room, lying on the bed, looking at the ceiling. The only thing keeping me company is my jumbled mind. Never a good place to be. I scratch at nothing while I shut out the whispers that haunt my thoughts. Constantly reminding myself they're not real.

After a while, I wander back out. I'm surprised to find it's already dark. I didn't think I was in there that long. Then again, I'm not sure what time it was when I went in there in the first place.

I'm barely five steps out of the room when a small voice calls out to me. "Why did you do it?"

I turn to see the petite blond standing there wearing nothing more than a tiny pair of shorts and a thin tank. I bite back a groan when my eyes zero in on her tiny nipples poking through.

Maybe she's part of my hell.

"Why did I do what, cher?" I ask, forcing my eyes back to hers. Not as hard as it sounds, considering her eyes have been in my dreams since the day we met.

"Bastian thought you were asking me to get you drugs or something." She draws her bottom lip between her teeth nervously as her eyes dance between mine.

"He did."

"Why didn't you let me tell him the truth? Why did you let him believe his assumptions?"

"Because he's going to think what he wants."

"Mmm," she nods, but something tells me she's not buying it. "Maybe he would have, but that's not why you did it."

"Then tell me, cher, why did I do it?"

"I don't know. I don't know you well enough to answer that."

67

Needing to deflect, I turn on the charm. It's not hard. In fact, I've had to dial it back. But now, it's the weapon I need to send her running.

"We can fix that," I give her my very famous smile as I go to where she stands in her doorway. I'm only a foot away from her now, and I already see the urgent need to run in her eyes. "We could get to know each other very well." I run a finger up her bare arm.

Her eyes go wide. The arousal I see in them nearly does me in. I want to grab her, place my mouth on hers. Taste every inch.

But the trepidation I also see is what I'm after. It's what has her backing up. "I—that's not a good idea." Her voice shakes with anxiety. "I—I'm not your type."

"Aww, now, cher. Haven't you heard? Everyone is my type."

She shakes her head as a couple of tears fall down her face.

Fuck! That was not supposed to happen.

"Hey, I didn't mean anything by it," I tell her, moving closer to her.

It doesn't matter, though. She's already in the room with the door closed, leaving me standing there feeling like the biggest asshole in the world.

CHAPTER NINE

Memories of you stay strong

Present day

I stare at the notebook, knowing what I need to write, what I need to confess. But putting pen to paper isn't the easiest thing to do unless I'm writing a song.

I've watched Lyra, Jake's daughter, since the day she was born. Though not his biological daughter, their bond is something I've marveled over. That tiny, little towhead brought the six-foot-something man to his knees with her first cries. Her smile and laugh are infectious, even on the worst days. She's such a happy kid despite not having a mom for so long. Hell, she's recovered from that crazy bitch of a mother kidnapping her better than I've recovered from any of the insignificant shit in my life.

Then Tyler came along. We didn't know he even existed, but the first time I saw him, there was no doubt that mischievous smile and tousled hair belonged to my best friend. The moment Ryder found out about his son was the moment that kid became an integral part of our lives.

Calling him rambunctious would be an understatement. The kid is fucking awesome. He is fearless and excited and has so much energy it's almost exhausting watching him. But more than that, like Lyra, he's happy.

Watching them made me realize I wasn't a happy child. I had no reason not to be, but I remember, even when I should've been happy, I always felt—in the way. Out of place. I suppose it didn't help that it seemed like I was the cause of so much contention between my mom and dad.

My behavior at school didn't improve. I couldn't sit still. The work, when I could focus, was easy. Once I figured something out, I knew it. Our family doctor believed the damage to my brain after the swimming pool incident played a part in the issues. My dad believed I lacked discipline and structure. By the time I was nine, my mom had quit her job to teach me from home.

If my dad had known how Momma handled my education, he would've been irate. What she did was the opposite of structure and discipline. Unfortunately, my ability to concentrate was lacking. Momma navigated like a pro. She navigated around me instead of forcing me into a rigid format. It was the only time I didn't feel like I was struggling in my education.

The feelings of contentment wouldn't last. They never did.

I pick up the pen and write about the day that everything truly started to go downhill.

Journal entry #2

April 2004

My routine—if you could call it that—began at 7:30 with breakfast. Half an hour later, I sat at the dining table with my work. With the exception of breakfast, Momma never started the day the same, but that day from start to finish will be forever ingrained in my mind.

That day started with math. Every twenty minutes on the dot, a new subject would begin. After the first hour and each subsequent hour, I'd have ten minutes to play, use the restroom, or do whatever I wanted to do.

In retrospect, I suppose that in itself was a structure but carefully crafted to meet the chaos of my erratic mind. And to prevent boredom from settling in too quickly. My momma knew me well.

At lunchtime, I sat at the counter eating the grilled cheese she made me. I can still taste it today. The buttery flavor with the melted cheese is seared into my mind. It was my favorite. I haven't touched it since.

She leaned across the table with a bright smile on her face. It was the smile she always saved for me. One I always had to return. It was compulsion. "You have piano lessons today."

I had different lessons every day. That day was supposed to be with Mr. Johnson. His specialty was Blues and Jazz stylings. Blues rapidly became my favorite. Three chords, twelve bars, and hundreds of combinations to pour your soul into.

"You've got a concert to prepare for, my little virtuoso."

I beamed at the remark. I loved that she was proud of me. The one thing I felt like I did right was the piano.

"We should've gotten you a haircut." She roughed my hair with a grin.

I pulled away, scowling. "It's not that long. I like it."

She laughed that tinkling, bubbling sound that I still hear when I close my eyes. I loved the way she laughed. It exuded pure joy. Happiness. Even then, I wondered how that felt. I had moments, but Momma seemed happy all the time. Even her fights with Dad never seemed to take away her cheer.

"It's adorable on you, Madsy. You're the most handsome little boy I know."

"Even more than Chris?" I goaded with a sly grin. At ten years old, I looked up to my sixteen-year-old brother. He could drive, was the star of the basketball team, and had a smoking hot girlfriend.

I was ten, not blind.

"Christopher isn't a boy anymore. He's the most handsome young man I know."

"Hmmm. Will I be that handsome when I'm older?" I pondered as any kid would.

"I can guarantee it," Momma answered with a wink. "You look just like your father. Now, how about some water to wash the sandwich down."

"Can I have a Coke? Please?" I batted my eyes with a grin.

I was such a manipulative little shit. Never afraid to turn on the charm to get my way. Something that has remained even all these years.

71

She scrunched her nose with a shake of her head. She pretended to be disapproving of my request, but I could see the twitch of her lips. I batted my eyes again until she couldn't hold back a chuckle. "Oh my, how am I supposed to say no to those bright blue eyes?"

I shrugged. "Easy. You don't." A wide smile spread across my face.

I lean back in my chair, scrubbing a hand over my face. That fucking smile has become synonymous with me. It's become a perfected mask. People don't look too hard when they see a smile, do they? If it reaches your eyes, they question even less.

Damn, that makes me sound like a sociopath. But they mimic because they can't feel. Sometimes, I wish that were my problem, but it's not. Mine is a carefully crafted façade perfected over decades of practice. It's a masquerade I live every day in an attempt to protect everyone I love from seeing the darkness inside me. They think it's just pain over the guilt I carry, but it's so much more.

I throw the pen down in frustration.

"You're drifting again," Bryan says as he perches on Bastian's motorcycle.

I don't even acknowledge him. He doesn't get brownie points for stating the obvious.

"Fucking genius, all right," I mumble. "So goddamn brilliant, I'm aware that I'm losing my mind."

I grip the glass of whiskey, tossing it back without tasting it. But it's not enough. My last hit was hours ago. I've long since fallen into the suffocation of sobriety.

That's when you know something is wrong. When sobriety feels foggy and congested.

All of Bastian's work to get me clean was wasted time and wasted tears. I knew with every agonizing minute it wouldn't last. Worse, I had no intention of staying clean even from that first excruciating ache.

But he tried. They all tried.

I grip my hair by the roots. My heart hammers in my chest, and my mind races. I need to get these words down, but until something calms the turmoil in my spirit, I'm going to struggle.

I pull out a stash from my pocket. Bryan watches as I break the drugs into a fine powder and then heat the spoon. My hands shake; whether in anticipation of relief or fear, it won't come, I don't know.

I wrap my belt around my arm then inject the poison into my veins. My eyes close as I wait for relief to come. As I wait for the effects to take over. To quiet the noise.

Seconds later, my eyes snap open, and my mind settles. My racing heart slows, and my hands stop shaking. The speedball has the power to get me through this, but my time is limited. Its effects never last long.

With a deep breath, I settle back, grab the pen, and pick up where I left off.

"What am I going to do with you?" she laughed as she ruffled my hair again.

"Love me until the sun stops shining," I told her with a grin.

"And the birds stop chirping."

"And pigs fly."

"I will always love you no matter what. You will always be my very special boy."

She always called me that. I once thought it had to do with the music. With the fact that they all thought I was some sort of musical prodigy. Now, I wonder if she didn't know about me even then. Did she know how inherently fuck up I would be? Could she see the signs?

But that wasn't what she told me when I asked her a few minutes later. "I call you that, Madsy, because we chose you. That's what makes you special."

"You didn't choose Chris or Callie?" I asked because I had no idea what she meant.

"We did, but not the same way we chose you. One day you'll understand just how much we love you. How much I love you."

"I already know, Momma. You love me because I play the piano the best, and you love the piano."

She laughed at my cockiness, about to say something, when she pressed a hand to her head and began to sway a little. My stomach flipped as unease washed over me. "Are you okay, Momma?"

She gave me a weak smile that did nothing to ease my mind. "I've got a bit of a headache. I think I'll lie down for a bit. The timers are set, and your lessons are on the board."

"Yes, ma'am," I nodded, then watched as she went upstairs.

I worked on my lessons for a while, but it was harder to stay on task without Momma. I wanted to go outside. When the alarm for my break sounded, I ran up to her room to ask permission.

She didn't answer my knock, so I let myself in as quietly as I could. She got headaches a lot. Every day, they became more and more frequent. I wanted to be quiet, so I didn't make it worse.

"Momma?" I called out softly. When she didn't answer, I tiptoed quietly to her.

I whispered her name one more time. When she didn't stir, I leaned over, kissing her cheek, noticing how cold she was, so I pulled her covers over her shoulder before going outside to play.

I was a child with no real concept of time. What child notices such things? Truthfully, though, even at twenty-nine, my perception of time is still skewed. I've never told anyone, but sometimes I lose hours and even days.

When my father, brother, and sister walked through the door while I sat at the piano, I knew everything was wrong.

After my ten minutes outside, I continued my work until I was finished. Then I sat at the piano. At the time, I didn't realize that I'd spent over two hours at those keys, lost in every note and chord as the melody wove itself around me. I was so focused on the song—the first song I ever composed—I didn't realize any time passed at all.

"Where's mom, Maddox?" my dad asked as he removed his suit jacket.

I blinked, the dread pooling deep in my belly. "She took a nap." It came out as a whisper as I felt the blood drain from my face.

74

Something was wrong. I knew it was. If I hadn't been so consumed, I would've realized sooner. I knew she wasn't feeling well, but I let my own interest take over.

On bated breath, I waited. It wasn't a long wait, but the moment I heard my father's screams, I knew everything was wrong.

"Amanda!" I heard him cry out. His tone made me shiver, and my tummy flipped.

He ran downstairs, carrying Momma with tears running down his face. I froze completely, not understanding what was happening, but I knew it was bad. It's so bad.

"Chris," he yelled out when he spotted him in the kitchen. "Call nine-one-one!"

"Wh — what do I tell them?" he asked Dad with a stutter.

"Tell them she's not breathing," he yelled.

Tears began to fall down my face. Everything around me felt like it was in fast forward and slow motion all at once. My heart hurt, and my head swam with so much grief. But not just my own. I could feel Callie's fear, Chris's panic, and my father's utter devastation. The weight was so unbearable that I slid off the piano bench to my knees on the floor.

The room spun. Everything was too much. I couldn't breathe.

A hand on my back soothed me. I looked to see Callie's pale blue eyes, the exact shade of Momma's, staring back at me. Unshed tears filled her eyes.

Somehow, with a heavy breath, I pulled my four-year-old sister into my arms in an attempt to console her. She sobbed softly in my arms while my tears continued to fall.

Eventually, she fell asleep. Chris took her from me and carried her upstairs.

My father knelt in front of me, taking in the river of tears flowing down my face. He wiped them away with his thumbs as he grips my face. "Maddox, stop crying," he orders, not harshly but firmly.

I look up through tear-stained lashes to my father's broken face. "I—I'm s—sorry," I sobbed. "I didn't mean to."

"Stop crying, son. You're a Masters. We can't afford to show weakness."

"I can't."

He gripped my shoulder with a hard shake. "Stop, right now. Stop your crying. Your mother is gone. Your tears will not bring her back. Be strong like she would want."

I wiped my face with the hem of my shirt. One last shuddering breath escaped me as I forced my tears to stop.

You'd think that day would've turned me off of music. Maybe for some, it would've been easier to walk away. For me—I immersed myself even further. It became my obsession.

Two weeks after my mom died, I performed at the River City Orchestra. I played the song I was working on the day she died. Full intricate weavings in a major second descending interval. I started that song for her—for my mom. I also finished it for her, then played it for five thousand rich, influential men and women gathered together for a charity performance she had organized.

But I didn't play for them. I played for her.

Tears seldom came after she died. Instead, I learned to let the music be my tears.

CHAPTER TEN

Are you ready for me!

Present day

I lean back in my chair with stinging, burning eyes, but the tears won't fall.

"Man, you've been at this for hours." Bryan tosses an apple, that I have no idea where he got, in the air. "Can't we go out?"

I stare at the clock on the wall. Hours? It feels like I just woke up.

I have so much left to say, but I am tired. I look out the window to see it's no longer raining, but— "Going out will leave me wide open for Bastian to find me."

"Maddox, if he were looking for you, he would've found you by now."

With a heaving sigh, I relent. Truth is, I need a break too. I can put on the hoodie and glasses, and we can go in Bryan's car.

"Fuck yeah! Strip club, man."

I roll my eyes at his enthusiasm. We're the same age. Shouldn't the excitement of strippers be a little less thrilling?

"Yeah. Whatever," I mutter. "I guess a strip club is good a place as any to stay low. Dark enough anyway."

An hour later, we walk through the doors of some high-dollar club with the door bouncer looking at me with a sneer. "Suit and tie are mandatory," he grunts as he folds his large, tattooed arms across his chest.

I reach into the pocket of my jeans, pulling out my ID. I hand it to him without a word. He looks me over with a raised brow then hands it back to me. "Am I supposed to believe that you're—"

I remove the sunglasses and push the hoodie back just enough to see that the person and the picture are the same.

"Holy shit!" he rasps. "You're supposed to be missing or something."

I slide the glasses back on and pull the hoodie up. "I still am." I let my tone convey the real meaning behind my words, then slip him a few hundred to ensure the message is received loud and clear.

"You got it, Mr.—uh—"

"Michaels," I give him Bryan's last name.

"Right this way, Mr. Michaels."

I follow him, watching as he murmurs into his phone. He hands us off to another tattooed guy that we follow up a flight of stairs into several sectioned-off areas. We walk through several men in suits that eye us suspiciously, probably because we aren't following their *dress code*. "Mr. Michaels, my name is Landon. I'm the floor manager here. Ms. Langley instructed me to bring you to one of our VIP rooms. You shouldn't have any problems with privacy. Do you have any preferences concerning girls?"

"I don't care," I wave. Then hesitate because that's not true. "Actually, no blonds."

"Understood. Anything else we can do for you? Beverages?"

"A couple bottles of Johnny Blue will be fine unless you have other refreshments on the menu."

He gives me a knowing smirk. "Anything specific you have in mind?"

"Surprise me."

He nods as he leaves the room, closing the door behind him.

Bryan and I fall into the expensive leather sofa sitting in the room. I cock a brow at him with a flick of my chin, gesturing to the chair next to the sofa. I'm not watching girls get naked with him sitting on the same cushion as me. I don't like him that much.

"So you gonna talk about the sudden issues with blonds?" Bryan asks me with a slick grin.

I feign ignorance, pretending the carpet is the most fascinating thing in the room. "Nope."

"I don't suppose it would have anything to do with the sweet little girl I heard you put a monster in, would it?"

My head snaps up. My brows fall between my eyes as my teeth clench. "Where did you hear that?"

He covers one side of his mouth with a hand as he moves to my ear. "I hear things," he whispers, then gives a slightly deranged laugh. "Just think of everything that poor girl will have to endure because of you."

"She won't endure anything," I grit out, ready for this conversation to be over. "I told her to get rid of it."

"Good thing. The world doesn't need more of your particular brand of fucked," he laughs again.

He's right. It's why I told her what I did. It's also another reason I left. She wouldn't let go if I was still around. And I'd never be able to keep up with the lie that I don't love her.

The door opens, and Landon comes in with another girl following behind, carrying a tray of glasses and two bottles of whiskey. "This is Holly. She's our best waitress and understands the importance of discretion."

The long-legged brunette gives me a coy smile as she places the tray on the table in front of us. "Anything you need at all, Mr. Michaels, just press that button. A light will come on, notifying me that you have a request."

I nod as she leaves the room. I turn my attention to Landon, wondering what he's brought me. He grins as he reaches into his coat pocket. "This is our best supply." He pours his offerings onto the tray the waitress just brought in. Uppers, downers, hallucinogens, and entactogens litter the surface. I have no desire for hallucinogens. Last time I used those, I ended up on a seventy-two-hour psych hold and another ill-fated encounter with fucking psychiatrists.

But the GHB and X are calling to me. Always preferring the push-pull over feeling the crap side effects, I choose both.

A few minutes later, I'm sunk deep into the comfortable sofa, watching some redhead swing around the pole. I watch with disinterest while Bryan drools on the floor. She dances in front of me, shaking her ass in my face, and I don't feel the slightest twinge of—anything.

When she reaches out, stroking a finger up my thigh, I grab her wrist. "Give him some of the attention, would ya?" I jerk my head toward Bryan.

She gives me a confused look before her face settles into a scowl. "Whatever," she huffs, stepping back from me. "My time's up anyway."

"Great," I flick my wrist, waving her off like some asshole. "Send in the next girl."

With my head leaned against the back of the sofa, I close my eyes, ignoring the sounds of Bryan's whining that he wanted the other girl a little longer. The music turns up to a Voodoo by Godsmack as the lights in the room change from blue to red.

I'm transported back several weeks to the girl I can't stop thinking about.

Two months ago

I walk through the doors of Red taking in the club Bastian and Rory opened up nearly a decade ago. It's changed a bit since I was here. The mirror over the bar is definitely not the same one. Zoey told me something about Bastian demolishing the place with a baseball bat when he thought Verity left him. I was surprised he didn't set the place on fire, considering how hot-headed he can be.

Tall stools with dark wood matching the antique bar fill the space. Men and women sit, enjoying their drinks and the music flowing through the room. There isn't a vacant seat to be found except a booth in the back that is clearly reserved, and I can guess for who.

I walk through the bar area to the second entrance that leads to the strip club side with Tristan hot on my tail. "What are you doing here, Maddox?"

"Came to see the show," I answer as I make my way to the door that divides the bar side from the strip club. I still don't know why they didn't just make two clubs, but it seems to work for them.

"Maddox, you're not supposed to be here." He grabs my arm as I reach the door.

I look at his offending hand then back to him with a raised brow. "Tristan, I know we don't know each other very well, but if you don't want me to rip off your arm and shove it down your throat, then I suggest you remove it. I don't like being touched without permission."

"Fucking hell," he mutters under his breath. "You really are Bastian's brother."

"No, I'm not," I growl.

"Maddox, seriously, you aren't supposed to be here. Bastian will—well, he won't kill me, but he'll do something to make me wish he did."

"Bastian isn't my warden, Tristan. You want to call him and tell him I'm here, by all means. He can find me in there," I nod my head toward the still unopened door.

"We won't serve you," he warns.

"I didn't ask you to." I walk through the door without glancing back.

Four small stages are circled with club chairs and sofas. The four small stages all meet in the middle forming one large stage surrounded by tables of men as some purple-haired girl twirls herself around the pole. Cages dangle from the ceiling with more smiling, dancing women.

I take a seat in a club chair that gives me a good view of the main stage without being front and center. I watch as the woman balances herself upside down, slowly lowering herself to the floor.

Since I haven't had a fix in almost three weeks, other needs have made themselves known. When I was high, I never knew when I would end up with a fantastic case of coke dick. Or which version I would get. The one where I couldn't get it up or the one where I couldn't get off. Both sucked, but not enough to deter my next hit.

81

Then again, it could also be Quinn. We haven't said a word to each other since the other day outside her bedroom. We've also managed a meticulous dance of avoidance, somehow managing to completely evade one another until Verity had supper ready. Even then, if we could help it, we didn't cross paths.

Bastian was suspicious, even cornering me to ask what I did. I wanted to punch him in the face for not minding his own business. I never realized how nosey he was before. Maybe Zane has worn off on him.

I've had a perpetual hard-on for days. No matter how many times I take care of it, it won't go away.

I guess I could've gone to the Playpen, Bastain's kink club, but somehow I ended up here. Which will actually help nothing since they have a strict hands-off-the-talent policy. But Delaney and I have been friendly in the past, and I see she's working this side tonight.

I catch her attention with a nod. Her face lights in a sexy grin as she struts her way to me. "Well, hello, stranger. I heard you were in town."

"I bet you did," I scoff with an eye roll. "I see you're still working here."

Delaney and I have known each other for years. I met her during my short stint at Sacred Heart after my near two-year-long expulsion from boarding school. During her first year of college, her father got arrested for corporate espionage, and the lifestyle she knew came crashing down. Somehow, she ended up working here at Red and never left. Although I hear Rory and Bastian pay well and take care of their employees like they're family, so I suppose that could be why she stayed, even after graduating from Loyola.

"I like the new hair." I nod to the long, cherry red ponytail hanging down to her waist. "It's sexy as hell."

She wraps it around her hand with a grin as she comes closer. Once she's within arm's reach, I grab her, pulling her to my lap. She throws her head back with a laugh. "Still just taking what you want?"

I shake my head. "I only take what I know I can have." She throws her arms around me in a tight hug. I notice Tristan glaring holes into both of us from across the room. "Still making him chase you?"

82

"I don't make him do anything. If he chases me, it's his choice." Her tone is light, but there is no missing the irritation. It's a touchy subject that I always touch.

"It's been years. Don't you think it's time to give him another chance?"

She leans back from me with disbelief etched over her pretty, angular face. "He was screwing everything that moved while we were together. Why should I give him another chance?"

"You told me yourself that neither of you ever claimed any sort of exclusivity."

"Yeah. We didn't. That still didn't give him the right to pretend I was nothing in front of everyone either."

"He looks ready to explode." I can't help but laugh at Tristan as his green eyes shoot daggers at me. His jaw is clenched so tightly his teeth are probably crumbling.

"Let him explode," she smirks.

I lean forward, dipping my head down to her ear. I intentionally make it look like more is going on than there is as I grip her hips, pulling her tighter against me. "You still like making him jealous?"

"I live for it," she says as she looks over her shoulder to the object of her disdain with a smile. She winds her fingers around my neck, coming in close. "It's my favorite part of this job."

I bite my lip to keep another laugh from passing my lips. We won't be very convincing if I guffaw for the room to hear.

After another few minutes of conversation and brilliant acting, she finally stands so she can get back to work. "What can I get you to drink, Mads?"

"I'm sure the warden has given you the dirt."

"They have. He's just trying to help, Mads."

"Everyone is always trying to save me," I chuckle. "One of these days, they'll realize I'm not worth saving."

Her sincere eyes meet mine, "Maddox, if no one in this world is worth saving, you are. I'll bring you a water."

"Thanks, Delaney."

A few minutes later, she returns with a couple bottles of water and a wink for the man still watching. He's probably supposed to be watching me. I know he's called Bastian. Just like I know Bastian told him to keep his green eyes on me for the night.

But it wasn't me he was watching. It was the every move of the scarlet lady openly flirting with me every chance she got.

I could only laugh. The guy had it bad and, apparently, was relentless.

When the lights go down, I turn my attention to the center stage. Voodoo cranks through the sound system as five girls float from the ceiling with aerial silks.

Color me impressed.

Perfectly synchronized, the girls twirl and spin on their way down in moves that are as graceful as they are sexy. Suddenly, I find myself wondering if Bastian and Rory didn't turn this place into a Burlesque show instead of a strip club. It's beautiful, but I'm not here for art. The hedonistic caveman in me wants ass and tits. With any luck, this case of blue balls caused by lush, wheaten curls and eyes the color of my favorite Macallan will be remedied at the end of the night.

But even I can't deny the sex appeal of five scantily clad women floating from the ceiling. I just hope the scanty becomes naked soon.

My eyes linger on the stage farthest from me, taking in every movement and motion before moving to the next. I sip on my water, watching with interest, my eyes feasting on the delectable bare flesh of each woman, until they find the stage closest to me, just as the girl spins to a halt.

And I lose my breath.

To loosely quote Humphrey Bogart: Of all the strip clubs in the world, I had to stumble into hers.

To say this is unexpected would be an understatement. She doesn't seem the type. Or she didn't until this moment when I realize the girl's body moves like a vision.

When our eyes lock, I see her pale flesh turn a beautiful shade of crimson. She doesn't falter, though. Her steps stay perfectly in sync with those of the other girls. Or so I assume since my eyes won't leave hers.

Those heavenly golden tresses fly around her face wildly as she moves her body with control and strength. Her eyes stay fastened to mine. Trepidation and fear fill them—and maybe a hint of lust—as she gyrates her hips in a bewitching circle that has me imagining her on top of me.

I watch with rapt fascination as she seductively climbs to the top of the pole. Legs that don't make sense on someone so small wrap around the slim metal as she uses strength that defies logic to lean back, tossing her top to the ground as she hangs upside down.

I am done. My brain has melted. All the blood in my body has left every other organ in favor of one particular muscle that is now acting as my heart.

I haven't been a virgin since I was twelve, but fuck, if she so much as breathes on me right now, I'd make the most desperate virgin look like he has staying power.

I sit, unmoving from that seat for four hours and dozens of dances. The only one that I care about is the willowy blond with the wild mass of curls.

When the last show ends, I'm out of my seat, heading to the backdoor. I walk through the crowd, rather uncomfortably since my pants feel about two sizes too tight, right past the two bouncers that are shielding the backstage area. I hear the giggles and murmurs of the girls behind the dressing room door along with my name once or twice.

Once I'm out the door, I prop myself against the building. Right across from the door. I want to be the first thing she sees when she comes outside.

They begin filing out of the building, one by one—well, actually in groups of two and three. I fight the urge to roll my eyes at their giggles and whispers like they're a bunch of teenage girls walking through high school hallways.

When Delaney comes out, she shakes her head at me with a big smile. "I figured you'd be out here waiting."

I cringe, thinking she must believe I'm waiting for her. "I—uh—Del—"

"I knew the way you watched her that something was up. I don't think I've ever seen you react that way to a woman."

I tilt my head, wondering exactly what she thinks she saw. Because the only thing I knew was I had never been so turned on in my fucking life. I blame it on the fact that I haven't had a fix in three weeks, and it's been even longer since I got laid.

"How do you think I reacted?" I ask, curious about what she thinks she saw.

"Interested, Madsy. You were actually interested. Not just looking for a quick fuck."

"Nah," I grin as I pull a pack of cigarettes out of my pocket. "I'm still looking for a quick fuck."

"If you say so, Mads, but you should know she's not the kind of girl looking for a quick anything. She's kind of had her heart broken."

My chest tightens when she tells me what I already suspected. It's why I know I need to stay the fuck away from her because all I have to offer is a quick fuck. "She tell you that?"

"No. But I heard her on the phone once. Her ex, I think. I don't know what he said, but she couldn't quit crying. Kept asking why she wasn't good enough."

"Fuck," I hiss, dragging my hand through my hair.

"Exactly. She's not in a place for anything," she tells me, then gets quiet for a second. Gears clearly turning in her mind. "Although, maybe a quick rebound with the hottest man on the planet will boost that self-esteem of hers."

I laugh even though it doesn't feel funny. In fact, the idea makes my stomach flip. I don't have anything to offer, but I also don't want to be her rebound. I want her to see how fucking gorgeous she is and how absolutely desirable, but I don't want to come in second place to anyone. Not again.

My arrogance is not lost on me.

"You know, I think I'll just take off." I jut my thumb towards the parking lot. "I don't need to cause anyone any more grief."

"Maddox, I wasn't saying—"

She gets cut off by the door opening. Out walks the girl who's been haunting my dreams lately wearing yoga pants and a hoodie with that blond mane piled on top of her head. She's just as fucking sexy in the oversized getup as she is with nothing but a G-string.

Her eyes lock on mine. In the pale glow of the moonlight, she looks like a damn angel.

She looks like salvation.

Delaney looks between us. The corner of her lips twitches as she fights a smile. "I'll see you later, Madsy," she says, tossing a wave as she walks away.

"See you, Delaney," I call out while keeping my eyes on the unknowing vixen. Because that's exactly what she is. She has no idea what she's doing to me.

"You waited for me?" she whispers, shifting nervously from foot to foot.

"Come with me," I tell her, ignoring her question. "I'll get you back to Bastian and Verity's."

"Can you not tell them about this? Please."

My eyes narrow as I remove the distance between us. I'm curious why she thinks Bastian doesn't know, but I'm more curious why she wants it to be a secret. And I need to be near her. "Why is it a secret, cher?"

"Why would I want anyone to know about this?" Her cheeks turn the color of cherries as she drops her gaze to the ground. "It's degrading and demeaning."

"Not saying I agree with you, but why do it if that's how you feel?"

"The money," she shrugs. "When my husband decided to toss me out, he tossed me with a lot of debt and no income."

"That doesn't make sense. How can he leave you with nothing?"

"Well, it's easy when he already had everything before we got married. I mean, he gave me a little money, but it barely made a dent in my debt. My parents have money, but not enough to handle all of my student loans and medical bills."

87

Finally, unable to stand her looking so ashamed, and going crazy to touch her, I gently grip her chin, tilting her head up to meet my eyes. "Quinn, there is nothing wrong with working here. Stop feeling ashamed for doing what you have to. Even if you didn't need the money, there's still no shame. Do you think those girls in there are all doing this for the money? I can guarantee a few do it because they want to. Because they love to dance and love their bodies. It's just expression like any other form of art."

She gives a wet chuckle as a tear spills past her lashes. "I'm not sure too many would agree with you. I can guarantee my dad wouldn't."

I nod with a laugh of my own. "That's not because you're doing anything wrong. That's because no father wants to think of his daughter naked. Much less naked with an audience."

"You won't tell them? Bastian and Verity? I just can't stand the thought of them knowing I do this. Not yet."

Then it occurs to me. "Quinn, what name did you give them when you started here."

"I gave them my name. Why?"

"Aww, cher, I can guarantee you Bastian and Verity already know you work here."

Her eyes grow wide as saucers as the blood leaves her face. "H—how?"

"Because, pretty girl, Bastian knows the name of every person that works for him."

"But I don't—are you saying that—"

"Yeah, cher, Bastian owns this place. Well, him and his friend."

She covers her face with her hands in mortification. "Oh, God."

"He doesn't care, Quinn. If he did, you wouldn't be here. Verity has worked here before too. Not on this side, but this is where they met."

"How did I not know this?"

"Does it matter?"

"No," she says, her breath coming in small pants.

My hand still on her face, I notice how close we are. Her breasts heave against my chest as her breath fans across my face. I watch as her pupils take over her eyes.

I fight for every ounce of self-control I possess not to take her right here in this alley.

Fight and lose when my lips drop to hers. Electricity ignites every cell in my body when she presses herself tighter against me with her hands fisted in my shirt. Her little moans spur me on as I move us until her back presses against the brick of the club.

I slowly lick the seam of her lips in a teasing move, wanting to see how she'll respond. When she opens on a gasp, I slide my tongue between her parted lips. Her sweet, cinnamon flavor exploding on my tongue lights my skin on fire.

I scoop her up, wrapping her slender legs around me as I press her further into the wall. She buries one hand into my hair, tugging the short hairs while she digs her nails into my neck with the other. I slide my hand under the thick hoodie, slowly trailing a path up her ribs. I trace a teasing thumb on the underside of her breast. She lets out a low moan as she begins to grind herself against me.

"You want me to touch ya, cher?" I rumble against her neck, my Cajun accent coming out thicker than it has in years.

"Mmm," she moans as her head falls back.

I rub a thumb over her nipple while grinding my hard as fuck but sadly covered dick against her hot, needy core. Clothes or not, there's no denying the inferno between us. It's a firestorm of want and need in the wide-open where anyone can walk up and see us.

I'd be lying if I said that wasn't a turn on itself.

"Oh god," she mutters as I slip a hand down the back of her pants, squeezing her firm ass as I make my way to her slick folds. A tight furnace of dripping arousal greets me as I dip a finger into her welcoming heat.

I work a finger, then two, in and out of her softness, gauging her reaction until I know I've reached her sweet spot. Her lashes flutter against her cheeks as her breathing picks up. "That's it, *cher*," I encourage. "I know it feels good. Savor it, embrace it."

89

"Fuck, Maddox, fuck," she shakes her head back and forth as her cunt begins to pulse around my fingers.

"You wanna come, pretty girl? You want to feel the fire and electricity that curls your toes? Makes your knees weak? Makes ya forget your name?"

"Yes. Please, yes."

I press my mouth against her neck as I grind my cock harder. "Then come, *cher*. I wanna hear ya scream." I bite the tender flesh of her neck just as her pussy clamps down on my fingers. Her cries are loud enough that they would draw the attention of passers-by. If there were any.

I continue my ministrations, drawing out every blissfully agonizing second of her orgasm while gently sucking away the pain of the bite. It'll leave a mark for sure. Not something I normally do to girls. Not where they can be seen anyway. With her? I want everyone to see it. Even if they can't know I'm the one who put it there.

I remove my hand from her pants, bringing my soaked fingers to her mouth. Her eyes widen in shock as I coat her lips with her juices. "Open," I demand. She does as I say nervously. I slip my fingers into her mouth with a smirk. "Now, lick them clean."

Slowly, she wraps her lips around the two fingers as her eyes fall shut. Her tongue slides over them, and fuck if I don't wish it were my throbbing cock instead. When I remove my fingers from her mouth, I slam my lips to her, needing to taste her. I lap and lick every inch of her mouth with a deep guttural groan. "You're the best thing I ever tasted, *cher*."

Her cheeks flame red. I can see the embarrassment in her eyes now that the post-orgasmic bliss is beginning to fade. "Don't do that," I command. "No embarrassment here, *cher*. It's just you and me."

"I—I don't—I—" she stammers.

I kiss her one more time then lower her to the ground. "I know, *cher*. I know you don't. But I needed to touch you. You're fucking beautiful, you know that, right?" She bites her lip with a shake of her head. "That's a goddamn shame. I don't know your ex, but if he made you feel like you're anything less than the most beautiful thing in the world, then he's an idiot because I swear to you, I've never seen anything more beautiful. Now come on. Let me get you back."

90

I take her hand, leading her out of the dark alley towards the car I borrowed from Bastian. I open the door for her to get in, but she stops, looking at the ground for a minute before casting those gorgeous amber eyes to me. "Maddox?"

"Yeah, *cher*?"

"Thank you," she whispers so low I almost miss it.

"Don't thank me for that, Quinn. It was my pleasure." I lean down, kissing her one last time, knowing it should be the last but hoping it's not.

CHAPTER ELEVEN

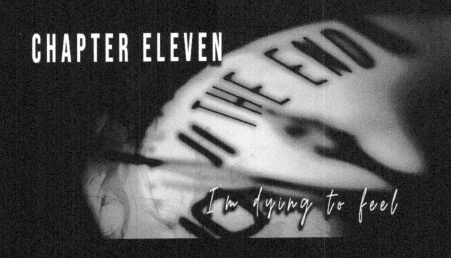

I'm dying to feel

Present day

"I can't believe you fucking did that," Bryan yells when we get back to the hotel. He's been bitching since we left the club, pissed that I dragged him out.

I'm disgusted.

Ignoring him, I head straight for the bathroom, barely making it before the contents of my stomach spill over. When there is nothing left, I go to the shower, ready to wash the stench and filth from my skin. I rest my arms and head against the tiny shower wall allowing the hot spray to wash over me. It does nothing to relax my tight muscles. The drugs wore off as soon as I realized I had some random chick's mouth attached to my dick.

I have never felt like this before. Never felt guilt about sex with someone, but right now, I feel like the lowest form of scum. I didn't even come before I shoved her off of me, but it doesn't matter. It already happened.

I slam my hand against the shower wall with a growl. "Goddammit!" I

Two months ago

I walk through the house to the kitchen for a drink. I lean back against the counter, looking at everyone. Rory and Bastian are playing a game of pool on the far-right side closest to the elevator. Layla, Rory's longtime, bombshell girlfriend and baby momma, sits with their daughters, fifteen-year-old Bella and almost-four-year-old Sophie, and Verity around the coffee table playing a game.

My eyes scan the room, looking for the other curly-haired blonde that I've developed a bit of an obsession for. When I look up toward the balcony, I see her leaning over the railing through the glass. I let my attention fall elsewhere but begin to make my way toward the staircase that leads to the balcony.

"Maddox," Bastian calls out before my foot reaches the bottom step.

I pause, looking over to him with an arched brow. "What?" I grunt out in irritation.

He jerks his head, beckoning me over. It annoys me more, but I go ahead because I won't start another fight with Verity, Layla, and the kids in here.

If the asshole had more walls...

I stand there without a word, making him roll his eyes. I find some wicked sense of satisfaction that I make Sebastian *L'uomo Nero* Delrie roll his eyes like a teenage princess.

"You need to talk to your friends," he tells me as he maneuvers around the table. "I'm tired of them calling me to talk to you."

I haven't talked to anyone since I got here. I make Bastian tell them no. He wants me here, then he can do this for me. I'm not in the mood to talk to any of them. If Bastian takes the fall, they are less likely to worry.

I don't respond to him, which I know pisses him off.

"Zoey wants to see you too," Rory tells me as he leans against his pool stick. His deep voice and cold hazel eyes convey no emotion, earning his title of Iceman. I'm sure he cares. Everyone cares about Zoey, but he won't show it. His cool façade is infamous, but I know Rory has a temper to rival most.

93

"No," I tell them both. "You want me to stay here and follow your little rules, then this is how it's going to be. Otherwise, I'm out."

"What makes you think you can leave?" Bastian challenges with a smirk as he aims for the nine-ball.

"Angle half an inch to the left with bottom English," I tell him as I start to walk off. "And what makes you think I haven't been leaving all along?"

"Dammit, Maddox," he yells. I smile to myself while throwing a middle finger over my shoulder.

I hear the balls clang against each other, and Rory chuckles. "Maybe you should've done what he said."

"Shut the fuck up," Bastian growls.

I'm still smiling when I step out on the balcony. I walk past her, sitting in the Adirondack chair in the far corner. Whatever she's thinking about has her undivided attention.

I watch her as I light a blunt, one of many I've got stashed like a fucking teenager. It doesn't give me the high I want, but it seems to take the edge off the constant feeling of panic. She looks at her phone, her fingers moving like she's texting someone. Her shoulders hunch forward in defeat, and I hear her sniff.

"Everything okay?" I ask, making her jump a foot. My heart jumps as I realize startling her wasn't the best idea, considering how she was leaning over the railing.

"I didn't know you were out here," she says breathlessly as she clutches her chest.

"Sorry." I nod towards the phone in her hand. "You looked like whatever was going on there was important."

Her bottom lip pulls between her teeth, making my dick twitch. I don't know what it is about that move that is so hot. She shakes her head, meeting my eyes. "It's not important. Thought you weren't supposed to do that." She gestures to the joint between my fingers.

I take a long hit, holding it until my lungs burn, then exhale the smoke. "I think I'm tired of everyone telling me what I should and shouldn't be doing."

Her cheeks flush brightly with embarrassment as her eyes drop to the floor. "Yeah—uh—it's not my business."

I should apologize. I know it was a dick thing to say, but it's also true. It's been a few weeks, and I am over everyone watching my every move.

"So you have no trouble taking off your clothes in front of a room full of people, but you can't sing." Another dickish thing to say.

The flushed cheeks spread to her hairline, and she begins to fidget. "It's not—I mean—I don't know. I've never been able to sing in front of anyone. I can't even sing if I know someone is in the same room."

"But you're good." She's more than good. A little coaching, and the girl has superstar potential. That smokey, velvety rasp she has is sexy and sultry, but I could tell if she reached deep down, she has power there too.

She shrugs her shoulders and turns around. I suppose I've embarrassed her enough, so I drop the subject while making a mental note to get her out of her shell. I've heard it. I can't unhear it. The fucking world needs to hear it

Yeah. She was that good. And I only heard a few notes before she saw me.

"So, about the other night." I stuff out the blunt and lean forward, placing my elbows on my knees.

"Oh, God!" She spins around with a squeak. "I'm so sorry. It shouldn't have happened. I shouldn't have done that. But I've never been kissed like that. Then you started—well, you know what you did. And it felt good, and then I—I—I'd never done that before, except, on my own. And I'm sorry. I should've stopped you. I just—I just—"

My head spins a bit more than normal, and it has nothing to do with the weed. This girl just spit out a whole lot of—well, honestly, it was a lot of word vomit. I don't think she took a breath.

And my emotions filter just as fast from pissed that she's apologizing for any of it to shock that—I think she just confessed that was the first time she had an orgasm that wasn't self-delivered back to pissed because what the fuck.

Her chest heaves rapidly like she's run a marathon. Whiskey eyes are wide with surprise. Like she can't believe she just said all of that. I notice when they dart to the door leading back inside, and I know she's a split second from bolting.

"Whoa." I'm at her side with my hand on her chin in less than a second. "First off, don't apologize. I kissed you, remember?"

"But..."

"No. No, buts. Did you want me to stop that night?"

"No, but..."

"Did it feel good?"

"Yes, but..."

"Then don't apologize. Don't carry guilt that doesn't belong to you. If anyone should apologize, it should be me. I initiated every second of that. But I ain't apologizing, *cher*. Ya feel me?"

She gives me a tiny nod as that bottom lip pulls between her teeth again.

"What I was going to say is don't say anything about it to Bastian or Verity. I don't think they'd be very happy to know I had a hand in corrupting you. I have a track record for breaking everything I touch except a guitar."

"I doubt that's true," she whispers.

"Trust me, *cher*, it's more than true. I'm the worst thing to happen to anyone. But I don't want to talk about that. I want to know about this orgasm thing. Have you really never had one?"

She turns that adorable shade of red again. "I—uh—I mean, I've given myself a few."

"That's a damn fucking shame." She sucks in a breath when she realizes I've backed her up to the railing again. "Because watching you fall apart was sexy as hell." I block her in with a hand on either side of her. Her breathing picks up, and I watch as her throat bobs as she swallows. Those whiskey eyes turn to nearly black. "I haven't been able to stop thinking about how that tight little pussy would feel coming around my cock."

"Oh," she gasps, shocked by my declaration.

I run my nose from her jaw to where her pulse throbs hard in her neck, where I bite lightly. "It's an epically bad idea. I can't do more than sex, and you're obviously not that kind of girl..."

"I'm—uh—oh God," she moans as a hand trails up the inside of her bare thigh through her skirt. "I'm still technically married."

"Mmm. Good thing I'm not asking for marriage. I am asking for sex. I want to fuck you, Quinn. I want to fuck you until we pass out and then fuck you again."

"Oh God," she gasps again.

"Let's get one thing straight, *cher*. I ain't God. But I'll give you a glimpse of paradise before I tarnish your soul."

Unable to stand it any longer, my mouth descends on her in a vicious attack of teeth and tongues. I groan when her nails dig into my flesh. Even through the fabric of my shirt, the slight biting pain brings a different type of euphoria.

Pain is an escape. It gives me something else to focus on, bringing other sensations similar to how I feel when I use. And sometimes, because I'm a sick fuck, I get the same rush from giving pain.

But it's been a long time since pain or sex brought any kind of actual release. Surprisingly, the small sting from her nails sets something free.

Not that I would engage in anything like that with her.

But still...

I grip her face, forcing her mouth to let me in farther, needing to taste every delectable, desirous inch of that enticing cinnamon flavor that could easily become my new addiction. Her hands move until she's reached under my shirt, those tiny fingers digging into my abs. I groan into her mouth when her touch feels like lightning across my skin.

I grip that mass of curls tightly, pulling our mouths apart. Staring down into her eyes, I see the lust as clearly as I feel my own. I spin her without warning or hesitation, forcing her back to my chest. I slide my hand up her skirt, cupping that hot as fuck pussy, and brush my thumb over her panty-clad clit. "I'm going to fuck you until the world disappears very soon, but I need inside you now," I growl in her ear. "I'm not waiting for later to feel you come on my cock, darlin'."

I wait, giving her a brief pause to refuse me. Instead, I'm greeted by the warmth of her arousal against my hand. I accept her body's invitation by wrapping the lace covering her heat in my fist and tearing the flimsy material away from her body.

"I'm gonna fuck you right here, *cher*. Right by the window where they could look up and see. Out on this balcony where they can walk out at any moment. I'm going to make you scream so loud, they hear you across the river."

She shivers in my arms but, once again, doesn't refuse me. Not even when I push her forward and tug that skirt up over her hips, leaving that glistening cunt on display.

I drop behind her. The sight of that dripping pink pulls a groan from my throat.

"What are you doing?" Her voice reaches a couple of octaves higher, panic more than apparent.

When she starts to stand, I grip her hips, applying a painful pressure to relay my message. "Don't fucking move." Her entire body ripples with nervous anticipation as her eyes lock with mine. "Not one fucking inch."

While keeping my fingers firmly buried in her hips, I nudge my nose through her slick folds, inhaling the succulent, heady aroma of her arousal. My dick throbs and pulses as my own becomes nearly unbearable, but for a taste of that delicious flavor, I will bear it.

I glide my tongue around her entrance, lapping those decadent juice as her sweet honey explodes on my tongue, making me see stars. Her soft moans caress the night in a challenge. A challenge to make them louder.

I dip my tongue into her sweltering heat, a smile tugging at my lips when her moans turn to soft, nonsensical mutterings. When I nudge her clit with my nose, she whimpers and pleads.

I can sense in the tightness of her body she wants to move against my mouth. Wants to ride it to the finish. But she's a good girl, doing exactly as I instructed because she never moves so much as a centimeter.

I feel her begin to throb and pulse, her climax so damn close. But this little *beb* isn't going to come on my tongue.

She whimpers when I pull away. Her breath comes in shallow pants as she looks at me over her shoulder with desperation. "Please," she cries out.

"Don't worry, *cher*, I'm not gonna leave you needin' a thing."

Before she can grasp the full meaning of my words, I'm buried deep inside of her. She cries out at the sudden, brutal intrusion. I don't give her a chance to adjust before I start moving hard and rough, pulling out then slamming back into her tight core.

I wrap my hand around her hair, yanking hard until she is looking at me over her shoulder. "You feel that, *cher*?" I grit out as I continue my vicious assault. "That's how you should be fucked. I can feel this tight cunt clamping down on me already."

"Oh—Mad—dear," she stammers as I continue to take what I want. And what I want is her finish.

I yank her back to my chest, my hand snaking its way to her swollen clit. I release her hair to press on her lower belly as I drive deeper inside of her. "Come for me, *cher*. Now."

With a pinch to her clit, she screams. Her voice carries through the silence of the night as her pussy strangles my dick with hot delicious torture until I find my own release. I carry us both through our orgasmic oblivion until all that can be heard is the mingling of our panting breath.

I drop my head to her shoulder, placing a kiss on her sweaty neck before I withdraw. "From now on, if it's not like that, then don't waste your time trying."

I dispose of the condom by throwing it over the balcony, hoping Bastian finds it. I tuck myself back into my jeans and turn around. My eyes are met by blazing multi-colored eyes and a hard-set jaw. I toss a middle finger to my brother with a smirk.

Despite what I said to Quinn earlier, I have no problem with Bastian knowing. I hope it pisses him off as much as his face pisses me off.

I turn around to face her again. She is gnawing on that bottom lip again, and as sexy as it is, I've realized it means she's nervous and embarrassed. Her eyes dart around for a second before finding mine. "I'm not easy, you know. I'm not like all those women you've been with."

I clench my teeth to stop myself from saying the wrong thing. Instead, I return to my seat in the Adirondack, bringing her with me. I pull her into my lap then force her to look at me. "I don't think anything like that, and it pisses me off that you think I would put you in the same category as the random women I fuck. I know I said I can't offer you more than that, but if it means you degrade yourself, it won't fucking happen again."

Her eyes drop to her hand. "I didn't mean—"

I jerk her chin to force her eyes back up. "I know exactly what you meant. I may be a fuck up, but unfortunately, I can't blame it on stupidity."

She shakes her head. "My confidence hasn't been the greatest lately. I guess I just thought, because you're you and all, that it was the only reason you could want to," she pauses to gesture between the two of us, "you know."

"Darlin, that's not even close to the truth. If that's all I was after, there are plenty out there for that purpose. If we'd met in a different life, maybe I could be better for you. This is just all I have to offer, and I mean it, *cher*. If a man can't give you that much—do that much for you, then they're not worth your time. Your pleasure should be theirs. It sure as fuck was mine."

Her skin brightens again, but this time there's a small smile on her lips. And I can't resist. I lean in for a kiss before I lift her off my lap. "Go inside before they send the calvary to save you from the big bad wolf."

I watch her hips sway as she walks off. My eyes linger even as I light the cigarette I've pulled from my pocket. When she's inside, I lean back against the chair, taking in the cloudless night. When I'm done, I stub out the

100

cigarette, flicking it over the rail. I start my way inside when a flash of red catches my eye.

I drop to pick up the thin, lacey material, bringing it to my nose with a smirk. I can't have the girl, but I can have fun with her body as long as she lets me. Or until the demons get too loud.

CHAPTER TWELVE

Regret is my home

Present day

Fuck up. If it can be fucked up, I'm gonna be the one to do it.

I don't know how it happened. I just know I thought it was Quinn. It looked like her. It smelled like her. It fucking felt like her.

Blaming the drugs would be easy enough, but I know it wasn't the drugs. It was me. My screwed-up head makes me see things that aren't there. Except, this time, I couldn't tell it wasn't real.

Probably because I want it to be.

I climb out of the shower, not feeling any better. I knew it wouldn't help, but I needed to wash the woman off my skin.

"Why did you let me do that?" I ask Bryan when I return to the bedroom. "You knew I didn't know what the hell was going on."

"Why the fuck do you feel guilty over that?" he throws his head back with a moan. "You dumped the chick. You made sure she hates your guts."

"Told you, I know things."

"That's fucking creepy," I scoff because I know he doesn't talk to my friends, and if anyone knew anything, it would be them.

"Whatever," he waves me off. "You gonna explain all the guilt over some fucking whore?"

I fly across the room, grabbing him by the shirt. I walk him backward until I have his back slammed against the wall. His head hits with a wicked thud, shaking the pictures on the wall. "Want to try that again?"

"She's a fucking stripper that let you in her pants faster than you can do a line."

"You fucking *coullion*. You stalking me? Or you stalking her?" He gives me a sleazy smirk without answering my question. "You say another word about her, and I'll cut your tongue out. Go near her again, and you'll learn the real meaning of go fuck yourself."

"You took yourself out of the equation, man. She's free game."

Anger, as I've never felt, consumes me. Wrath. Vengeful fury courses through my veins until my fist connects with his face. He won't go near her if I have anything to say about it.

He grins wider with blood on his teeth which only incites me more. I swing again and again until he slumps onto the floor. I want to keep going but somehow find the power to stop. I don't actually want to kill him. Not yet anyway.

If he goes near Quinn again, I won't hesitate.

I'm wound up. My mind is racing in a million different directions. Frustration and anger. Disappointment and confusion. They're at war for space in my head.

I drop onto the bed, my head in my hands. I begin pulling at my hair. It's so loud even though the only sound in the room is the air conditioning. Desperation fills me until I know there's no other choice. I've got to quiet the monster in my head.

103

Minutes later, I feel relief, but it's not nearly enough. Not what I need. So I do a little more. Until the numbness I seek finally washes over me like the ocean over the sand. Each wave takes a bit of the noise with each pass.

"Can't believe you did that, motherfucker," Bryan hisses as he attempts to stand.

I lean back in my chair as bliss and comfort wash over me. "Lucky I didn't fucking kill you," I mumble.

"You're a fucking lunatic, Maddox," he spits.

"Well established."

He continues to mutter and mumble, but I tune him out. The itch to write comes over me for the first time in a long time. Words I haven't felt in a long time fill my head. I grab the notebook and pen and begin writing. The words flow out so fast I can't write them fast enough.

I hear the melody in my head. The lyrics come until I've written several songs and my hand cramps.

Two hours pass in a blink. I sit back in the chair, wanting to feel proud of what I've done. It's been so long since I was able to write a single word.. Every time I'd try, I'd slip further into the darkness.

I want to be proud, but I'm not. There's this niggling in my gut, this overwhelming feeling of dread.

I start to flip the pages back to the first song I wrote when Bryan stirs from across the room after falling asleep shortly after I started writing. "Are we leaving any time soon?" he groans as he stretches his arms over his head.

"I've already told you that I can't leave until I finish telling them goodbye."

"Why haven't you finished? We've been here for two days. You've been writing in that notebook for hours."

"I was writing some songs."

He walks over to me, grabbing the notebook before I can stop him. "Why are you writing songs if you are leaving it all behind?" He flips the notebook open, looking at it then at me. His face grows dark as his eyes dart around the pages. Finally, he tosses it back on the table in front of me. "There's nothing there."

My shoulders hunch forward as he confirms my suspicions. Everything I've just written is shit.

"I'm ready to blow this joint. Get your goodbyes done so we can go."

He's right. I need to get this done and forget about the songs. They don't matter anymore. The one thing I always had left me a while ago, and I can't bring it back.

I rip out the songs, toss the crumpled paper to the floor, then start to write the next god-awful chapter of my story.

Journal entry #3

July 2004

Everyone thinks the first time I ever saw Zoey was at Darien Whitmore's party my junior year. It seems our first encounter only left an impression on me. Makes sense since I was only ten, but the memory lasted.

I suppose it would be more significant to me, given the circumstances leading up to and after that encounter. It was the only bright light in a shit load of pain.

Momma had been gone for a few months, and I was lonely. So damn lonely. Dad started working more, which was an amazing feat. Chris was anywhere but home. With his girlfriend and his friends so much, we barely saw him. Callie was only four, so she couldn't provide me with a lot of companionship.

It was too late in the school year to transition me back into the classroom setting, so my dad hired a tutor to continue with my education. Fortunately, mom had my entire curriculum planned, and I was accustomed to the routine. Unfortunately, it wasn't the same without her.

When summer rolled around, I hoped it meant we would do more. Vacations, summer camps, anything, but it continued just as before except with a nanny that rarely paid attention to us.

So when I opened the door to see Jewel, my favorite aunt in the whole world, standing on the other side of the door, I was ecstatic. She handed me a guitar case that left me bouncing. My first guitar.

God, I was ten years old, and the woman gave me a damn 1938 Martin D-45. That guitar meant everything to me, but when I got old enough to understand how rare it was, I couldn't help but wonder where she found it. Ninety-one guitars made over ten years. Impossible to find.

I also wondered how she afforded it. Jewel had blown through the biggest bulk of her trust and inheritance before she turned twenty-one.

But at the time, I didn't know any of this. I just knew the coolest aunt in the world had just gifted me with another instrument and a trip out of this house.

Our first stop was at a drive-thru for food. I couldn't contain my excitement at the idea of French fries and milkshakes. As I sat eating my food, I watched as she poured out cocaine onto the center console of her car. I watched in fascination as she crushed the substance with her credit card then quickly inhaled it with her rolled-up dollar in change.

"What's that?" I asked with wide eyes.

She gave me a wink and a grin as she rubbed her nose. "That's candy."

"I like candy," I shrugged.

"This is adult candy, but when you're older, I'll share."

I gave a nod, wondering how much older I needed to be before I got to try it out.

The day seemed perfect. Right until I exited the bathroom and Jewel was nowhere to be found. My head dropped with disappointment, but not surprise. It wasn't the first time she'd taken me somewhere then forgotten about me.

I knew the drill. I had to find the gate and an adult. Then I'd have to tell them what happened and watch as they gave me pitying looks while they called my dad.

I sat in the chair once Dad was called. All I could do was wait. Waiting made my tummy flip and my heart feel like it was galloping. I gnawed on a nail while my foot tapped the floor. I fidgeted in the chair to the point I knew it was driving the lady behind the desk crazy.

Lost in my own thoughts, thinking of the trouble I'd caused by going with Jewel, I never noticed the door open and more people file in. My anxiety and guilt so consumed me I didn't see the girl that sat next to me until she spoke. "Are you okay?"

I turned my head to see the palest of blue eyes and animated face framed by long dark hair, the color of chocolate hanging in waves to her waist. I was mesmerized, especially by eyes so similar to my mom's. Then she smiled, warming me from the inside out, making me feel less alone.

"My aunt forgot me," I said honestly. There was no point in lying, after all.

Her face scrunched in confusion. Not surprising. What kid would expect an adult to forget a kid? "Forgot you?" she asked.

My face heated to my roots with embarrassment. I could only nod, turning my gaze to the floor. She reached across, grabbing my hand. "I'm sorry," she said, eyes glassy with unshed tears.

I didn't know what to think about that. The simple gesture of having my hand held or the sympathy on display. It wasn't something I'd seen before.

"Come on, Zoey," a woman called out before I could respond to the girl's kindness.

"He's all alone, Momma. Can we stay with him?"

The woman looked at the girl. Then at me, her eyes softened in understanding. I should have been more embarrassed, but I was too busy trying not to cry because all I could think about was how much I missed my mom.

"Stay here," the woman told Zoey. "I've got to take your father his phone, but I will be right back."

Zoey nodded vigorously with a smile.

Her mom looked down to the two boys on either side of her, telling them to come along. The dark-haired boy glared at me like I'd taken his favorite toy. "I'm gonna stay with Zoey," he declared like he was an adult instead of a kid.

Her mom quirked a brow, but I saw the corners of her mouth twitch in amusement. "Want to try that again, Jaxon?"

"May I stay with Zoey?" he huffed.

Jax was so fucking protective—possessive of her even back then. It's pretty funny if you think about it. Or it would be if I didn't understand it. He was born to protect her like a knight protects the queen. I just wish I wasn't the villain he was always protecting her from.

"You can stay," her mom nodded, then turned to the blond-haired boy. "What about you, Zane?"

He rolled his eyes petulantly. "I'll stay," he grumbled as he trudged behind Jax. "He follows her. I follow him."

Jax sat next to Zoey. Not in the vacant chair beside her, but in the same seat, like some type of territorial dispute.

"I'm Zoey," she smiled wide and sweet. "That's Zane," her head tilted to the other side of me, where Zane had taken a seat. "He's my twin. And this is our best friend, Jax."

I ignored Jax because his glares were getting on my nerves. Instead, I looked at Zane. His annoyance had quickly faded into a wide, lazy grin. "You don't look like twins."

They both rolled their eyes with annoyance, and my stomach plummeted with worry that I'd said the wrong thing. "Yeah. Everyone says that," Zoey replied with a huff.

"Do you live around here?" Zane asked as he leaned back in the chair. Apparently, he thought he was the coolest kid in history. He must've been born with that cocky arrogance.

"Yeah. I live outside the city."

"Where do you go to school?" Zoey asked.

My face began to heat. I was embarrassed to admit that I didn't go to a school. It made me sound weird.

"I—uh—I used to go to Sacred Heart," I muttered, hoping they wouldn't press farther.

108

"Rich kid," Jax muttered under his breath which turned to a groan when Zoey elbowed him in the ribs. "What was that for?"

"That was mean." She stuck her tongue out, and I laughed.

"Technically, we're rich kids too." Zane's eyes narrowed until an evil smirk crossed his lips. "You're just jealous because Zoey's giving somebody else attention."

I watched the three of them banter quietly. A feeling of longing settled in my belly. I wanted what they had, even if I had no idea what it was exactly.

My dad walked in a few minutes later, and I wanted to be sick. His face was red, hair disheveled, and his jaw clenched so tightly I thought his teeth might break. "Maddox," his voice boomed across the room, making me jump, "do you know how worried I've been? How the hell did you get here?"

My head dropped as guilt and remorse washed over me. I knew better, but I—I don't know. "Jewel brought me," I whispered.

"Of fucking course," he muttered. "You know you're not allowed to go anywhere with anyone without permission.

"She told me you said it was okay." My head continued to hang lower, my shoulders hunched forward because I knew better.

"Dammit, Maddox."

"Trey, maybe you should take this home." I looked up to find another man standing behind him with his hand on my dad's shoulder. I knew it was Zoey and Zane's dad because their mom stood next to him. I just didn't know how they knew my dad, but kids seldom know all the ins and outs of their parents' lives.

"Yeah." My dad said, extending his hand to the other man. "You're right. Good to see you, David."

They shared a few words, mostly sympathies about my mom before we all parted ways. I watched as they walked toward their cars with sadness and so much envy. Zoey turned before she climbed into the backseat with a slight wave, making my chest squeeze. I wished we could be friends, but I knew it was unlikely.

The ride home with my dad was so silent it made my heart race at unimaginable speed. I was nauseous, and it hurt to breathe, but I worked hard to hide it, refusing to meet his gaze. Yelling would have been better. At least then, I wouldn't have to wonder what he was thinking.

When we walked into the house, his hand gripped the back of my neck in a firm hold. I knew I wouldn't wonder for much longer what my punishment would be. I steeled myself for the lecture I knew would come along with the belt on my ass.

But the lecture and spanking never came.

"Maddox, go to your room." His tone left no room for argument even while his eyes stayed firmly fastened on Jewel.

I went upstairs quickly, but as soon as I knew they wouldn't notice, I slipped down the back stairway.

"What the hell is wrong with you?" Dad demanded. "You know you can't see him, much less take him, if I am not here."

"Why are you so upset? He's fine, Trey." I recognized the flippancy in her tone and cringed, knowing it would piss Dad off even more.

"Goddammit, Jewel! Don't you stop to consider what could've happened to him?" he yelled even louder. "You know what? It doesn't matter because you are no longer welcome here."

"I have a right to see him. He's—"

"No! You have no rights. What you had was a privilege, and that privilege has been revoked."

"You can't do that!" she shrieked loudly.

My heart was racing, not that it ever really slowed. I hated that everyone always seemed to argue about me. I didn't know how to stop it. How to be better.

"Jewel, you are my baby sister, and I will always love you, but it is my job to protect him, even if that's from you. I mean it. I'm done. You are not welcome here anymore."

"I'll tell him, Trey," she hissed. "I'll tell him the truth, and he will hate you."

My breath hitched, and my chest squeezed tight. I have no idea what they were talking about. Had no idea why she thought I could ever hate my dad.

110

I slapped a hand over my mouth. I wanted to run in there and ask what they were talking about.

"It wouldn't change anything, Jewel. And remember, I won't be the only one he hates."

That was the end of their conversation. Jewel left without another word, and I didn't see her again for years.

A few weeks later, the new school year began, and I was shipped off to New York. I assumed I'd done something wrong. That it was a punishment for running off with Jewel.

It was the start of many new things for me. It set the stage for my life to unfold as it has. Because without it, I wouldn't have found my true family. The ones who have my back no matter what.

It was also the beginning of trying so desperately hard to prove myself to everyone. To prove I wasn't a massive fuck up or a burden. That I could be something more than my last name.

It was also where I learned I would never accomplish that goal. It was when the truth that I will never be enough became apparent.

More than all of that was the changing of the season. It began my descent into the abyss. My season in hell. A season that has never ended.

CHAPTER THIRTEL

Can't forgive and can't erase

Present day

I stare at the words on the page, recognizing the truth in them. If I'd never been sent to New York, I wouldn't have met Ryder, and I'm not convinced I would have made it this long without him. Later came the rest of the guys. My friends—my real family.

But as much as they have kept me moving forward for so long, I know I've been a hindrance to all of them.

And if I'd never been sent to New York, maybe, just maybe, other events wouldn't have unfolded. Events that taught me to keep everything close to my chest. For my protection and for others.

To this day, I've never spoken about any of this. Not even to Ryder. No one needed to know. I didn't want the pity, and I didn't want anyone else getting hurt because of it.

I debate if I want to tell them now. If I want anyone to know the secrets I've kept hidden for so long.

I started this to say goodbye and relieve them of any blame they may try

With a sigh, I pick up the pen. I already know it is unlikely any of them will see this anyway. The shrink wanted me to write it all out. To expunge the demons through the pages. So far, it has felt like very little expungement has occurred, but I've written this much. I may as well continue. Maybe that will cure my broken psyche, after all.

Unlikely, but I'm on a roll.

Journal entry #4

2004-2006

Boarding school was when I changed from difficult to eccentric. From musical prodigy to overall genius.

I didn't entirely understand it then. I fucking hate it now. I've called Tyler a virtuoso a few times without thinking and wished every time I could take it back. No one deserves that kind of pressure.

God, I hope I didn't set that kid up for failure.

My father was dumbfounded when a few tests showed I didn't suffer intellectually, but rather the poor performance and disruptive behavior was because I'd been bored.

"That's exactly what we're telling you, Mr. Masters," Ms. Collier, the guidance counselor, explained with a strange smile. Now I know that's the smile of someone ready to suck any dick they have to in order to win the prize. In that case, it was me.

They thought I would bring some kind of accolades to the overpriced school. They were sorely disappointed.

I watched as my dad dragged his hand down his face with a clenched jaw. I didn't know who he was angry at, and I really didn't want to know.

"We would like to give Maddox a more challenging curriculum. If he progresses as I believe he will, he could be a graduate by next year."

"No."

113

Ms. Collier's brows shot to her hairline, but there was no doubt my father meant what he said. His tone conveyed it all with a single word, but she still asked, "Pardon me?"

"NO!" Dad boomed. He was no longer speaking as a concerned, bedraggled father but a man of power and not to be trifled with. It was his CEO voice, even if I didn't totally recognize it at the time. "There is more to school than what you learn in a book. My son will one day run Masters Corp. If he's—as you put it—gifted, he will excel in academics without much assistance. He needs to learn how to work with people and lead. Navigate the world around him. He won't learn that in books, but by interacting with people. Thrusting him into an adult environment would be counterintuitive to that goal."

The woman seemed taken aback at his tone. One would think working at the pretentious school, that she would be well accustomed to the rantings of the wealthy and powerful. Still, she didn't seem to understand my dad.

My dad, who would be considered uneducated by most, was not CEO of Masters Corp because of his last name, but because of his cunning business savvy and sharp mind. He didn't go to Harvard or some other ivy league institution. He'd learned to be a shrewd businessman long before he graduated high school. Then attended a state college while working side-by-side with his uncle until he took over the company just after Chris was born.

"But without the proper challenges, he will become more restless and disruptive. Just as before," she argued weakly, but there was no point. Once my dad said something, it was final. The only exclusion to that rule was my mom.

"I never said do not challenge him. As much as I'm paying you, I'm sure you can figure something out."

The woman had gone from smiling to frowning to nearly cowering since the conversation started. Wiliam Masters III only had to speak, and his will would be done. All she could do was nod her head in agreement.

I didn't care what they agreed on. I didn't want to be there. I'd already lost Momma. Being sent away felt an awful lot like losing everyone else too. But there was nothing I could do.

I thought he was sending me away because my mom's death was my fault. He could barely look at me before she died. Of course, he couldn't bear to be in the same house with me after she was gone.

Adjusting proved to be problematic. I was a sad, lonely kid whose mother had recently died, ripped away from his family. I withdrew from everything and everyone, yet still struggled to stay still and focus. My mind buzzed all the time with noise I couldn't explain, and what had been my only time for escape was unceremoniously taken when dad refused to let me bring my guitar and the school would only allow me an hour in the music room a week.

The worst part was that I was hyperaware of all of it but couldn't seem to shake it. I just knew I couldn't talk to anyone. It would've been another burden.

I made it through the first year mostly unscathed and excited for summer. Ready to see my family. I'd missed them so much. I didn't even care that I would get lectured and reprimanded for my grades and conduct.

I was looking forward to not having a panic attack every day. Every fucking day. Panic because I missed my family. Over not getting my work done. The constant social stimulus that proved to be overbearing most days. Knowledge of what that stupid label they'd placed on me meant. And sometimes, panic over nothing at all.

I was eleven years old and losing my shit. I needed something familiar.

Didn't happen. Dad had Callie and me at every two-week camp available. I saw my brother and sister for a total of four days that summer.

The day I had to return to school, I had another damn panic attack. Of all times and people to have one, it had to be on the way to the airport with my dad. One more thing to disappoint him.

"Get ahold of yourself, Maddox," he demanded.

"I—I'm sorry," I wheezed out.

He grunted and growled a lecture I couldn't hear over the roaring in my ears. Eventually, he pushed my head between my knees, waiting until my breathing returned to normal.

Twenty minutes later, we stood at the gate. He placed a hand on my shoulder with stern eyes and a firm tone; he said, "No fucking off, Maddox. I expect you to represent this family and show them the man that will run the company one day."

I was a damn kid with a mountain of expectations and an ocean of pressure added to my very small shoulders. And I knew I was going to disappoint everyone.

Early into the semester, the school had me at the doctor after days in bed with headaches and stomach aches. The doctor decided my issue was not physical but psychological. He said I was suffering from separation anxiety and panic disorder and ADHD. I was given prescriptions and ordered to see a psychologist, which the school had available three days a week.

A few weeks later, I felt like a new kid. I was getting my work done, made a few friends, and no longer felt like a weight was crushing me. Everything was still too fast some days. Sometimes there was still a lot of noise in my head. But the panic attacks were less frequent, and I almost felt happy.

Although, I wasn't allowed to spend hours upon hours in the music room, they did allow me time every day. The music teacher also allowed me to take different instruments to my room to learn.

The school psychologist was helping me too. For the first time, I felt like I could talk about things—some things. I could talk about missing my family, my mom's death, and how everything was just too much sometimes. I knew better than to tell him about the noise.

For the first time since my mom died, I felt like I could breathe.

Until that, too, ripped me apart, taking a piece of my soul with it.

I walked into Murphey's office for our appointment just like every week. It started as a monthly ritual, but he increased them to bi-weekly after the first few visits. I was nervous that day because what I wanted to talk about was embarrassing for a twelve-year-old boy, but I didn't have anyone else.

I suppose I could've talked to my dad, but I thought it would be one more thing he'd be disappointed about. And Chris never had time for more than a quick hello when I called.

I sat in the chair across from Murphey, my eyes darting across the room, looking anywhere but at him. My knees bounced uncontrollably as I shifted in my chair.

"You seem anxious, Maddox," he astutely observed. "Why don't you tell me what's bothering you?"

I felt my entire body flush, causing me to sweat from the heat of embarrassment. "I—uh—I've been having these dreams."

It was so hard for me to understand. I had wet dreams before. That wasn't what bothered me. It was the star, and sometimes stars, of these dreams.

Before, it was usually Charolette Wayland, a high school sophomore I'd seen a few times in the music room. Then one night in Charolette's place was Cian MacDonnell, another high schooler I'd bumped into a few times. The night before the visit with Murphey, it was both of them.

"Have you had these dreams before?"

I felt my face heat even more. It felt like my head was about to explode. "Yeah. I mean, yes, but not like this," my voice cracked. and I wasn't sure if it was nerves for the sound of puberty that had been apparent in my voice for the last six months.

"They're perfectly normal, Maddox, but perhaps you'd feel better if you told me about them."

My heart began to hammer so loud all I could hear was the roaring in my ears. I leaned forward with my head in my hands to hide my face and the fact my pants were getting tighter as I recalled the dream. Before I finished my recollection, a moan and a grunt cut through the room, drowning out my voice.

My head snapped up as I leaped from my chair in mortification and terror, knocking the chair over as I did. Murphey didn't even stop, his eyes locked on mine.

"What—what—" I couldn't even finish my thought. All I knew was this was wrong, and I needed out of there fast.

I turned to run. To get the hell out of there as quickly as possible, but I didn't make it. He stood in front of the door, blocking my exit.

"Don't run, Maddox. That was perfectly natural. It's what we are made to do."

I shook my head quickly in denial. "That—no—I mean—" I stammered over my words as my knees shook violently.

"You can't go out there like that," he gestured to the erection straining my pants. My humiliation grew, wishing the ground would open up and swallow me whole.

He moved towards me, and I backed away. It didn't deter him. He kept backing me up until my back hit the bookshelf across the room.

"Let me help you, Maddox."

I shook my head again, only finding a single word. "No."

He placed one hand on my shoulder, holding me in place with painful pressure, making me wince. The other hand dropped lower. "Perfectly natural," he repeated as he dropped to his knees.

I was frozen. My muscles were stiff. My voice wouldn't work. I threw my head back against the shelf, squeezing my eyes shut, and I retreated deep into my mind. Pretending I was anywhere but there.

Shame. So much shame engulfed me. They were right. I was smart. So, logically I knew I could not control my body's response.

That understanding did nothing to ease the torment in my mind, to stop the torrential downpour of emotions—guilt, shame, humiliation, confusion, anger—that flooded my soul.

Tears stung my eyes. I swiped with fury when one escaped. At that moment, I felt anything but strong, but I was a Masters. We did not show weakness. Even in our weakest moments.

I started to run for the door again, ready to call my dad—to beg him to bring me home, when Murphey called out to me. "Before you get any ideas about telling anyone what just happened here, I want you to think about how embarrassing all of this would be for your father. How disappointed he would be for you to cause him more trouble."

I swallowed hard, knowing he was right. This would cause so much trouble.

"See you next week, Maddox," he winked and smiled.

I was out of the office, down the three flights of stairs, and out of the building in thirty seconds. Soon as my feet touched the landing, I threw myself over the railing and emptied the contents of my stomach.

The rest of that week, I told everyone I was sick. It was a lie.

Except every time I closed my eyes, my stomach turned. Every time my eyes were open, I was afraid the truth could be seen.

By the next appointment with Murphey O'Dell, I was hyperventilating. Terrified that a repeat of the week before was on the horizon. When I took my seat across from him, I was shaking so violently the chair vibrated.

"Take these, Maddox," he demanded as he thrust pills into my hand.

My fist tightened around them, but I didn't attempt to take them. I shook my head over and over until he gripped my hair painfully, yanking my head back with jarring force. "Take the pills, Maddox. It's the same thing you're given every day."

When I still didn't comply, he grabbed the bottle from his desk. He squeezed my jaw until I opened, thrusting the pills into my mouth. "Swallow them." He didn't give me a choice, holding my nose and mouth until I swallowed.

"Good, Maddox." He sounded so fucking pleased I wanted to scream. "Now, why don't you tell me what has you so upset."

"Fuck you, asshole," I spat, my panic giving way to anger.

The sadistic smile that crawled its way onto his face made me regret my choice of words as a cold chill set throughout my body.

An hour later, I left his office with tears running down my face, the pill bottle in my hand, and in so much pain, walking was agony.

I wanted to die, and the pills taunted me, but I was too afraid of the consequences if I didn't succeed.

Instead, over the next few months, the pills became a crutch. My way to deal with the hell I was subjected to.

So did sex. Because I was no longer the innocent little boy, I used what was taken from me as a way to regain control. To use my body on my terms.

119

I was as aware then as I am now that nothing I was doing could be construed as healthy, but I saw no other choice. I still see no other choice. I was in quicksand, trying not to sink in the muck and the mire that wanted to drag me into its depths. I should've known it was a battle I could not win.

My hands shake as I grab the whiskey bottle from the middle of the table, turning it up until the last drop hits my tongue. As it burns its way to the pit of my stomach, anger—so much suppressed rage burns its way to the surface. The guilt and shame of what I endured eats away at me.

I grip my hair tightly in my fist with a roar as I throw the bottle across the room, watching the glass shatter to the floor. Bile rises in my throat, and I force the putrid flavor back down as I lean over with my hands propped on my thighs. My lungs squeeze as I struggle to breathe.

I have never told anyone about Murphey O'Dell. I never meant for it to make it to the pages. Never intended for the lock to be broken. It wasn't a conscious decision I don't think. Maybe it was. I don't even know anymore, but it was a secret I intended to carry to my grave. I've shoved those memories into the farthest recesses of my mind, vaulted under locked and key. But now Pandora's Box has been opened, and the agony and pain are as unbearable as they were all those years ago.

I go to the bathroom, stripping off my clothes. I don't look in the mirror, knowing the demons that riddle my mind and soul will be more apparent.

I step into the shower for the second time in a few hours to, once again, wash the filth away. I stand beneath the freezing spray as it runs over my body, wishing it could wash my sins away.

My eyes sting as the over-chlorinated water runs into them, but I don't dare close them, knowing what awaits me in the darkness.

Logic holds no place where a broken spirit resides. Where a soul has been made black, not by your own actions but the actions of others.

I don't shirk my responsibility in the darkness that consumes me. I've made plenty of mistakes. My choices have never been driven by wisdom or selflessness. The black hollowness that consumes me belongs to me. Consequences of my actions.

But the biggest seed was sown into my soul by someone that was sworn to do no harm. Someone that gained my trust that was already so tentative and fragile during a time in my life when I desperately needed a friend. Someone to confide in.

It doesn't matter how many times I've told myself that I didn't do anything wrong—that I didn't deserve what was done to me, the voice in my head says I caused it. I was weak to my thoughts and emotions. I trusted too easily. That weakness left me vulnerable to predators.

"Fuck," I cry out as tears stream down my face. I scrub my skin until it's raw and burning, then I scrub some more.

This life I've lived was always doomed. I've already lived beyond what's tolerable. I've tried hard to cling to the love of my friends and fight for them. But I am so goddamn exhausted, tired of this war that will never fucking end. That I will never win.

CHAPTER FOURTEEN

Truth alone

Present Day

Another hit runs through my veins like fire. I release the tourniquet and relish the burn. I sink into the chair, praying for the relief it brings to come quickly. To rescue me from the images I cannot get to stop replaying in my mind.

The images are soon replaced by other memories. Thoughts of all the fuck ups in my life. Of every time I let something terrible dictate my decisions and actions.

I suppose that's what I'm doing now. Holed up in this hotel to get high, running away from the people that love me because I couldn't handle the news. Because when something bad happens in my life, it's never just one thing. And more often than not, I'm the cause of it in the first place.

All of this started with my overdose months ago. It was stupid, I know. I realize how much it terrified my friends.

It's why I've tried to create separation these last few months. It's been a dick move and a contradicting one considering how Quinn slipped into my life. Still, I wanted them to stop worrying about me.

hospital room most vividly. I smiled and joked, but the absolute terror in Ryder's face nearly killed me. I was afraid I'd broken my best friend. It has never been their job to take care of me. It's not their job to worry about me, but there they were with so much worry radiating off of them, it was suffocating.

Ryder has Heaven now. He will be fine without me, but for a long time, I knew he needed me. No matter how bad we were for each other. Over fifteen years of friendship had not only created a lifelong bond, but it had also created the most fucking unhealthy codependency. I was killing Ryder, but I knew it would have been so much worse without me. When Heaven came back into his life, I knew he would be okay. It would be a long hard road, but he would be okay.

Ryder was my saving grace at that school, and he never knew it. At first, I withdrew into myself again, but then these kids started approaching me. Older kids who liked to have fun. That was when I realized what my last name meant to people. I seized the opportunity when they began inviting me to their home and to parties all over Manhattan. The depraved debauchery of New York's debutants and social elite sucked my twelve-year-old self in. It was the escape I thought I needed.

I dove headfirst into all of it. I appreciated the relief I found in smoking weed. I loved the way alcohol would take away my worries and care for anything. And I soon learned sex was a great stress relief. It didn't hurt that between the ages of twelve and thirteen, I shot up seven inches, the innocent baby face began to change, and I no longer looked like a sweet kid. At thirteen, I was passing for a few years older already. And I learned how to use my smile. I was well aware I was being used. Male or female, they wanted to be attached to my last name and use me to make their significant others jealous.

That, of course, led to fighting. I got my ass kicked on a few occasions by jealous boyfriends until I learned how to handle myself. Soon enough, I'd earned a reputation. It was insane, considering I was so young, that older, bigger guys considered me someone not to be messed with, but it was survival of the fittest. I was already a pro at surviving anyway, right?

On breaks at home, I would still beg Dad to let me stay. Except when he said no, I would lash out. He was replacing things I destroyed on a regular basis, and then I was suffering the consequences. I knew I was disappointing him, but I couldn't find it in me to care. I also couldn't find it in me to stop.

But the summer before eighth grade started, I didn't bother asking to stay. After he found me fucking Callie's babysitter in the kitchen, I knew there was no point.

I walked into the school, a fake smile plastered to hide the fact I wanted to vomit. Being back there meant being subjected to torment for another ten months.

After dropping my bags off in the student apartment, I went in search of some *friends* to help take my mind off the fact I'd returned to hell. For some reason, that led me to the locker rooms of the gym. When I walked in, there was a brawl. Three guys going at it like it was a fight to the death while all the other kids stood around, encouraging the bloodshed.

As I looked closer, I realized two of the kids were entitled little pricks who made it a point to bully anyone they could get away with, and the other kid was someone I'd never seen. The anger and fury on the kid was scary. He fought the other two kids like a street brawler. Nothing like the two preppy misfits that thought they were thirteen-year-old badasses.

But two on one wasn't fair. I wasn't going to stand around cheering for the kid who was in an unfair fight like the rest of the overprivileged heathens. So I grabbed Richie Lerner by the collar of his shirt, pulling him out of the fight. I flung him to the ground then stood my lanky body over him. Although I wasn't as lanky as most of the kids here because I also learned if I was going to continue drawing the ire of all the boyfriends of the school, then I needed some meat on me to handle myself.

Richie attempted to get up, but my fist connecting with his nose kept him down. Without the two on one disadvantage, the new kid made quick work of Josh McFarland. I watched as he stood over the other boy, blood dripping from his nose, bruises already forming on his cheek, panting with a look of war in his deep hazel eyes.

And his spirit called to me, like kindred souls meeting for the first time. I recognized the pain in his eyes. I felt the anguish that he harbored in his heart but refused to show the rest of the world.

He looked over to me with a nod and a bloody smirk.

124

The first time I met Ryder Jamison would be forever ingrained in my mind. From that point on, we became as inseparable as two people could be. It didn't hurt that he was also my apartment mate that year and every year after.

We bonded over many things. Our fucked up childhood—or the parts I shared anyway—our love of music and the rage and the pain we both endured. Even when we said nothing for hours, just plucked away at our guitars, we felt at peace.

We even began sharing breaks. We went home with each other for holidays and summers. I'd finally had that friend I'd always wanted. Someone who got me without me needing to explain a thing. He just knew.

And Ryder was there for another fucked up day in my life when we were in Louisiana for Christmas break our freshmen year.

Journal entry #5

December 2008-March 2010

This time, Dad sent a driver to pick me up from the airport with the excuse of working late. Chris wasn't coming home from Texas Tech this break with the excuse of finals. Truth is, I think he just didn't want to be there. His trips home were getting less frequent every year.

When we walked through the heavy oak doors, voices carried throughout the house, angry and resentful. I froze with my arm thrown across Ryder's chest to halt his movements.

I recognized my Dad's voice, as well as his new wife. He'd married Callie's nanny, much to my displeasure the spring before.

But the third voice was one I hadn't heard in a few years. One I'd missed but knew better than to mention.

"You're a fucking asshole, Trey!" she yelled out in a high-pitched shriek. "I have a right to be here."

"I'm not having this discussion with you again, Jewel. You don't have rights within this family. You had privileges that you lost because you couldn't keep your fucking nose clean."

"Maybe you should both calm down," I heard Jamie say softly as I slowly made my way to the kitchen. Each step felt like I was walking to my doom, but I couldn't stop myself. In my heart, I knew something was about to shake my world. Rip apart everything I thought I knew. Something that had been niggling at me for years. Since the last conversation I'd overheard between my dad and my aunt.

"I am calm," my dad said, and I could tell his teeth were clenched tightly. *"I have to protect my son. Even if that means protecting him from family."*

"Protect him?" Jewel laughed an unbelieving, sarcastic sound. *"You ship him off for months at a time, and you want me to believe you're protecting him?"*

"That's exactly what I'm doing. I send him away because of you. Because you never listen. I knew you'd come around eventually, and every time you do, he gets hurt."

"When has he ever been hurt? When have I ever hurt him?"

"He almost died *because of you!"* Dad booms like thunder. *"If you hadn't been so fucking wasted, you would've noticed he'd slipped off. If I hadn't come home when I did, he would've drowned."*

"Are you going to punish me forever, Trey? It was a mistake. He's fine now."

"Fine? Are you kidding? He hasn't been fine since that day. No. You're not staying. You're not getting another chance to hurt him. I have to protect my son."

"He's my *son, Trey. I have a right—"*

"You have no rights! You forfeited those rights the day you dropped him off at my doorstep and vanished! You left him without so much as a second thought, and Amanda and I had to take care of a newborn that was going through fucking withdrawals. You couldn't even be bothered to take him to the damn hospital."

I couldn't have stopped the gasp that escaped my lips if I had wanted to. The entire room began spinning, and I thought the floor under my feet was about to collapse. My eyes darted back and forth between my dad's suddenly ghostly face and Jewel's smirk.

126

"Maddox," my dad breathed, and for the first time in what felt like forever, I wasn't subjugated to his harsh glares of disappointment but a look of absolute terror and remorse.

"What did you say?" I asked, my voice cracking with each word as tears threatened. But I knew better than to let one fall.

"Madsy, I'm your real mom," Jewel said with excitement. Like the revelation would send me straight into her arms.

I shook my head, backing away slowly.

"Maddox, you—you're my son, Maddox. Always have been. Always will be," my dad said as he walked toward me. "You are my blood, even if I didn't create you."

I couldn't hear this. No. I didn't want to think about what it meant. Because what it meant was that my momma was not really my mother. It meant the woman who made me feel like the most important person in the world didn't really belong to me.

It also meant my dad had never actually been mine either. I was just a souvenir of how his sister fucked up her life. Because I knew if Jewel was my mom, she couldn't have been more than fifteen or sixteen when she had me.

Jewel had always been a train wreck. She ran away the first time when she was thirteen, only to do it again when she was brought home. She went to rehab five times before she was twenty-one. She disappeared for weeks at a time, with no one knowing if she were dead or alive.

Then I understood why my dad couldn't look at me most of the time. I was the reminder of her mistakes and the burden left behind for my dad to take care of. Another mistake for him to have to clean up.

I bumped into a post about the time my dad reached me. He grabbed each side of my face, forcing me to look at him, but I couldn't see him. I couldn't see anything but the millions of thoughts running through my head. So many things made sense now. Why I was always so different from Chris, and Callie too. Neither one of them seem to have the issues I did. They were normal.

127

"Maddox, look at me," my dad demanded, and for the first time in what felt like ever, my dad was actually looking at me too. "This does not change anything. Do you understand me? Breathe, Maddox."

My eyes finally focused on him as I tried to do what he said. I focused on his words and not on what felt like fifteen years of rejection.

But it all finally made sense. I was the fuck up, always causing problems for him. I was the reason his wife died. I was the constant reminder of his baby sister that he'd tried to help so many times over the years, only to be disappointed over and over.

"Trey, let him go. Come on, Madsy. You can come with me now."

Dad whirled around to face her, keeping himself between us. "Have you lost your mind? He isn't going anywhere with you."

"Don't you think that's up to him now?" she said with a smile. Like she thought the world was that simple.

"No, Jewel, it's not up to him. He's fifteen years old. He's not going anywhere with you."

"You can't control him any more than you could control me, Trey. Give it up."

I'd moved from behind my dad to stand closer to Ryder. I needed to be near someone I could trust. Someone I knew wouldn't fuck me over.

But Jewel was deranged. Truly deranged. Not because of anything she said, but because she believed it.

She reached for me, I suppose, in an attempt to get a hug. I really don't know.

"Don't touch me," I belted out as I jumped away from her.

Her face fell, for the first time realizing that her big reveal didn't have the effect she wanted. "Madsy, I'm your mom."

"No," I spat. "My mom died. You're the aunt that forgot about me at the zoo. You're the woman that tried to sell me off to her drug dealer."

128

"Excuse me," Dad blurted out in shock.

I turned to look at him with anger and frustration. "Momma tracked her down just as she was making the hand-off."

"Don't be so dramatic, Maddox. I wasn't actually going to do it."

"I was eight," I bit out. "I didn't understand it then, but I sure as fuck do now."

My dad looked like he was about to explode, but I was done. I couldn't stay in there with them any longer. My only option, though, was to go upstairs to my room.

"You okay, mate?" Ryder asked, that British accent full and thick and on display.

"Not really," I answered truthfully. "I don't know what to do with any of this, Ry."

"I don't reckon there's much to do with it. It bloody sucks, that's for sure."

I lay on my bed, looking up at the ceiling while he sat in the chair across my room, plucking at the strings of my guitar. The one Jewel gave me.

Dark thoughts swirled around in my mind, getting heavier with each passing minute. The burden I was to everyone never seemed more real. I was such an inconvenience to Jewel, she couldn't be bothered to keep me. Hell, apparently, she couldn't even be bothered to stop using while she was pregnant. I wondered if that's why I was such a damn mess.

I was a burden to my dad. Although, technically, I guess he was my uncle. He'd taken on raising a kid that wasn't his. A kid that caused him more headaches than a person should have. From withdrawals as a newborn to staying in trouble at school. Because lately, it was more than just a little disruptive behavior. He was doling out money left and right to make sure I didn't get expelled for fighting. If he found out about the rest, boarding school would've been the least of my worries.

129

I wondered who my biological dad was. Did he know about me and not want me too? Was he some random hookup of Jewel's? Or worse, was I the result of how she paid for her drugs during that time in her life?

My stomach began to churn violently, and my heart started racing. I wondered what the point was. All I'd been was a nuisance my entire life. A constant inconvenience and burden to all those around me. When I left there after the break, all I would have was a fucking school where I was fucking raped by the person in charge of my mental health, a bunch of kids who cared more about my last name and what I stood to inherit one day, and Ryder.

I loved Ryder, but I couldn't keep it up anymore.

CHAPTER FIFTEEN

Your day will come

Journal cont...

I spent a week in the hospital that break. A few days of it was strapped to a bed. They wanted me to talk about my feelings and shit. That wasn't happening, so I began tossing out bullshit. I didn't like manipulating people, but I knew the right things to say to get them to let me go. I also blew a lot of smoke up their asses. I heard the doctor tell my dad that I was attention-seeking and questioned him about several things. I also heard the word narcissist thrown out a time or two as well.

Even if it was my own fault they said it, that one stung.

I felt bad. I felt bad that Ryder found me. Ryder has stuck with me through everything. All I've ever been able to offer in return is the same courtesy. But it's a courtesy I know he's grateful for because he's been through some fucked up shit too.

I also felt guilty that my dad, once again, had to deal with my shit. That I'd disappointed him, God only knows how many times.

But mostly. I felt bad that it didn't work.

couldn't. If I was breathing, I had to go back. For Ryder. There was no way I was letting Murphey O'Dell anywhere near him.

The first few weeks back, I barely left the apartment. My routine was class and my room, my room and class. I sat in the dark day in and day out with nothing but the new Fender my dad bought me for Christmas. I tried to write new music, but nothing would come to me. So I simply played what I already knew.

Ryder spent nearly all of his free time with me. It wasn't fair to him but fuck if I didn't appreciate it.

"There's a party going on at Preston's place. His parents are in Greece for—well, who knows how long, but they're not home." We sat back to back on my bed in the dark, playing our guitars. I played a piece of a song, and where I dropped, he'd play a piece of a different song that started with the same chord. Sometimes we'd add our own twist or a different style, but Ryder and I played together like it's what we were born to do.

"Not feeling it Ry." I strummed out a few bars with a heavy sigh. He wanted to go, but he didn't want to leave me. He hated leaving me. Not that I could blame him. I knew he was scared that he'd walk in and find I'd finished the job back in River City, but it wasn't fair to him. "I think you should go. You don't have to stay just because I'm here. I'll be okay. I swear."

"No, you won't." A dark chuckle fills the air. I can feel the muscles in his back tighten against mine. "I'm not going without you, but I think we should go. You need something besides these four walls in the dark."

"Why? Me and these four walls have become very good friends," I joked.

"Mads," he sighed heavily.

I leaned my head back against his with my eyes closed tight. "All right, Ry. I'll go," I told him.

Soon as we got there, I hit the liquor and the X. If I had to be there, I wanted whatever it took to make me feel like I was anywhere else. It wasn't a huge party. Preston Montgomery-Wilkes was an elitist, and if your last name didn't mean you were automatically a multimillionaire by birth, he didn't have time for you. So his guest list was always on the small side.

Unless you were a tall, leggy blond exchange student from Germany that spoke very little English. Preston had been after her since she appeared at the beginning of the semester.

But when I locked eyes with her that night, I knew it wasn't Preston who would get her. She wanted Ryder and me. Soon as we entered the room, her eye-fucking began. The next morning, I woke up with my legs tangled with both of theirs.

That was the first time Ryder and I shared. It wouldn't be the last, but that's what opened the door to our very unique relationship.

I didn't go home at all that year. Instead, I went with Ryder. My dad argued at first, so his sudden change of heart made me believe Jewel was still around. Spring break and summer, we stayed with his grandfather, who took us and Ryder's sister, Rayna, to Australia with him while he was there on business. That summer, we both fell in love with surfing. Every waking moment was spent in the water.

Come Christmas break, my dad was resigned. He didn't ask me to come home. I supposed my stunt scared him enough that he didn't want to push.

We spent that Christmas with Ryder's mom and stepdad. His grandfather was away on business again, so there wasn't much choice. A few nights into our stay, his mother hosted a Christmas party. I was shocked at the indulgence of it. My family could be over the top at times. It was always for appearances—to promote the Masters' name and brand, but what his mother put on was insane. Gold and crystal were everywhere. She even boasted the ornaments were 24 karats and handmade by the designers of her father's company. It was gaudy, in my opinion, but I was sixteen, so what did I know?

I learned that night that Ryder's mother was possibly one of the worst human beings on the planet. She didn't deserve to have kids. Especially not Ryder and Rayna.

She spent the entire night putting them down every chance she got, but always when she thought no one was looking. When all eyes were on them, they were beautiful reflections of the hard work she'd put in as their mother.

At some point, I watched as she berated Rayna to the point of tears then proceeded to slap her hard across the face. Ryder was beside himself. He yelled and threatened his mother until she said something that made him

133

stop. To this day, I don't know what that something was, but with blazing fury in his eyes and fists clenched by his side, he walked away.

I followed a few minutes later. I heard Rayna's soft sobs and paused at her door to knock. I tapped lightly, asking that she let me in, but after several minutes of no response, I gave up. I understood what it was to want to be left alone.

I entered Ryder's room to the thundering sound of destruction. He'd taken one of his guitars and used it as a weapon against everything. Glass was shattered. The drywall was damaged. The guitar was in pieces.

The anger gave way to defeat when he saw me, and he crumpled on the bed. I sat next to him in silence. Neither of us moved or said a word for the longest time until he decided to break it. "You're not the only one with family issues, Mads," he told me sadly.

"Never thought I was, Ry. My problems just go beyond the familial. I'm the one that's fucked up."

"You're not fucked up, Mads. You're you."

He looked over at me, and I swear he saw through me. Right to my soul. And I saw him too. We were both so damaged and broken on the inside even though the world saw us as perfectly untouchable.

We'd both developed a reputation for being trouble. But the rich sort. Tabloids and paparazzi wanted to catch us at every turn. Of course, it hadn't been hard lately. We were always in some sort of trouble that my dad had to get us out of, but Dad didn't complain. I knew I was treading thin ice, but I was determined to push it as far as I could.

But at that moment, there were no flashing cameras. No audience. It was just two very lost, lonely, broken boys that felt each other's pain in ways no one would ever understand.

We just stared at each other. It could've been seconds, minutes, or hours. I had no idea. Then he crushed his mouth to mine in a kiss like I'd never experienced. It wasn't passion or fire or heat. It was dark and tormented, much like my soul.

When he pulled back, I didn't say anything, but I tilted my head in question, waiting on him to explain. "I'm sorry if that was weird."

"Not weird. Unexpected."

He nodded and blew out a breath. When it came to sex, Ryder and I were both gender blind. Some had referred to us as pansexual, but we hated being labeled as anything. We were just us.

But we'd never gone there with each other.

He gripped my head, leaning until our foreheads touched. "I want to fuck you."

All the hairs on my neck stood on end, and I closed my eyes. For a brief moment, my mind revolted. But when I opened my eyes, I knew my answer. "Only if I get to fuck you too," I told him with my lips pressed in a thin tight line.

Within moments, clothes were gone, and so were any boundaries or inhibitions between us. Secrets remained, and they always would. But we were as close as any two people could be, sharing our battles and our demons in a way that two teenagers shouldn't even comprehend because nothing about it could've been construed as gentle lovemaking. He was the first and only person I've ever willingly let inside me, even if it was brutal.

Soon after, we returned to school early. We spent much of it at every party we could. Getting drunk and high had become my favorite pastime, along with fucking anything and everything that moved. It was how I coped with O'Dell.

He'd been drawn to Ryder for a while and didn't hesitate to taunt me with him. I had to protect him, so I offered myself as a sacrifice to the sadistic motherfucker to keep him away from my best friend. But he'd gotten extremely more aggressive with his demands, and his blackmail knew no bounds. I didn't mind the physical pain. It kept my mind off of the mental agony each encounter left on me. But the aftermath was a little worse each time. Either my anger would grow, or I'd withdraw into myself. I was a mess of emotions that were getting harder and harder to control.

The tipping point came just before spring break. Ryder and some other guy had gotten into a horrible fight over the other guy's girlfriend. Dudes were funny about their girlfriends. Never seemed to have the sense to know they're the ones spreading their legs. Although, there were also a few girls that would quickly claim force. Ryder and I made sure to keep far away from those psychopaths.

But the counselor wanted him to see O'Dell for anger issues. I lost sleep for days over that. I knew what would happen if Ryder went into that office. Not only did I not want him to suffer the torment I'd been suffering for three years, I didn't want him to find out about me.

I just didn't know what I could do to stop it. I wracked my brain for days with no solutions.

Finally, the day of Ryder's appointment, I went to O'Dell's office. I planned on offering myself in hopes of satiating the man's disgusting need for underage boys.

As I reached the door, feeling cold, numb, and dirty, he called out to me. "I sure hope Ryder is as satisfying as you are, Maddox."

Livid fury burned in my chest as I spun on my heels. I couldn't see anything but red. I crossed the room in three long strides, grabbing the puny, pudgy man by the lapels of his suit. I planted him on his desk in one quick motion and began to pound his face with my fist.

He begged and pleaded and cried, but I didn't care about his wailing and moaning. I just continued to hammer, inflicting every ounce of acrid rage that had been building inside for years on his face and body. Blood flew, cartlidge crunched, flesh broke as I delivered my punishment.

The doors flew open, and hands grabbed me, pulling me off the man. I think I heard someone yell to call an ambulance, but I couldn't be sure.

I turned to see Ryder standing in the door, a look of total disbelief on his face as he looked to O'Dell and then back to me. He didn't know. He would never know. But I did it all for him. I would never let anyone hurt him the way they hurt me.

An hour later, I was taken into custody by the police. When my father showed up that night, he was irate, demanding to know what had gotten into me.

"I did what needed to be done," I told him with my chin tilted up.

For the first time, the look of disappointment in his eyes didn't hurt. I didn't care who was disappointed in me. I didn't feel even the slightest bit guilty that Murphey O'Dell would need reconstructive surgery and therapy for months.

But I did feel guilty for one thing. That he was still breathing, and I vowed to myself that one day, I would rectify that problem.

CHAPTER SIXTEEN

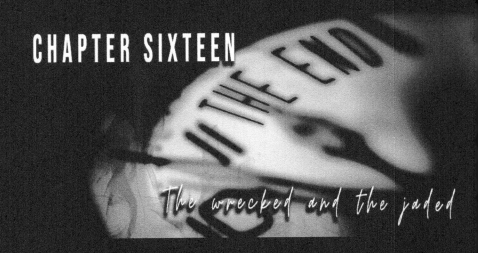

The wrecked and the jaded

Present Day

I look over everything I've written with a sigh. The urge to rip it all out strikes again. Not like anyone will actually see this. It's just another fabrication my brain has conjured that keeps me from leaving this place. Because I quite literally cannot make myself move on from here.

Maybe somewhere deep inside, I'm hoping Bastian does show up. That he drags my ass, kicking and screaming all the way back to River City.

All the way back to the girl I am missing so much it hurts. It's been a couple of days since I left, and my already broken heart keeps breaking. I just keep reminding myself it's for the best. Not like she would want me now anyway. Not after what I said. And the idea of being near her but not having her is like swallowing a vat of acid. It's burning me up from the inside out.

She's not the only one I've hurt these past few weeks. I may have spoken to Ryder before I left, but I've been avoiding him and everyone else for weeks. I know they're worried about me, and I don't mean to add to that worry. I've just—I didn't want to see their worry and pity. I didn't want them to see the truth. That I'm not any better now than I was before.

And Zoey. I never meant to hurt her. I've caused her enough pain over the years. I've hurt her more times than I can count, but I just couldn't see her. I didn't want to look in her eyes and see the fear I knew would be there.

But, of fucking course, Jax—fucking Jax—ever her protector and defender couldn't leave it alone. She sheds a tear, and he's ready to blast the world. I don't blame him. I really don't. How could I when I feel the same way? But this time, I needed her to stay away. I just couldn't see or talk to her. My head just wasn't there.

I was also not in the mood for Jax. He and I had an uneasy alliance of sorts. He knew how I felt about Zoey and how she felt about me. We had a connection he didn't understand but tried to accept. Just like I accepted she was and would always be his. Something I'd known probably from the moment I met her.

But there was always this underlying tension between the two of us. Neither of us fully trusted the other for a long damn time, but we co-existed for her.

Then he had to blow it all out of the water with his damn hot head. And Jax didn't know it, but I was not in the mood for his bullshit. For the first time in over a decade, I had no intentions of being his punching bag, verbal or otherwise.

But that wasn't all he accomplished that day. I denied it to myself, but that was the day I fell for the girl.

Seven weeks ago

"Oh, God!" Quinn erupts on my tongue for the third time that afternoon. I grinned as I lapped every drop she offered to me. Like a sacrifice of milk and honey. "Please, no more."

I crawl up her tight little body, my grin still firmly in place. Her wild curls sprawl out on the pillow like a messy halo, and sweat beads on her flushed face as she fights to catch her breath.

I drop my mouth to her in a long, sensuous kiss, allowing her to taste her bliss on my lips. The head of my cock teases her entrance, making her writhe beneath me. She says no more, but since the moment she came on my hand, the little siren has been insatiable.

"Masters," a deep voice carries through the renovated warehouse on a boom.

Quinn's eyes grow wide with worry and fear. It pisses me off because who the fuck does he think he is?

"Wh—who is that?" her voice quakes with worry.

"Just a pain in my ass." I kiss her lips one more time before I crawl from the bed. I snatch my sweats off the floor, pulling them on as I leave the room. "Don't fucking move from there," I tell her before I walk out. "We're not done."

"Masters!" the fucking asshole yells out again.

"What?" I demand as I walk into the main living area where Jax and Zane stand with arms crossed, waiting on me.

"Jesus, Maddox, you could've handled that first." Zane gestures to my crotch with a grin.

Fucking clown. Zane and I had issues for a while too, but those issues are in the past. We get along fine.

"Well, I was planning on doing just that before someone burst in, uninvited, I might add, bellowing my name like a fucking bear," I taunt Jax with a smirk. His shoulders heave and nostrils flare. I almost expect him to start pawing the ground, preparing to charge. I haven't even started waving the red cape yet. "What the hell do you think I've done now?" I direct the question to both of them.

"Not me," Zane grins as he leans against the sofa. "I'm just here because Zoey thinks I can control him. She's the one who sucks his dick, not me. Though he knows I wouldn't mind." Zane waggles his brows like a damn fool, and I laugh because it only pisses Jax off some more.

"Shut the fuck up, Zee," he grunts.

"Always so *en colaire*, Jax. Always hangin' a *bahbin*. Maybe you should try smilin' once in a while." Now I wave the red right in front of him, knowing he has no clue what I've just said. But I also know he has an idea. It's also so far beyond how we've been with each other for the last few years, it throws him off a bit.

"Cut the shit, Maddox."

I've taken every beating he's dished out for years because I believed I had it coming. I still do. That will probably never change. But I've been miserable for a long time. Anxiety, guilt, pain, fear, worry—they grow and fester if you don't deal with them. Mine morphed into anger and frustration, and self-destruction a long time ago. And I'm tired. I'm tired of it all, but today, I'm tired of everyone trying to run my life for me.

I will admit, though, there has been one bright spot in all of this. Hell, probably the brightest spot in years, and she's in my temporary bed, naked under my sheets, waiting for me, while I'm out here with a throbbing dick, talking to a cranky giant and his way too laid back cohort. I don't feel like being the dog he kicks today.

Besides, I know why he's here, but I'm not talking to Zoey. She's like Ryder. Maybe not quite as in tune with me as he is. That comes from being together practically every day for nearly two decades. But we still have this inexplicable connection. No matter how often or little we see each other, that connection never wanes. Not even during the time she tried to hate me.

I love Zoey. I have always believed I would never love another, but it's not a love I can't live without. Because as much as it hurts, I have lived without her. As much as it ripped me to pieces, I've willingly watched her live her life with Jax and their kids. As long as she is part of my life in some capacity, I'll be okay. Mostly. Sure, I've gone on some pretty serious benders after being around her, but for a little while, just seeing her smile, I'm happy.

And it's for all those reasons and more that I can't see or talk to her any more than the others. They may not know everything about me, all the parts I've kept hidden, but they know me. They know what's important, and they'll see through the bullshit that I'm getting better. They'll know I'm just as fucked up as I ever was.

Which is why I intend on pushing Jax's last buttons. Maybe if I do that, he'll keep Zoey away.

"And what shit is that, Jax?" I walk past him with an eye roll to the fridge. I grab a carton of orange juice and a glass from the cabinet, then pour myself a drink.

I turn to see him rolling his neck from side to side. The muscles in his jaw flex as he clenches his teeth, and his fists are balled tightly at his side. One

141

thing I've never doubted is that Jax McCabe will raze the world for Zoey. Even when we were kids, that day at the zoo, I knew. I could see it then, and I can see it now.

But he's trying to contain his animosity for her sake. "Call her," he grits out. "You've been here for weeks. You won't see her, so just fucking call her."

"I thought you'd be ecstatic that I left her alone." I raise a brow, challenging him to deny.

And the fucker does just that. "Why would I want that, jackass? I know you two share some sort of bond. Why would I be happy that you're hurting her? Again. I want to fucking kill you every time she cries, but I want you to call her."

A knot forms in my chest, knowing she's crying over me. I'm not worth her tears. But I keep my face neutral and my tone emotionless. "I'm not calling her," I tell him as I turn up the glass, driving home that I don't care. The bittersweet liquid does nothing to wash away the guilt and lies from my soul.

"What the hell is wrong with you?" he bellows loudly. "I thought you cared about Zoey, but I guess you really are a narcissistic, self-centered bastard. You don't care about anyone but yourself."

And a switch flips. He hasn't said anything I haven't thought about myself. He isn't saying anything that I haven't heard before. But for some reason, hearing him say it sets something off inside me. Anger because Jax doesn't know a thing about me. He's never tried to know anything except maybe what Zoey has told him.

"What's the matter, Jax?" I ask as a devilish smile forms on my lips. One I don't remember permitting, along with the words I'm about to say. It's like an out-of-body experience. I'm watching myself as I unleash verbal venom that is meant to inflict the harshest pain and incite the fiercest rage. Also knowing, if he tells her, it will hurt her deeply. But I cannot stop it. "You got the girl and the kids. You have the happily ever after. It shouldn't bother you that I got all her firsts. That my dick was in her mouth, cunt, and ass before you grew the balls to make a move. I popped every cherry she could imagine and then invented a few more. She was a good little slut for me. Pretty sure she'd go for another round too. What do you say, Jax? Want to tag team that pretty little ass? She sure did like it when it was Ryder and me. Don't think I've ever heard anyone scream as loud as she did."

I know what they mean by hell in his eyes because it's all right there in Jax's dark ones. They blaze with the fire of a thousand suns—yeah, that's the best analogy I can come up with right now, sue me. Zane stands straight with a string of muttered curses looking back and forth between the two of us.

But none of that is where my attention is. If I didn't wish I could stop the uttered garbage that slipped from my lips before, I sure as hell do now as I stare into whiskey eyes that are full of confusion and disappointment. I'm so focused on her I don't see the fist coming from the six-and-a-half-foot quarterback until it lands on my jaw, knocking me backward.

I've felt the power behind Jax McCabe's right hook more times than I can count. Fuck, if every time doesn't hurt more than the last. Good thing I enjoy physical pain almost as much as I like cocaine and sex, and I'm still not happy that he ruined my fun times earlier. Even less happy that after my verbal vomit, it's probably finished for good.

But in all these years, I've never fought back. I shouldn't fight back now. Not after what I said. And definitely not after the gasp from the girl standing in the corner.

As always, I logically know that she would probably think better if I just stayed down and took what Jax dealt. It might earn me back a few points after hearing what she did. But logic isn't motivating me. Aware or not, it seldom does.

When my fist connects, the satisfying crunch beneath my knuckles makes me grin. I've been waiting to do this for over ten years. If I'm going to do it, I'm going to fucking enjoy it.

Jax is stunned for a minute, probably from shock that I hit him back. But it lasts less than a breath before we are both swinging like two prizefighters. I connect with his face. He lands a hard shot to my ribs. I feel the cartilage of my nose crunch as I connect with his kidney.

Blow after blow, we are relentless. Furniture gets broken. Pictures fall from the walls. There is no fancy footwork. No elaborate grappling for kicks. Just flesh on flesh. Blood pours and flies and bones break. Neither of us backing down. Until we're both pulled away and pushed to a corner.

Bastian stands in front of me while Rory blocks Jax's path. Blood runs down Jax's face from his cut eyebrow and nose. Dark bruises are already forming beneath the nasty swelling. I'm certain my face is as bad as his.

"Had enough yet, Jax?" I spit out the blood in my mouth on the floor. "Not the same when I hit back, is it?"

With teeth bared, he moves quickly past Rory, only to catch the heel of Bastian's boot to his stomach, making him fall to a knee. "Stay there," Bastian growls when Jax starts to get up.

Jax's eyes narrow with a challenge as he continues to his feet. When we both start for each other again, the slide action of a gun halts us. "If either of you moves, I will shoot you both," Rory grunts.

The gasp from across the room catches the attention of everyone. "*Che cazzo.* What are you doing here, Quinn?" Bastian asks before leveling me with a dirty look.

I roll my eyes at him, then turn my attention back to Quinn, who is wrapped firmly in Zane's arm. Her long bare legs dangle inches above the floor as she squirms against him. My eyes travel up to see her wearing my old Nine Inch Nails t-shirt, and I'm betting nothing else.

A strange possessiveness rolls over me like a tidal wave, nearly knocking the breath out of me as I take in her wild, whiskey eyes and unruly curls that say she's been doing a lot more than sleeping. I bite the inside of my cheek to keep myself from demanding he stop touching her.

"I don't know why women always want to protect you," Zane drawls thickly. "And always the little, bitty things with the pretty eyes." He tilts his head to the side with an arched brow and a cocky, knowing grin.

Jax growls, inciting a smack to the head from Rory as I choke back my own guttural response. "Enough, Jax," his brother tells him.

"He had it coming," Jax barks out in argument.

"I don't care." Bastian slices his hands through the air dramatically. "What I care about is your damn wife calling me while I'm in the middle of business." He points at Jax with narrowed eyes. "In hysterics, no less, with kids screaming in the background, to tell me you are on your way to my house. I would ask why, but it's pretty obvious you can't let the damn past go."

144

Jax slaps his hand away from his face then gets chest to chest with Bastian. "She's been upset for days because he's a selfish asshole," he accuses. "I can't sit back and do nothing. He can, at least, call her and tell her to leave him alone."

Bastian looks at the space between him and Jax, or lack thereof. A dangerous smile forms on his face as he looks up to Jax, who stands a few inches over him. He stands a few inches over everyone in the damn room.

"Bastian, don't," Rory calls out in warning, but I'm pretty sure it's Jax he's warning.

"Get your brother to back off before I end his career." Bastian's smile never drops, and his eyes never waver from Jax's.

"You know I'm not afraid of you, Bastian," Jax says with his own sick smile. "Never have been."

"You've never had a reason before, but I might need to give you one."

"That's enough," Rory yells as he pushes them apart. "Jax, grow up. You know if he'd done what you said, you'd still be right here."

"Can't believe you're letting him come between us," Jax hisses at Bastian.

"I'm not letting anything come between us. He's my brother. Just because you didn't know that doesn't change the fact. Or the fact that I take care of my family, which you are part of. And for the record, he hasn't talked to anyone since he's been here. Fair or not, it's how he wants to handle things for now."

I don't show it, but I'm more than a little stunned at Bastian's defense of me. We may be blood, but Jax is more of a brother to him than I'll ever be.

"He's going through hell," he continues. "If he wants to do that without his friends witnessing it, so be it."

"Nobody forced him to be a junkie," Jax sneers in my direction.

His words don't affect me. He's right. No one forced me to stick a needle in my arm. But Bastian isn't quite so forgiving. "Lotta big talk considering your wife is an addict, Jax."

Jax's eyes flare with anger again, but this time it isn't him who responds. I've watched this tennis match play back and forth. Listening to them talk about me like I'm not even in the room. I don't care, but… "Don't talk about her like that," I snap.

There is one obvious difference between Zoey and me. She's clean and has been for years.

"Want me to enlighten you to when he fell off the wagon?" Bastian continues like I never said a word.

I go rigid. He doesn't know that. Does he? He can't possibly know, but I don't want to take a chance either. "Bastian, shut up," I warn with a hiss.

He turns around to face me. I silently plead for him to keep quiet. He knows. I can see it in his eyes, but I don't want him saying it. Not now. Not ever. "Always playing the asshole," he shakes his head in disapproval. "All your secrets are what's eating you alive, Maddox."

"But they're my secrets. Mine to carry. Mine to share." My jaw sets, and my lips press into a thin line, but my heart begins to pound as my mind begins to race with the beginnings of a panic attack.

"Get out, Jax," Bastian tells him.

"You're kidding, right?" Jax shouts with surprise.

"I brought him here to help him. Not to fight with you or be made to feel guilty because Zoey is upset. Until he's ready to see her, don't come back."

"This is ridiculous," Jax yells again.

I watch as Rory pushes him toward the elevator gate. "Go, Jax. He's right, and you're out of line."

If this were any other time, I'd want the image of Jax's absolutely dumbfounded face framed, but all I want to do is get out of this room before they see me in a full-blown panic attack because I can feel it coming.

I leave them all standing there, still arguing. I walk into my room, slamming the door behind me. For a minute, I consider leaving. Packing all my shit and walking out the front door.

Bastian can't keep me here. Not really. Well, unless he takes me back to the basement.

Sebastian Delrie may be the boogeyman to some of the more unsavory people in River City, but the truth is, he's only scary if you are a degenerate piece of shit or if you double-cross him. And even then, only if you fear pain or death.

Most days, I welcome both. He knows it too, and that's why I frustrate him. He can't intimidate me into falling in line.

But I won't leave. Not yet. I may not want to be in this city, but I'm not ready to go back to New York. To the smiling, worried faces of my family. I'm sure as hell not going to my dad's. And I don't want to be alone.

Bastian is my best option.

I sit on the bed, head hanging low between my shoulders, hands pulling hard on the back of my neck. What does Bastian know? Did Ryder and Dane tell him about when I started using again? Did they tell him what happened after? What else does he know?

Panic makes my throat begin to close as I begin to imagine. Does he know about... Oh, God!

I slide to the floor as my heart hammers. I fall to my side, clawing at my throat and chest, trying to rip the constriction out until I am unable to do anything but succumb to the paralyzing anxiety I know won't kill me, but I wish would.

The voices scream loudly, tormenting me with every dark thought I've ever had or heard. The reminder that I'm a monster—evil taunts me as my body shakes. My vision blurs as the memories and dreams dance in my mind. Even my fucking skin crawls with memories of unwanted touch.

Then a soft humming fills my ears. It's low—so low I miss some of the notes. Still, the melody of "Fix You" is clear, surrounding me like a warm, heavy blanket, and the haunting memories of my past morph into the first time I heard that song.

I was thirteen, and it had been a bad day, as most were at that age. I had a small radio in my dorm room, playing music, hoping it would help me forget the day, week, and the last year. My mind was bogged down with the desperate desire to just fade away into nothingness when the song came on. It wasn't the type of music I gravitated to then or now, but the words resonated as I imagined my momma singing it to me. And it helped me that day.

147

Just like now. Her voice cracks with nervousness and fear, but with every note, it becomes more clear and vibrant. Her sweet, soulful voice soothes my tattered spirit, and I finally feel like I can breathe.

I turn my head to see Quinn kneeling next to me on the bed. I only imagined crawling to the floor, unable to move. I've been in this spot the entire time.

She rubs my back in slow, sure circles as she continues to hum. Even as her cheeks flush, she continues to hum the song. Her eyes stay firmly latched to mine with a quiet confidence and warmth that I feel in my bones.

"You're singing," I croak out, my throat still tight from the attack.

"I'm humming." Her cheeks brighten more as she ducks her head.

I tip her chin back up so I can see in those mesmerizing eyes and brush the hair from her face. "You're splitting hairs."

"You said it helps. I get it. It's why I became a music therapist. I know music helps. I also know panic attacks suck. You looked like you were having a bad one."

I release her with a frown, dragging my hand down my face with a groan. "Everyone is a bad one." And every fucking one drains me for days. It's part of why I fell in love with cocaine. "I didn't know you were a music therapist." I'm not sure where I thought she went every day, but I assumed she had another job. I just didn't guess it was music-related.

Although, if anyone understands the power of a song—of a melody, it's me.

She shrugs her shoulders with a smile. "I can play instruments in front of people. I just can't sing."

She climbs off the bed, I assume, to leave. Good deed done and all.

But she surprises me when she grabs my hand, pulling me to my feet. She leads me into the bathroom connected to my room. "Sit," she commands firmly as she points to the side of the tub. I raise my brows in surprise at her assertiveness. She rolls her eyes as she begins to rummage through the cabinets. "I know you don't like being told what to do, but do it anyway."

148

I press my lips together tightly to stop a grin because bossy Quinn is cute as hell. Then I do as she asked—told—me. When she turns to see me sitting, she gives a serious but satisfied nod. I hide my looming chuckle behind my hand when she sets the first aid kit next to me, digging through until she finds what she wants.

"You don't have to do this," I tell her, gripping behind her knees when she steps between my legs. "I'm a big boy. I can take care of it myself."

Her eyes meet mine, hard at first but softening with each second that passes. My stomach flips when she gently cups my bruised cheek. "It's okay to let people help you, Maddox. You don't have to be the one to take care of everyone all the time."

My fingers flex against her skin. The urge to push her away is strong, but strangely, the urge to lean on her—let her take care of me—is stronger. The desire to keep her close.

Always a conflict of emotions raging inside of me, never just one thing I can grab hold of. Even though I know I can't keep her, I won't push her away. Not yet. I'm not ready to let her go. But that doesn't mean I won't give her the option to run away. "Did you not just hear me out there? Did that sound like someone who cares about other people? You heard Jax. I'm a selfish asshole."

"Jax was wrong," she tells me with conviction, once again surprising me. "I saw someone trying to push everyone away. You think it's for their own good, right?"

"I'm not that altruistic," I mutter.

"Aren't you?" This girl is blowing my mind. I'm not used to people reading me so easily. Only two people have ever seen beyond the bullshit. But she's also wrong. I'm not protecting them. I'm protecting myself from their pity and worry. "You pretend a lot, Maddox, but I can see how much it bothered you when Jax told you Zoey was upset."

"Which should prove that I'm a selfish bastard. I know it's hurting her, but I still won't talk to her." She needs to see that I'm not a good person. I steal, kill, and destroy everything good.

"It proves that you think cutting the people who care about you off is what's best for them. I don't know why you would think that, but I know that much. Now be still; this might sting."

149

I chuckle at her warning. "Darlin', you've seen me naked. Do I look like a little alcohol will bother me?"

Her nose curls up, and she pokes her tongue out. "I get it, tough guy. You like pain."

"It's a good distraction," I nod as she cleans the cut beneath my eye.

"This needs stitches," she mumbles softly, "but I already know you won't go to a doctor, right?"

"Nope."

She nods with a huff. "I'll use this glue stuff."

I sit quietly as she continues to play nurse. I stroke the skin behind her knees, waiting on her to finish. A strange feeling of not quite peace— contentment maybe—washes over me.

"So, what you said out there? Was it true? You slept with his wife?"

"She wasn't his wife at the time," I grunt with a hard eye roll.

"Well, I would hope you wouldn't sleep with a married wo—" Her sentence drops. Her face has turned ashen as she chews on her cheek.

Her face is always so expressive. It's never hard to tell what she's thinking or feeling. But even if it weren't, it wouldn't be hard to guess where her head just went.

I pull her to my lap, tucking a stray hair behind her ear. I grip her chin firmly, making her look at me when her eyes drop to her hands. A sure tell that she's embarrassed. "No, *cher*, I do not make a habit to fuck married women. I won't say it hasn't happened, but I didn't know it at the time."

"But you are—I mean we—" She stammers over her words, and I can see her embarrassment growing.

I get it. Guilt is a filthy monster that consumes every inch of your mind until you can't breathe. But this girl has nothing to feel guilty about. "Where is he? Your husband?"

"Back in Springfield with his new girlfriend," she says quietly as a tear falls down her cheek.

150

I brush it away with a thumb, then lean my forehead to hers. "You may be married, but only on paper. He is an idiot to have tossed you aside."

"You don't know that. Maybe his new girlfriend is everything I never could be for him. I mean, she's already—" she trails off, leaving me curious about what she was going to say. But I don't ask. If she wanted me to know, she would tell me.

"No, darlin'. I don't have to know his new woman to know he's an idiot. You're beautiful, Quinn. And brave as fuck to leave everything you've known to start over."

"Yeah," she says with bitterness. "So brave, I take my clothes off, so men have something for their spank bank later."

I swallow the putrid vitriol that wants to be unleashed. I may be into exhibitionism on occasion, but the thought of everyone seeing her like that makes me a bit murderous, even if I've been witness to it. But it is not my place or business to say anything to her.

The truth is that's one more way she's brave. She is doing what she needs to do to get on her feet on her terms. I can't fault her for that. Not everyone has access to trust funds and inheritance like I did at her age.

"Yeah, *cher*, that makes you brave too. And what we're doing?" I point between us. "There is nothing wrong with that. You and your husband have filed for divorce. He kicked you out, though why the hell you just left is beyond me, and moved in his new girlfriend. You have nothing to feel guilty about."

"We had an ironclad prenup." She drops her head again. "I was such a stupid kid."

"Did you love him?"

"Yes. I'm not going to cop out and say I didn't. I did love him."

"Do you still love him?" I have no idea why I ask that.

My stomach drops when her eyes glaze over. Suddenly, I want to take the question back. I don't know why, but I do not want to hear her say she still loves the guy. "You don't have to answer that," I blurt out, hoping she won't.

151

"I don't love him as I did," she admits, "but it's not something that just goes away. I have loved him since I was seventeen. But he broke my heart and my trust. Sometimes I think he broke me."

Fuck, this feels weird. Almost like déjà vu but not quite. I feel like a condolence prize, but I know I shouldn't. She's not mine. I'm not hers. We're just having fun for now.

So I deflect. "Maybe a good rebound was just what you needed." I waggle my eyebrows with a forced grin.

"Shut up," she laughs, wiping her tears away. The sound washes some of the tension in my chest away. "Tell me about Zoey. She must be pretty special if you still talk to her after all this time."

This is usually where I throw out a vague statement or two. Cover the entirety of our relationship about how I had her, I fucked it up and lost her, and how I'm still not over her.

But that's not what I want to tell her at all...

CHAPTER SEVENTEEN

Remember the years

Seven weeks ago

"What do you want to know?" I ask her quietly. Talking about my time with Zoey isn't easy. Zoey is proof that I destroy everything. I took a sweet girl and corrupted her as much as I could, then left her for dead.

"I don't know. There must be a reason that you stayed so close."

I chuckle, but there's no humor behind it. "Because Zoey is truly the kindest, warmest, most forgiving person in the world. I fucked up on a supreme level, but she not only forgave me, she let me continue to be part of her life."

"I doubt it was that bad." She gives me an unbelieving, doubtful look.

"I gave her a drink laced with drugs after she told me she didn't want to do them with me that night, and when she started having a bad reaction, I left her."

Her gasp fills the bathroom with an echo. She doesn't say anything, but there's nothing she can say. How do you argue with irrefutable evidence that I'm scum?

"Why would you do that?"

"Anger? Stupidity? I was already trashed out of my mind? It doesn't matter. There's no excuse for it."

"It still doesn't explain a lot. For her to be so upset that you're not talking to her, it can't be that simple. Tell me."

"All right," I sigh. "I'll tell you, but not in here. It's a long story, and this tub is killing my ass."

She stands, taking me by the hand. "My room? I kind of need some pants."

I slide my free hand up her leg, under my shirt to find her bare ass. "Think I like you like this," I grin as I grip a handful.

"Such a romantic." She rolls her eyes sarcastically. "Come on, Romeo. You promised me a story."

She leads me out of the room where Bastian is leaning against the wall with his arms crossed over his chest. "We need to talk," he grunts as he eyes Quinn's and my joined hands.

"Later," I tell him and keep following Quinn.

"Now." He grips my arm with a scowl.

I look at his hand on my arm then at him with a snarl. "No." I shrug out of his grip. "I promised the lady a story. You can wait."

We walk into the room and shut the door behind us.

"You could've talked to him," she says as she grabs a pair of shorts from the dresser.

"I could have, but I didn't want to." I watch as she pulls on the thin cotton over her legs. "I told you I liked you better without them."

She smiles with a shake of her head. "No, sir. I was promised a story. I don't want you to have any distractions."

"You think those little shorts will keep me from getting distracted?" I arch a brow in question.

She ignores me, pulling me to the bed. Climbing onto the bed, she tugs me with her. "Not helping with the distractions, darlin'."

"You're incorrigible. You know that?"

154

"Oh, absolutely. Incorrigible, irredeemable, habitual, reprobate. That's me perfectly." I lean back against her headboard with my hands propped behind my head, waiting to see what she does.

She crawls beside me, curling into my chest. It catches me off guard. Really off guard because once she's there, I realize I don't want her to be anywhere else.

I run my hand through my hair at the thought. I want her, but I can't have her. I can't fall for her, but I think I have. I've fucked up. I've fucked up thoroughly.

My only saving grace is that she hasn't fallen for me. I can take a broken heart, but I can't handle breaking another. It would be inevitable if she did.

"Now tell me the story."

"All right, canary, I'll tell you."

"Canary?" she raises her brows with surprise.

"Yep. You're a tiny, yellow, singing bird. Canary."

"I don't sing."

"You did for me," I remind her of moments ago. The exact moment I fell.

"Don't get used to it, Romeo. It was a one-off because I couldn't stand seeing you suffer. Now tell me the story."

Her words hit me hard. She couldn't stand to see me suffer. If she only knew.

I suppose it's as good a time as any to give her a glimpse into the darkness inside of me.

I start at the beginning, right after returning home from my expulsion. Dad had me on lockdown. He was disappointed in me again, but this time I didn't care. I accepted his disappointment because if I gave him what he wanted, he would've been even more so.

I just couldn't tell him why I beat the shit out of O'Dell. Dad knew something was up. Said until I told him the reason I wasn't allowed to leave the house. I took the punishment, and my dad stopped speaking to me.

155

A few weeks later, I was lying in a hammock in our backyard since I wasn't allowed more than fifty feet from the backdoor with my guitar in hand when a shadow fell over me. I looked up to see a face I hadn't seen in months.

March 2010

"What are you doing here?" I asked.

"What? That's all I get? No, how ya been? Good to see you?" Bryan taunted me with a devious smirk.

"Last time I saw you, I got arrested for trespassing," I grunted. "You know how much hell I caught for that stunt."

"But it was one hell of a party."

"That is was," I nodded, remembering the massive warehouse rave that turned out to be very illegal. "The music was shit."

"But the party favors were the best."

"What do you want, Bryan?" I rolled my eyes even though I silently agreed.

"There's a party on the Island."

"How did you know I was here? How did you even get in here?"

My family's property was two hundred acres with a massive gate and stone wall around the main property that consisted of my grandparents, father, and uncle's homes. To get through, you'd have to drive through the main gate where security would allow entry or climb the wall, which was a bitch. Bryan didn't look like he'd climbed any walls, and I knew my Dad wouldn't let him in. I had to fight to get him to let Ryder in the week before.

"I know things," he winked at me. Bryan always seemed to be around when everything felt like it was going to shit. And it never failed that he would cause more shit to explode. I just couldn't get rid of the guy. I tried, but he always came back like fucking herpes.

"It's fucking weird," I told him as I went back to playing my guitar. "Besides, I'm locked in here like a prisoner. Daddy Norton won't let me have any yard time."

"I'm sure it's going to be insane. I hear Zoey Valen will be there."

I raised a brow. I'd never forgotten the girl from the zoo. I hadn't had the chance to see her again. Not really. I wasn't around enough. But we shared a few friends and had been to a few of the same parties. I'd heard about her, her brother, and her friend. Even saw a few pictures online through social media. She was a knockout, and I'd been dying to get to know her. I never saw much of a point since most of my time was spent in New York.

"What time is this party?" I asked, trying to feign indifference.

"Starts at ten."

"I'll see what I can do," I tell him with a nod. "Now get out of here before my dad sees you, and I'm confined to my room."

"You're dad isn't here."

"Again, how the hell do you know that?"

He shrugs his shoulders with another grin. "Think I'll just go for a swim."

I didn't argue. I didn't have the energy. Bryan exhausted me.

That night, I slipped down the back stairs hoping no one would be there. I knew dad was in his office, but I wasn't sure where Jamie was. I thought she was in bed, but she was also pregnant with my new sister/cousin, so her trips to the kitchen were frequent. As far as they thought, I was locked in my room being broody. I grabbed the keys to the truck my dad bought me (like I was ever around) and made it all the way to the backdoor when a voice called out.

"Thought you were grounded."

I turned around to see Jewel standing in the kitchen with her arms folded across her chest. "Thought you weren't allowed here," I snap.

"I was visiting my mother, and she told me you were here."

"Yep. I'm here. Now you can go."

"Aww, come on, Madsy. I'm your mom."

"No. Fuck no. My mom died six years ago. You? You're just the drug whore that didn't want me."

157

"What do you know about drugs, Madsy?" She reached into her pocket and pulled out a baggy. "Give me five minutes, and you can have it. Ever had coke? I know you do stuff, Maddox? Remember last year? Your drug screen had way more than mine would."

"Why? Why do you want five minutes?"

"I miss you. I always miss you."

I felt bad. I really did. But my anger with her trumped any guilt at the time. "You've got thirty seconds," I snatched the bag from her fingers because even though I hadn't done it before, I wanted something to get me through this party. Without something to take the edge off, parties were always sensory overload for me. I knew there would be alcohol, but I didn't want to be wasted and drive two hours home and knew coke didn't last as long as other stuff.

"I can always tell Trey that you snuck out." She threatened like she was still a teenager herself.

"And I can tell him about this," I waved the bag. "Where else could I get them? I've been under house arrest for weeks. Besides, you told me you'd share all those years ago. Looks like you're sharing."

"I'm not sure I like this version of you, Maddox." Her lips pulled into a frown, and disappointment swam in her eyes.

"Good thing you gave up the right to like any version of me," I spat out like an asshole as I climbed in the truck, praying my dad didn't hear me leave. His office was soundproofed and on the opposite side of the house as the garage and the driveway, but if he heard me, all bets were off.

He didn't hear me, and two hours later, I was pulling up to some person I didn't even know on the Island. Fortunately, it didn't take me long to find a couple of friends. Bryan spotted me before I spotted him.

I wandered around for a while when I spotted her. She was so sexy, but unlike most girls, she didn't flaunt it. She seemed completely oblivious to her beauty. I watched with envy as Jax kept his arm thrown over her shoulder, laughing. I wondered if they were together, considering the way they were. He moved, she moved. She moved, he moved. It was awkward to watch considering I was there to see if I could get her to go out with me.

When he kissed her head, I rolled my eyes and took off for the bathroom. Coke definitely didn't last as long as the other things I'd tried, but I liked the effects a lot more.

When I exited the bathroom, they were in my line of sight, and this time Zane was there too with a girl under each arm. I watched with curiosity as the girls flirted with the two guys and Zoey began to drift into the background.

I'm an idiot. A massive glutton for punishment. A fucking masochist.

Because when the girl pulled Jax away, I saw it. I saw the way Zoey watched him sadly, and I saw the guilt in his eyes as he walked away. It was obvious they wanted to be together.

But for whatever reason, they weren't. That meant I had a chance.

I went to her, rubbing my nose to make sure nothing was left behind, and tapped her on the shoulder. She turned around, and those eyes that looked like lightning against the night sky floored me with how sad they were. I was going to turn on the charm, but with the look on her face, I couldn't do it. "Are you okay?"

A bright smile flashed across her face like she didn't just watch the guy ditch her for another girl. It was probably a convincing act for most people, but I knew a thing or two about wearing masks. Plus, I could feel her sadness. The emotions of people around me have always affected me, but with Zoey, it was different. I couldn't explain it if I tried, but it was like her soul spoke to mine. I'd only felt that with one other person.

"I'm fine. Just enjoying the party," she waved her drink at me. "I'm Zoey."

I smiled even though a part of me was sad she didn't remember me as I did her. Of course, those eyes would make anyone hard to forget. But it wasn't fair of me to expect her to remember a few moments when we were kids.

"Maddox. Would you like some company, Zoey?"

"Sure." She jerked her head for me to follow. We walked until we found a semi-private location several feet from the bonfire lit near the water. "I've never seen you at any of these things."

159

"I've been to a few, but I'm not around much."

"You're not from here?" I watched as she turned up her cup, fascinated by her delicate throat swallowing the liquid. My mind went to all sorts of places it had no business going because I could tell Zoey was not that kind of girl.

But fuck if I didn't want to dirty her up.

That was my biggest mistake.

We talked all night about everything, it seemed. She talked about art while I talked about music. She talked about Jax and Zane while I told her all about Ryder, Callie, and Chris. I told her everything. Well, everything that was public knowledge.

"Oh, wait." She tapped her chin with her finger as her brows dropped between her eyes. "I do know you."

Part of me hoped she remembered, but I could tell by the tease in her eyes she wasn't talking about our first encounter. "You're the bad boy billionaire on the cover of the magazines."

I flinched. I couldn't help it. For the first time, I wished I hadn't been so recognized. I ran my hand through my hair and looked at her bashfully. "Yeah, that's me," I chuckled awkwardly. "Except, I'm not a billionaire. That's my dad."

"So, you're as much of a player as my brother and Jax," she smirks.

I didn't know what to say. I mean, I couldn't deny it, and it was a little funny this pint-sized girl was calling me out.

As the night rolled on, she began to yawn and nodded off a couple of times. "Maybe you should find your brother and friend, so you can go home," I suggested.

"We're supposed to stay here tonight, but I would kill for my bed right now."

"I could take you home," I quickly offered, then instantly regretted how eager I sounded.

"Fuck no," a deep voice called behind me.

160

Zoey's eyes flicked up, and her eyes lit with a combination of swoon and fury. I had no doubt who stood behind me. "You don't get to tell me what to do, Jax," she snapped.

"You came with us. You'll leave with us." I turned around to see the local football hero standing with his arms crossed over his chest, glaring at the girl sitting across from me. He looked down at me with a hard scowl on his face. I smirked while casually scratching my nose with my middle finger. His scowl morphed into anger, and it was obvious he was ready to start swinging.

"What's going on?" Zane strolled up, looking like that cat that swallowed the canary with a blond firmly attached to him.

"Tell her she can't leave with this tool," Jax gestured to us.

"Zane isn't the boss of me any more than you are," Zoey stood to her full five-foot glory with hands on her hips. "If I want to go home, then I will go home. If he's nice enough to take me, I see nothing wrong with that. It's a whole hell of a lot better than standing around here by myself while you two ditch me."

Jax flinched, knowing he couldn't argue with what she said. She didn't give him a choice either. She walked over to me, grabbed my hand, and began pulling me behind her. "Thank you for your offer. I would be glad if you could take me home," she told me but kept her eyes firmly on Jax.

I shrugged with a bigger grin, loving that the guy was so pissed. "Sure thing, darlin'."

Jax started after us, but Zane stopped him. "Let her go, man."

I heard them argue as we left. I had this strange satisfaction that his night was ruined. The way I saw it, he deserved it if he couldn't pull his head out of his ass for the girl he clearly wanted.

The drive back was quiet. She sang along to the radio, horribly out of tune I might add, and stared out the window. I knew she didn't like leaving like that, but who was I to argue.

I pulled into her driveway shortly after three in the morning. "Thanks for bringing me home."

"Anytime." I meant it. "You're not going to get in trouble for coming in so late?"

161

"I was supposed to stay there, remember? They'll be thrilled I came home."

We sat there for a few seconds staring at each other until I finally cleared my throat. "You better get inside before they think I'm trespassing or something," I nodded toward the house.

She surprised me when she leaned across the console and kissed me. Once my brain caught up with the rest of me, I kissed her back in earnest, relishing the tiny moan that came from her mouth. But when she began to climb over the console, somehow, I found the restraint to stop her. "Don't think that's such a great idea, beautiful." The look of rejection on her face made me panic. I didn't want her to think I didn't want her because I did, but I also knew she was reacting to how Jax had made her feel. I gripped her chin to make sure she heard what I said next. "You're not that kind of girl, Zoey. It's late, and you're pissed, even if you're keeping a smile on your face to hide it. But I'd like to get to know you better. Can I call you?"

She bit her lip shyly with a nod. I pulled out my phone so she could put her number in, then call herself. "Thank you," she told me as she stood outside the door of my truck.

"For what?" I asked, but I already knew the answer.

"For not taking advantage."

I laughed. How could I not? Because under any other circumstances, I wouldn't be leaving here with a hard dick. "I'll call you, Zoey. Okay?"

She nodded, and I watched as she walked to her front door, then inside. I left there excited to get to know the girl that helped my day feel a little less shitty all those years ago. The girl who didn't want me to be alone.

162

CHAPTER EIGHTEEN

never the right one

Seven weeks ago

I tell her everything. Including when Zoey walked in on me doing a line in my bedroom and Ryder coming out in a towel. That was fun to explain since she knew about the other side of Ryder's and my relationship, but nothing was going on there.

I tell her about Zoey wanting to try the drugs with me. How I was a fucking idiot and let her. I even told her about the few times she asked for Ryder and me together. That was probably the biggest mistake and the beginning of the end.

"You know you didn't force her to do any of that, right?" Quinn asks as she strokes a finger over my abs.

"I know that here," I tap the side of my head. Because that's what it always boiled down to. The logical and the emotional. "But here," I slap a hand over my heart, "I know if she'd never met me, the shit she's been through wouldn't have happened."

"How did it end? You said she almost died."

"That night was a fucking disaster," I groan.

"You know I'm technically adopted, right?"

She nods against my chest as her fingers continue to rake over my skin. She has no idea how fucking hard it is to concentrate when she does that, but I'll be damned if I tell her to stop.

"I was supposed to meet Zoey that night at her friend's party. I walked downstairs and heard my dad and Jewel arguing again. It had become a regular thing. She was pissed I wouldn't have anything to do with her and blamed Dad. Dad was pissed she kept coming around but couldn't seem to get her to stay away. That night she said something about my birth dad, who I now know is Bastian's dad. She was telling Dad that he wanted to see me, and he told her that her rapist would never see me."

A small gasp escapes her. My fingers involuntarily flex against her hip where I've been holding her. I know it's got to be painful, but she doesn't say anything.

The absolute horror and anger I felt that night is as real now as it was then. Knowing you're a product of rape—of some coward forcing himself on another—it really fucks with your head.

It definitely fucked with mine. I left there without letting my presence be known. Before I even got to the party, I was already wasted. I don't even know how I made it in one piece. Bryan met me at the door, and we went in search of Zoey.

She knew something was off. Kept asking me to tell her what had happened, but I couldn't. Instead, I did my damnedest to convince her to get high with me. She didn't want to. Not when she knew I was already so fucked up.

A while later, Bryan handed me a glass with a wink. He told me what he did, and I gave it to her anyway. I just didn't expect her to have the reaction she did.

When she told me she wasn't feeling well, I went with her to the bathroom. She couldn't stop throwing up, and minutes later, she started seizing.

I fucking panicked. I don't know why, but I did. I left her there like a damn fool. I could only be grateful I had the forethought to call Zane.

164

I raced home as quickly as I could. When I got there, no one was home. They probably left for Florida right after I did for a long weekend in Miami.

Or I thought no one was home. I sure as hell didn't expect to see Chris's girlfriend walk downstairs wearing nothing but a towel.

"Thought you were at a party," she said as she swayed her hips in my direction.

Tasha and Chris had been going out for a while, but I didn't trust her. For good reason, considering she appeared in my room one night sans towel a few months back. I shot that shit down fast. I wanted to tell Chris, but Tasha was a professional skank. She had Chris wrapped around her little finger, and I knew he'd never believe me.

Suddenly, I resented that fact too.

I was still reeling from Dad and Jewel's conversation, freaking out about Zoey, worried if she would be okay, and totally, completely trashed out of my mind on everything.

I was in a death spiral of bad decisions that night and thought one more wouldn't hurt.

So when she ran a long finger across my chest, I didn't think twice about ripping that towel from her body, bending her over the arm of the couch, and fucking her like an animal.

With her folded in two, her hair wrapped around my fist, and my cock deep in her ass, she screamed out my name over and over. I had no idea if she was begging for more or begging me to stop, and I didn't care.

Until I heard Chris's voice yell out across the room.

I pushed off her, raking a condemnable hand through my hair with a curse. I started toward my brother, who looked absolutely mortified, while his girl tried to pretend she wasn't a willing party.

Turns out, my brother had more faith in me than I thought. Or he just knew her better than I believed. Because he didn't believe anything she said.

But he still left in a fit of rage.

The next day, I found out Zoey was okay, but I had a lot of consequences to pay. The disappointment on my dad's face was almost more than I could take. But when he said I was leaving River City for good, the guilt turned to resentment. I couldn't believe he was letting Jax's brother strong-arm him into making me go.

Worse still, they wouldn't let me see Zoey before I was forced out of town, and she wouldn't answer my calls or return my texts.

"Finally, Bastian helped me get back into town for her graduation, and I apologized to her for everything."

"Wow," Quinn whispers quietly. "That was some breakup."

I pull away from her and climb off the bed. The regret and shame of what I did that night will always haunt me. I hurt two people I cared deeply for, and I can never take it back. Zoey may have forgiven me, but Chris and I haven't said much to each other since. Of course, I'm sure the fact that I avoid him aids in that.

I don't tell her about the part where, if not for me, Zoey would never have been raped. How it's my fault she spiraled into addiction afterward because I gave her the first taste of drugs back when we were kids. Or if I'd just called Jax and Zane when I found her, they could've helped her sooner. Instead, I kept her safely hidden with me for a year because I was afraid she'd disappear.

The night of the first anniversary of her rape, I found her in the bathroom, arm sliced open from wrist to elbow, bleeding out on my bathroom floor. Cocaine was scattered all over the bathroom counters. I had no idea how much she'd consumed, but I had a feeling it was a lot more than anyone should take, no matter their tolerance. Especially someone her size.

I made yet another hard as hell phone call that night. It seemed like the only time I called Zane or Jax was to tell them something awful.

When I left the hospital the next day, I went to the bathroom to clean it up. Her blood was everywhere, and as hard as I tried not to, I broke. I couldn't stop the tears, the all-consuming guilt, and the pain of knowing if I'd done something different, it wouldn't have happened.

For the third time, because of me, Zoey nearly died. And that was my undoing.

I'd already started drinking again after finding her in the alley that night. Seeing her face so beaten and bloody and watching her scream and panic

166

every time the paramedics tried to touch her was more than I could take. I needed something to help. And in my warped brain, I thought I was addicted to drugs, not alcohol.

Alcohol wasn't going to cut it though, so I raked the remnants into piles and did them all, waiting for it to take me to oblivion.

"You loved her." Quinn's eyes meet mine in the bathroom mirror.

"Love, Quinn. I love her. I will always love her."

I almost expect to see a flash of jealousy, maybe even anger, at my admission. Instead, I am met with understanding. More than I deserve. Such sincerity and warmth blows me away.

I turn around to face her. "Where did you come from, canary?"

"Springfield," she quips with a shrug. "And just so you don't get any ideas, I have no intentions of being shared with anyone. I'm a one at a time kind of girl."

I grin to hide the fact that the idea of sharing her with anyone pisses me the fuck off.

It's definitely a strange fucking feeling. I've never had a problem sharing with anyone before. I have always liked multiple people during sex. But the thought of anyone else touching her, even Ryder, is making me very angry.

"No sharing, *cher*," I pretend like I agree with her when it's actually a fucking decree. Something I never thought twice about with anyone else. Hell, I shared Zoey, the girl I believed was the love of my life. Yet, here I am mentally declaring no one else will ever touch her again. Not with me or without me. For as long as she's mine.

"You're too hard on yourself, Maddox. Give yourself a break once in a while. Let some of that burden fall off your shoulders. The only person you're responsible for is you." She reaches up, cupping my face. When it feels like those beautiful eyes are staring straight into my soul, I fight the urge to run.

This woman has power over me as no other has ever held. She makes me want to make promises I can't keep. It's only a matter of time before I blow all of this up, but I want to keep her.

Even when I know I can't.

CHAPTER NINETEEN

Express all the feelings

Present day

I wake up from the vivid as hell daydream with pen and paper in my hand. It felt like I was right there with her, reliving the fight with Jax, my damn panic attack, her singing, telling her Zoey's and my story. Realizing I'd fallen in love with the girl in such a damn short amount of time. Yeah. It felt so real.

I look at the pages in front of me with shock. Lyrics upon lyrics fill so many of the pages. Lyrics I don't remember writing. Pages of songs pour from me, and I swear I can hear the melody of each one. I don't even need my guitar. Don't need to find the notes. Every note and chord are as clear as if I were playing it.

Turning the pages, I begin to write out the notes and the chords and note the arrangement. I can hear the tap of the drums, the beat of the bass. I see each string on the guitars and the keys on the piano. I imagine each instrument's part as if I'm surrounded by an orchestra. Each bar is intricate. Delicate and beautiful in places. Angry and roaring in others.

I write until I have a few completely composed songs with the best lyrics I've ever written before me. I sit back, looking at what I've done with

"Holy shit," I run my fingers through my hair as I sit back in my chair.

For *months,* not a word or a note. For *years* they were few and far between. An album's worth sure, but my part only contributed to about half on the last one. Ryder and Angel were the other half. At one time, I could whip out a song in an hour. Have it fine-tuned and performance-ready in a week or two, but never anything like this. In hours, I had no less than six full compositions.

Maybe all I've needed was just to get the fuck away from everyone.

"Here, asshole," Bryan walks in after being gone for more than a day. He tosses the guitar—*my guitar*—on the bed. One I haven't seen in years because it's been at my dad's house.

"How did you get that?" I ask him, my brows pinched in suspicion and confusion.

"Because I'm you, idiot." He pulls out a chair, sitting next to me, stretching his legs out in front of him. "Thought having it might help get us out of here faster." He reaches inside his jacket and pulls out two envelopes. "This too, since you seem to be using the stuff like it's going to disappear if you wait too long."

"You didn't answer my question. How did you get the guitar?"

"I answered. You don't listen."

"Whatever," I grumble with an eye roll. He's working my last nerve. I think I realize now why we've never spent a lot of time around each other. A few hours at a time, at most. "I don't even know why I keep you around."

"Because I'm the only one that knows all your dirt." His face lights with an almost malicious smirk, and I swear it changes for a split second. I have the urge to punch him again, but I ignore it.

"Half of my goddamn dirt is your fault." My fist slams on the table, rattling the unstable surface.

"Name one thing that is my fault," he responds with wide eyes, baiting me.

169

"Zoey." I dare him to deny it.

Of course, he accepts that dare. "Isn't part of recovery accepting responsibility?"

My jaw drops at this asshole. "You're the one that put the GHB in her drink." I throw my hands up in exasperation. "You are the one that kept feeding me the drugs all night."

"And you are the one that handed her the drink and took the drugs. You asked me to help you forget, so that's what I did. I provided the means. You're the one who executed the plan."

"Are you kidding me?" I stand abruptly, knocking the chair to the floor. The already weak back falls to pieces on the floor.

I begin to pace erratically around the room, nearly knocking Bastian's bike to the ground. I step around the drip from the ceiling and the puddle forming on the floor from the rain outside. "She could've died because of you." I grip my hair tightly, pulling at the roots until my hands come away with fists full of hair.

"Again, you're the one who gave her the drink, buddy, and you are the one who ran."

"Because you told me to!" I yell.

He tuts at me while shaking his head in disappointment. "You ever told anyone this story?"

"Just Quinn." I stop my pacing to look at him. "Why?"

"I was going to suggest you share your brilliant theory in your little book." He points at the notebook I've been filling with a smirk. "Sure, they'd love to hear you blame someone they don't even know exists."

"Zoey saw you," I grit out as I begin to pace again, stepping around the puddle.

"You sure about that?" His grin is wide and patronizing, and I want to knock it right off his smarmy face.

But for some reason, I suddenly can't step over the puddle that's been growing. I look at it and back to him as frustration begins to rattle me.

"For fuck's sake, Maddox. It's not fucking real."

170

"If it's not real, then how do you know what I'm looking at?" I challenge.

"Because you've been avoiding stepping in that spot for twenty minutes. Not to mention you keep staring at it like it will attack you. Just step over it."

I squeeze the bridge of my nose with a shaky hand. "I can't."

"You've lost it. Like you've completely lost it this time." He guffaws at me like I'm the most hilarious thing he's seen all week. "You have really fallen down the rabbit hole. Seen any talking caterpillars. Oh wait, you probably shared his bong."

"Fuck you," I spit.

But he's right. I've had some pretty bad moments in the past. Paralyzing anxiety. Moments when the noise is so loud I can't think. Seeing things that I know aren't there. Losing time. All of it has been hell. Trying to ignore the shit when I'm around everyone, so they don't know, is enough to cause a panic attack on its own.

I blame my past. All the times I slipped into my own head to escape the sadness, the pain, the guilt, and the humiliation, began to take on a life of its own when I was around sixteen or seventeen I think. Although, at this point, I don't even know if that's right anymore.

But I've always *known* what a hallucination was. I've always known what was real and what wasn't. I've also never felt so compelled by one as I do right now by this puddle that I'm being told isn't real.

And even if it is, why the hell can't I step over it? It's just a fucking puddle, so why was it controlling me?

"It's not real. It's not real," I whisper over and over, hoping to get logic and reality to take over. I squeeze my eyes shut, praying that when I open them, it will be gone. Except it's not. And now it doesn't just look like water.

"Maybe you should've done another line," Bryan laughs again. "You're a little less insane when you're high."

Except, I am. Or I think I am.

"Not real. It's not fucking real. Get a fucking grip, Maddox." I whisper again, trying to ignore him and the fact the puddle is growing, and it has turned thick and red. Like blood.

171

Shit! Why the hell is this happening again?

"Jesus Christ," Bryan grunts, standing from the table. He walks over to me, grips me by the shirt, and pulls me through it. I know it's not real now. I know there isn't really blood on the floor. But I swear to God I feel it slick under my feet, making me nauseous. He pushes me to his vacated chair with a huff. "Do whatever the hell it is you need to do to stop this shit. So we can leave this shit hole. Since you seem to be as trapped here as you were by whatever the hell you keep seeing on the floor."

I drop my head in my hands. The urge to pull my hair out comes over me strong.

"These are shit," he pushes the notebook to me.

My head throbs relentlessly. To the point of blinding pain. "I can't write. I can barely fucking see."

He pours me a drink and slides the envelopes to me. I imbibe in the poisons hoping they'll work fast to stop my racing thoughts. A hundred thoughts come all at once. Reality and fantasy—or nightmares—blend together into one picture in my mind with all the colors running together.

I toss back another drink, stumbling my way to the bed. The room spins as I nearly collapse on top of my guitar. My stomach flips, the contents threatening to spill. I close my eyes, fighting back the bile, and wait for sleep to take me.

CHAPTER TWENTY

never to ask why

Seven weeks ago

I slip out of Quinn's room later that night. After sharing the dark and the dirty, we got dirty in the dark. But it's just sex. It has to be. So sleepovers are out of the question.

Even if I want to stay.

I pull her door closed and make my way to the kitchen for something to drink and food. As I'm standing at the counter dressing my sandwich, the hairs on my neck stand on end. "You can stop playing boogeyman, you fucking creeper."

"Aww, but your forced acknowledgment is more amusing, *little* brother," he quips.

Even with my back turned, I could see the smirk on his face. "You're annoying as hell, you know?"

"Yeah? Must be in our DNA."

"I'm trying to eat a sandwich."

"Don't pretend with me, Maddox. You know damn well what I'm asking. What are you doing with Quinn?"

"My memory is a little foggy. Maybe with a little play by play I might remember. But don't worry that pissy little head of yours. The fuck up won't break the princess. She knows it's just sex."

"Never called you a fuck up."

"You didn't have to. You see the magazines? I'm front-page news. Maddox Masters breaking hearts and destroying pussies worldwide. Good shit."

"Done feeling sorry for yourself yet?"

"Just stating facts."

He looks at me with an arched brow. He's irritated, but he's like a dog with a bone. "Like it or not, Maddox, I know you. I know all there is to know about you."

My skin begins to crawl with his words. The panic from earlier threatens to reappear. I clench my jaw tightly in an effort to keep it contained. "You don't know shit, Bastian. You only think you do because you've always had some lackey watching me."

"Yeah, the memory must be bad if you forgot all our conversations. I don't need lackeys to know you, only to keep tabs on your bullshit so I can keep you safe."

"Fuck you."

"Sorry, but I don't swing that way, *fratello*."

A slow, sly grin crosses my face as venom prepares to spew. "Don't knock it 'til you try it, *brother*. Maybe you and Verity should try a little role reversal some time. You both might enjoy her fucking you for a change." I turn to put the containers back in the fridge. No quicker than I have the fridge door

174

shut, I'm pressed up against it. He's glaring at me with murderous intent, steam practically pouring from his ears. "You better watch it, Bastian, brother or not, being manhandled like this gets my dick excited. Who knows whose bed I'll end up in when you let me go."

Bastian bares his teeth, an attempt to look menacing. I'm sure to anyone in their right mind he would. But I'm not in my right mind, and his display of aggression makes me smile wider. "I can't figure out if you're stupid or if you just want to die," he growls just as a smirk crosses his face and lets go of me. "Actually, that's not true. I know exactly what you want, but you won't get it from me. Also, don't forget that you didn't know a clit from a g-spot before me."

"Oh, I knew. That's why Zoey keeps Jax so satisfied. He's welcome. You all are."

"Dammit, Maddox. Can you stop? For one minute, just stop with this bullshit, asshole act. Stop pretending and playing games. I meant what I said, I know you. This isn't you. You're not me."

"Then who am I, Bastian? Who is it that you think I am?"

"You're a guy that got dealt a shitty hand in life and has suffered, Maddox. Far more than anyone at your age or any age. And you push people away because of it but push all you want. I'm here today, tomorrow, and every day after. I don't turn my back on family. Even if that family acts like a little shit."

My gut churns at what he's trying to say, but I don't want to hear it. "Yep. That's me. Poor little rich boy whose momma died, daddy shipped him off, and then he finds out they're not actually his parents at all, and he's stuck with a dick for a brother. Sounds tragic, right?"

"I know, Maddox. I know everything you're trying your fucking damnedest to hide."

My shoulders heave with a heavy inhale. I swallow, trying to force the knot in my throat back down while pushing the sandwich away, my appetite long gone. "You don't know shit," I rasp out.

"O'Dell? Alton? Rossi? I know about them all. You were never supposed to be like me, Maddox, but I guess that runs in the blood too."

175

Shaking my head, I walk around him, trying to get away. I don't want to hear it. My secrets are mine. He's not supposed to know. And I am not fucking talking about it.

He grabs my arm as I shove past him. "Stop running, Maddox. The more you run, the worse you get."

I jerk away with a growl. "Back off."

"Have it your way," he tells me, letting me go. "By the way, tonight we are going to my dad's for supper."

I spin around with a glare. "What did you say?"

"You heard me just fine the first time. No reason to pretend you didn't."

"If you think I am going there, you are bat shit. There's no fucking way."

"Oh, you're going if I have to knock your ass out all over again, so be ready."

He walks away from me without a backward glance, leaving me fuming.

Sweat drips into my eyes as I swing the rope around twice, jump for ten reps, and repeat. Rage Against the Machine blasts loudly in my ears as I push my body to its limits. Every muscle in my body screams as I fight the urge to get high.

In less than two hours, Bastian expects me to be in the same room as Paul Delrie. To Bastian, he may be dad, but to me, he's the man that raped Jewel. How the fuck am I supposed to reconcile that.

I finally stop with the rope to grab a bottle of water and a towel for my face. The music still blasting in my ears helps me shut off the world—to focus as I try to wrap my head around what Bastian wants.

If Bastian knows so much about me, and as much as I hate to admit he knows anything, I'm not naïve enough to believe otherwise, then how does he not know what his dad did? Was he just too young? Has he never felt a need to check into his father's past. Didn't he wonder how I came to be?

What I do know is that going to that house is not a good idea. When I see the man, I am going to want to do what I've dreamed of for years. I smile at the thought of snapping the bastard's neck, watching the light flicker from his eyes. Bastian will probably kill me, but that's okay. I'm not afraid to die. It will all be worth it if I can take that sick fuck with me.

I am so lost in my thoughts, reveling in hearing Paul taking his last breath, that I don't think, only react when a hand begins to travel up my back. Reflex takes over, and I spin, gripping them by the throat and forcing their back against the wall. Wide eyes stare up at me as tiny hands grip at my wrist. I loosen my grasp, but I don't let go as I offer up a warning. "Do *not* *ever* sneak up on me again," I grit between bared teeth.

Her eyes dart between mine as her pulse throbs against my hand. I narrow my eyes at her with a smirk because even though I can tell she is nervous, that's not fear I see in her eyes. "Are you turned on, *cher*?"

"No," she whispers as I stroke my thumb over the thrum in her neck, noticing the way her heart skipped a beat.

"Mmm." I drop my nose to her jaw, tracing it slowly to her ear. Squeezing her neck a little tighter, I grin when her already peaked nipples cut like diamonds through her dress. "You're lying. I don't like being lied to," I whisper. "I can smell it on you."

"I'm not lying." I might believe her if not for the skip of her heart and the way her tongue darts between her lips.

I kick her feet apart and slide my hand up the inside of her thigh. Her chest rises and falls rapidly as I stop inches from her core. She sucks in a breath when I breach the edge of the lace covering her hot cunt. "Wanna try that again?" I tease. "Gotta warn ya, darlin', lying is a real trigger for me. Now, tell me, are you wet right now?"

When she shakes her head in denial, I slide my hand from her throat to her jaw. I grip it tightly until her lips part enough for me to slip my thumb into her mouth. I slide a finger through her wet folds, watching as her eyes roll back into her head. "Don't you know bad girls get punished? But I think that's what my little canary wants, isn't it?" I smirk when her pussy clenches around my fingers and her pupils blow wide. "I just wonder if you're gonna like what I do to this lying little mouth."

177

I step away from her with a grin, sucking her flavor from my fingers. "Get on your knees, *cher*," I order.

Heat rises to her cheeks as she bites her lip. Her eyes dart to the door, then back to me. She opens her mouth to say something, then snaps it closed.

She has no idea how much of an open book she is. From her expression to her body language, I can read her as easily as the pages in my maw maw's hymn books. She was turned on as hell at the thought of me commanding her, at my use of force. She loved it when my hands were around her throat, her life essentially in my hands but knowing I wouldn't hurt her. And the idea of getting caught on her knees excites her.

But people are trained to think something is wrong with that. That you shouldn't want to see people fuck or have people watch you. That being aggressive, dominant, submissive, enjoying pain are all shameful and deviant.

So I don't miss her hesitation.

I raise a brow at her. "I'm waiting, canary. I won't say it again. Or maybe you want me to make you."

She lowers herself to her knees. Her lashes flutter as she looks up at me. I stifle a groan as I watch her throat bob with a nervous swallow.

"Pull my dick out."

Her eyes dart to the door again for a split second before she pulls my shorts down far enough to let my throbbing cock spring free. She licks her lips when she reaches for me. Nervous or not, she wants me, which is why those golden eyes fill with confusion when I bat her hands away.

"Hands behind your back," I tell her, my voice dropping an octave from my own desire. "Keep them there. Understand?" Her head bobs in acknowledgment, but that's not what I want. "Do. You. Understand?"

"Yes," she says softly with her eyes still on my cock, making it twitch with anticipation.

"Yes, what?"

"Yes, I understand. Keep my hands behind my back."

"Good girl," I grip her hair tightly in my fist, jerking her head back. "Now open wide, *cher*, and take your punishment."

I slide my cock through her parted lips, forcing her to take all of me. Using my free hand, I rub the head against the roof of her mouth with a groan. I thrust again to the back of her mouth, staying there for just a moment, enjoying the way it contracts around me. "Use your teeth," I growl. When her teeth graze my aching flesh, I begin to fuck her mouth in earnest. My grip on her hair tightens as I pound into her throat. The feeling of her gagging around me and the tear that runs down her face spurs me on more. I watch as her hands begins to creep back in front of her. I know what she wants, but that's not punishment.

"Hands, canary," I bark.

She whimpers but puts them back behind her. A few more thrusts, and I release a euphoric roar as I spill down her throat. I hold myself there as my cock pulses in her mouth. She swallows around me, taking every drop.

I pull away, tucking myself back into my pants before dropping to eye level with her. "You did good, *cher*. If you're a good girl, I might let you come later tonight."

"Or I can do it myself," she says with a she-devil grin.

I grip her face, planting my mouth on hers. I kiss her mouth nearly as hard as I fucked it before I release her, leaving her panting. "If you touch your pussy, next time it won't be your mouth I fuck."

Her mouth falls open, but once again, her pupils blow wide. I chuckle, knowing she's curious. "Don't worry, darlin'. We'll get there. Just don't give me a reason to do it before you're ready."

I stand up, bringing her with me. We walk to the door when she stops me. "You made me forget," she says, placing her hands on my chest.

"Forget what?"

"I came to make sure you were okay. Verity told me you guys are supposed to go to Bastian's dad's tonight." She places one of her tiny hands on my cheek.

I grit my teeth. For a moment, I'd forgotten all about that. "No. I'm not okay, but big brother, as usual, thinks he's in charge."

"I wish I could help."

My eyes close as I lean into her hand, finding comfort I have no business seeking. "Come with us," I say before I can stop the words. I don't know where this comes from. This need to have her there, but I know that's exactly what it is. A need.

"I wasn't invited, Maddox. It's a family thing."

When she starts to pull her hand away, I place mine over it, keeping it there. "I'm inviting you. And you are Verity's family. Please come."

"All right. I'll come. For you."

And with those words, I know this is more than just sex for her too.

CHAPTER TWENTY-ONE

How could I be wrong?

Seven weeks ago

I walk into Bastian's childhood home with more anxiety and tension than I've felt in years. I fight against the urge to light the place on fire or run as far as I can. Quinn's hand in mine is the only thing keeping me in place.

When I told Bastian the only way I would go was if Quinn came too, I thought another lecture was coming. Instead, I got a nod of acceptance.

That doesn't mean I haven't noticed the way he keeps watching me. All the way to his dad's, he's observed me with curiosity and amusement that's been both irritating and unnerving. Like he knew something I didn't.

Newsflash. I knew too. Didn't mean I could admit it.

When we made it past the foyer, Verity took Quinn with her to the kitchen. I could hear boisterous laughter billowing nearly as soon as they went through the door. I couldn't stop the scowl that pulled at my mouth. I didn't want her away from me or near that motherfucker.

I followed Bastian until we stood next to a small minibar. I stared at the variety of liquor. I knew what each one was despite being in crystal decanters. My mouth watered with need. The need to feel the burn, to let it

Honestly, I wanted more than that, but the alcohol was closer.

Bastian hands me a glass, and I'm disappointed but not surprised that all I get was fucking water. "Why did you bring me here, Bastian?" I finally snap.

"You know, I thought when you first objected so strongly to coming here a few weeks ago, it was out of resentment that you weren't told who your dad was. I got that. I was pissed when I first found out about you. I was an asshole to keep it from you for so long, even if I understood."

He turns up his drink, watching me closely. He knows I want what's in *his* glass, and he's a son of a bitch for taunting me. "Then the other night, I was listening to you talk to Quinn."

My hackles rise that he was eavesdropping on my private conversation. "Aren't you a little old to be snooping like a teenager?" I snap.

"Not in my house. And not when you don't shut the door all the way. Anyway, you can imagine my surprise when I heard you tell Quinn about the night everything went down with Zoey. We all knew you were trashed, but Maddox Masters trashed still doesn't screw people over. I just never understood what made you snap. What made you do everything you could do to cause all of your relationships to implode."

"They didn't all implode."

"I'm not sure you could actually do anything to make Ryder abandon you. I may disagree with this unhealthy codependency you two have, but I know he's loyal. I get that. I have that with Rory."

"Get to the goddamn point, Bastian, because I'm still trying to decide if I want to light this fucking house on fire or not."

"The point is that you have it all wrong." He says it so casually I know he believes it.

But I know what I heard, and I tell him that. "You think I'm going to take that piece of shit's word for it," I hiss. "When's the last time you heard someone admit they raped a fifteen-year-old girl."

182

"Maddox, if you don't know anything else about me, you know I don't tolerate that. Father or not, do you think he'd still be breathing if I thought he did something like that. I just need you to hear him out."

I turn away from him, already tired of the bullshit. I walk around the house until I come into a room with a piano. A beautiful, antique Steinway and Sons' Rocco grand piano sits next to floor-to-ceiling windows overlooking the lake.

I run my hand over the smooth wood, trying to remember the last time I played a piano of this caliber, and realize it was the last time I was at my dad's. Bastian, of course, follows like the prison warden he's trying to be, probably afraid I'm going to sneak out. He sets his glass on the rail wood, making me fight the urge to slap it off.

He runs his fingers over the key, tapping out a few bars. "This belonged to my—our grandfather. His mother was a concert pianist in Italy. Called her a virtuoso because she played her first concert when she was twelve." He looks over at me knowingly. "Said she was composing her own music when she was just a little girl."

"You play?" I ask, still looking at the glass sitting on the beautifully preserved wood like it's a demon. I'm not sure if it's because of my anal, OCD obsession about not damaging instruments, or the fact I really want that fucking drink.

He doesn't answer. Instead, he moves his fingers across the keys. I smirk as the intro to Enter Sandman fills the room. "At least your taste in music doesn't suck."

"Seems we're more alike than you think," he mutters as he continues to play the song.

"Funny, Zoey always told me she was attracted to me because I reminded her of someone. I assumed it was the football star, but maybe it was just my long, lost big *brother*."

He stops playing to glare at me with a hard scowl. "No. Just... Don't say that again."

I start to respond when the doorbell rings. My eyes narrow in suspicion. I have no idea who's at that door, but my skin begins to tingle with the sudden awareness that I'm being set up.

Bastian leaves to answer the door, so I sit at the piano to distract myself from whatever is going on. My fingers fly across the keys, playing a song I wrote long, long ago. A song with no words but with the deep sorrow of a kid lost in his own mind.

I close my eyes as each chord and note reverberates through the room, echoing off the walls and the high ceilings. Someone sits beside me, and tension leaves my body as I absorb the warmth radiating from them. For a minute, the anger subsides, and the chaos settles.

When I finish the song, I look over to see beautiful eyes staring at me, full of tears. "That was beautiful," she whispers.

"Didn't know the rock star had it in him, did ya, *cher*?"

"I did," a deep voice booms across the room. "You've always had so much talent."

I turn to see my dad standing in the entryway of the room, staring at me with respect and admiration. It's a foreign look I don't think I've ever seen on him.

I take in his dark hair, now heavily peppered with gray, the lines on his face more prominent. When I was a kid, he seemed so formidable. He's aged a lot over the years. Time is funny that way. But I'm a little stunned at how much he's aged since I last saw him two years ago.

"What are you doing here?" I growl. Our relationship always seemed so tenuous, but it's practically been mercurial the last several years at best.

He lets out a long, weary sigh. "Bastian called me. I think it's time we talked, son."

"I think it's past time," Bastian barks as he follows his father into the room. The sight of Paul Delrie incites a murderous rage I've only felt a handful of times. I stand from the piano, in the man's face in two long strides. Bastian is quick, though. He puts himself between us, ready to defend his father.

"Sit down," he commands, pointing at the piano bench where Quinn sits, looking at me with worry and fear.

"I can sit when I'm dead," I grind, my eyes boring into Delrie's.

184

"You can sit now. I will fucking make you, Maddox. Don't try me." Bastian's warning is clear, but he seems to forget I am not afraid of him or his threats.

"Then make me," I dare, never taking my eyes from his father's, who is looking at me with remorse, guilt, and shame. Expressions I am all too familiar with. But they mean nothing from him.

A small hand wraps around mine, pulling gently back to the bench. "Just hear them out," she whispers. "Then you can leave."

I look into her pleading eyes and nod. I'll sit. I'll even listen. But when they finish saying what they need, I'll do what I need.

"Maddox, why didn't you come to me? I never knew you overheard. Is that why you went crazy that night?" Dad's eyes plead with me to help him understand. Except he doesn't make any sense.

"We've barely had a full conversation in twenty-nine years except for when you tell me to suck it up because I'm a Masters. In fact, if I remember correctly, the last conversation we had, you told me I was wasting my life on music, and I wouldn't ever amount to anything."

"That's not what I said, Maddox. I only meant that you were too brilliant to throw it all away on chance."

"No, you meant you needed me to take over your company since apparently only a Masters by blood can, and Chris isn't yours either. Nice to be reminded you didn't take me from Jewel out of love or a sense of duty but for that fucking company."

"You know that's not what I did. Maddox, you were always the best at everything you did, but I didn't want you to take that risk and be disappointed if it didn't work out."

"So, let me get this straight. I'm the best, but being the best means nothing since I was doomed to fail?"

"You are the best, son. But you are also the most self-sabotaging man I've ever met."

"Yep. That's me. The fuck up."

"Maddox, shut up," Bastian snaps at me. "You know that's not what he meant."

185

"Do I? Because most of my life, he avoided me. He shipped me off, pretending I didn't exist, until the day I went to college, then suddenly, he was invested. I didn't know why then, but damn if he didn't let me know on graduation day."

"Maddox," he lets out a long, heavy sigh, "I messed up with you, but I was just trying to protect you. If I'd known you'd heard what I said, I would have—"

"What? Kept me from blowing everything to hell that night? To answer your question, yes, that's exactly what pushed me over the edge. Zoey wasn't—I..." I shake my head, having no idea how to finish that sentence. "It shouldn't have happened. I shouldn't have fucked Tasha either. But I did, and I can't take any of it back. But tell me why I would've come to you. You have done nothing but lie to me my entire life."

"I didn't rape your mother, Maddox," Paul tells me, looking absolutely sincere. "It's not an excuse, but I was trashed that night. I don't remember anything at all, and Trey knew that." He turns an accusing finger toward my father. "I came to your house wasted when Caterina threw me out. I don't even know how I made it to the door. I went to the guest room and passed out. I woke up, still fucking drunk with your very underage sister riding my dick. I would *never* have gone after her. She was like a damn sister to me too, and you knew it. But I let you blame me because I knew it was easier than blaming her. She was the child, and drunk or not, I should've known better somehow. Then I played your family's game and stayed away from my son because you threatened to ruin my life if I didn't. And just so you know, I didn't do that for me. You know who I am, Trey. It would've been so much easier just to handle *you*. I did it for *your family* and for Maddox. So I want to know why the fuck you would say that shit?"

He shows no signs of lying. I don't know if it's the truth, but he damn sure fucking believes every word he just said. Which is so much different than the scenario that has played in my head for the last fifteen years. My skin begins to itch and tingle, and the noises begin to roar.

"I said it because she was a fucking kid. You were the adult and my best friend. You should've known better," my dad yells out.

"What?" I say but it comes out tight and garbled, but they don't acknowledge me.

186

"I didn't know what zip code I was in. It may be a shit excuse, but I was too drunk to give a shit who was riding me. Too pissed at Caterina to care. I didn't know it was Jewel. Hell, I didn't even know she was in the house. Do you *not* remember the next morning? I didn't even remember coming to your house. I realized after the fact that Jewel was infatuated with me, but it falls on you too. All of you. Jewel had problems. You blamed it on rebellion and drugs, but she had so many more problems than that, and none of you would acknowledge them."

"How the fuck would you know? She was my sister, not yours."

"Because Caterina and I were the ones who helped her when you wouldn't. Even after what she did, she came here, and we tried to help her. Did you know she heard voices, Trey? Just like your father? You know as well as I do that he didn't fall off the roof. He jumped. But all your family was concerned with was making sure it didn't cause a scandal."

I collapse back onto the piano bench as I take everything in. It's too much. Too much information too fast. It seems it's the only way I ever find out anything. "Paw Paw Br—," I shake my head because I don't remember much, but I remember how much I loved my grandfather. I was five when he died, and after the day I nearly drowned, the memories of him became fuzzy. But I remember he was my best friend. My favorite person in the world. I even remember when he fell off the roof. "He killed himself?"

My dad's head snaps to me, his face as white as a sheet before he turns back to Paul. Sebastian looks at me curiously, like he doesn't understand. Paul shoots daggers at my dad, who gives him a subtle shake of his head.

"What? What was that?" I point at him. "What else are you fucking hiding?"

"Nothing, Maddox. We're not hiding anything."

"Did he fall, or did he kill himself?" I ask, finally tired of the avoidance. "Because I was there. I remember being on the roof with him. We were playing a game."

"What the hell?" Bastian jerks back with surprise.

My dad lowers his head sadly. "You weren't trying to play a game, Maddox. He wanted you to jump with him. I pulled up to get you, and you were on the roof crying. He was floating face down in the pool. You told me he wanted you to fly with him."

Quinn gasps as Bastian and Paul curse. I just sit there in silence. I don't know what to say. I don't know what to think. What I do know is that it is getting hard to breathe, and I fucking hate that I can't process emotions and information like a goddamn normal person.

My grandfather *and* mother heard shit that wasn't there? What the hell does that mean for me?

My hands begin to flex against my legs as I fight the urge to claw at this itch I know isn't really there. My head starts throbbing with noise that no one else can hear.

And the desire to get high is stronger than ever.

"I'm outta here," I announce as I practically jump to my feet.

I don't wait for them to stop me. I ignore the calls for me to wait. I'm out the door before they can decide who should come after me. I hope no one does.

Once I'm outside, I walk to the end of the driveway and bend over at the waist as my heart pounds in my chest.

Why? Why is every part of my life lies?

My pawpaw wanted me to jump with him? I don't remember that. Why don't I remember? Is it because of when I was hurt as a kid? Or is it because I blocked it out?

"Maddox?" a familiar, feminine voice calls to me.

I turn to find fire engine red hair coming my way. I want to tell her to go away, but the words won't come.

"What are you doing here?" she asks as she looks over my shoulder toward Delrie's house. "Are you okay?"

I shake my head as I try to get the voices to quiet and my heart to slow. "Do you want to come over?" she jerks her head over her shoulder to the house next door.

"When did you move here?" I finally rasp out.

"A couple of years ago. Layla rents it to me. Why don't you come inside?" Her blue eyes shining with worry.

188

"I'll be fine," I tell her. "I just had to get out of there."

She nods in understanding then throws her arms around me. "I don't know what's going on, Maddox, but you know I'm always around if you need someone to talk to."

"I'll be fine, Delaney. I always am." I lie. I've been lied to so much in my life that it's turned me into a liar myself.

I'm fine? I'm never fucking fine.

But they can't know that. I definitely can't let them know that I hear and see things too.

She looks me over, and apparently, my act is pretty good because she gives me a satisfied nod. "I'll just get back home then," she tells me as she looks over my shoulder. "Looks like the calvary is coming anyway."

I look over my shoulder and roll my eyes. "Or the firing squad," I mutter.

She gives me another hug and walks away. I turn around to face Bastian.

"You come to make sure I didn't run off?" I snap.

"Something like that," he says as he looks me over. "Were you about to run off?"

"I wasn't going to run. I was going to walk off. Got caught by Delaney."

"I forget you two know each other sometimes," he grins widely. "Tristan know how well you know her?"

"Doesn't matter to me if he does," I shrug.

"I want to ask you something, and I want an honest answer." He pauses for a moment, waiting for me to respond. I roll my hand through the air, telling him to continue, which causes him to roll his eyes. "I saw your reaction in there when they talked about Jewel and your grandfather hearing voices. Do you hear them?"

He's right. I did let a moment of panic slip through my façade, but I'm not letting it happen twice. I'm sure as hell not admitting it after all of that. "No."

He watches me carefully, looking for a tell that I'm lying. He won't find one. Bastian is great at spotting a liar, but I'm better at hiding the shit that

189

gets you locked away. Finally, he seems to accept my answer. "You know I'm not letting you leave, right?"

"You can't fucking stop me, Bastian. I'm done here. I'm just done with it all."

"What does that even mean, Maddox?"

I shrug and begin to walk off. He grabs me, slamming me against the side of his truck. "Not letting you go, Mads." He says it casually, but his eyes flare with anger.

"Will you just stop? Stop trying to save me from whatever it is that you are trying to save me from."

"I'm trying to save you from yourself, *stronzo*. Your dad was right. You are your own worst fucking enemy, but you're my brother, and I'm not going to watch you kill yourself."

It's still weird to think of him as my brother, but over the years, he really has become a friend. He was someone I could call when I needed help. Or rather my friends. I've never asked for any myself. And I've seen the change in him since he met Verity. He's still Bastian. He still loves peeling the skin off of assholes, but he shows his heart more. He isn't afraid to show he cares anymore.

I know I should appreciate that he does care about me, but he's been another liar in my life. And that has had my mind turning since last night.

"Let me ask you something, Bastian. You said last night that *you know*. What is it that you think you know?"

"I know everything, Maddox. Everything you've done and everything that's been done to you. Well, except for your grandfather, I guess."

"So, the night you and Rory decided to do whatever it was to my dad to make sure I left town, did you know what I was going back to? Did you know why I was expelled in the first place?"

"Of course not. You know me, Maddox. Do you think I would've let you go back there had I known?"

I lean my head back, looking up at the stars lighting the sky, trying to collect my thoughts, and process the fact that he knows my greatest shame.

I fight back the sting in my eyes, refusing to shed a damn tear. I'm not that kid anymore. "When did you figure it out?"

"I didn't know until just now. I only had suspicions. I'm the one who made sure it couldn't be linked back to you, then I had Christian do some digging."

I close my eyes with a heavy exhale, trying to expel the memories and demons. "I didn't think I was. If they hadn't stopped me, I would've killed him that day in his office."

"How long?"

"For years."

"Why didn't you tell someone, Maddox?"

I look at him with raised brows. "Would you have told anyone?"

"No," he shakes his head. "I would've done exactly as you did."

"All those years protecting me. Guess it didn't do much good, did it."

He lowers his head. Frustration rolls off him in waves. "You are not *me*. Stop thinking you are. O'Dell, Alton, Rossi? They suffered the consequences of their depravities. Only reason I didn't do it is because you got there first."

"You tell anyone?" My stomach churns at the possibility that he did.

"No one else knows. I haven't even told Rory. That's why they're still looking for Rossi. It doesn't make you evil, Maddox."

"If you say so, Bastian."

I agreed because I didn't feel like arguing, but I didn't believe it. I knew better.

CHAPTER TWENTY-TWO

The cycle of suffering goes on

Journal entry #6

September 2013

The years following my return to New York were uneventful and normal. I still struggled like hell with the desire to get blasted. There were days the noise in my head was so loud I struggled to concentrate. But it was mostly normal.

Well, for me anyway. Ryder had been in hell for months. He was on his own bender of alcohol, drugs, and sex. Lots of sex with anyone he could get. Then there were the times he only wanted me. No one else would've been able to handle him like that. He was angry, and it seemed he was only getting angrier by the day.

He hid it well, but not from me. He told me everything. Which was why I always felt like shit because I hid so much from him.

I thought returning to New York would be hard. And it was for a bit, but I'd spent more time there in the last ten years than I had in Louisiana. It didn't feel like home exactly, but it was familiar. I had my friends, including

We clicked instantly over music and ink. We started a band, and I made it my mission to make sure we played as many gigs as we could. Once Jake left for college, we continued, but we refused to replace him, so his spot was always there whenever he was home for breaks.

Shortly after he graduated, Dane opened a tattoo shop. He'd given me my first ink when we were still in school. He was a tattoo master. Almost as good as Sebastian, but I'd never tell him that. All of my ink had been done by him but one. That one he refused. Years later, his sister did it for me, and his reaction to Tori tattooing my dick was hilarious.

One not very special day in September, Dane was slammed in his shop, Ryder was back at his apartment with a hangover, and wrapped around God only knew how many women and men, and Cara, Dane's baby sister, needed to be picked up from school early. I had been in class all morning and was just walking out of class when I got a text asking me if I could get her.

I had no problem swinging by and getting Cara. I loved that brat like my own sister, and if she needed me, I was there.

I walked into her school's main office, signed her out, and went back outside to wait on her. I was listening to the latest from Alice in Chains, not really paying attention to anything, when a man walked out of the office with Cara. The sight of his hand on her shoulder sent chills up my spine.

Since that day in his office, I hadn't heard or seen anything of Murphey O'Dell. I knew he sued the school and my dad. I also knew they all settled with him because I wouldn't give them a reason for what I did. Dad was irate, but I didn't care. It wasn't their business.

When Dad sent me back to New York, I knew he wouldn't be at the school. He resigned shortly after his settlement, citing some post-traumatic bullshit— he didn't know the fucking meaning of the word—and I knew I wouldn't see him since there was technically a restraining order in place against me. I was not allowed within one hundred feet of him.

Cara smiled at the man and began walking to my SUV with a smile. I gave her one in return, but my eyes were firmly locked on the predator she'd just walked away from. When his eyes locked with mine, my stomach churned violently with nausea but also with red hot fury. He jerked his eyes to Cara and back to me with a smirk. My fingers wrapped so tightly around the steering wheel I thought it might break.

"Who's that guy?" I asked Cara once she was in the car and belted in. That wasn't what I wanted to ask. I wanted to ask if he fucking touched her, but I couldn't.

"He's the new school psychologist," she said cheerfully. "I'm supposed to start seeing him next week."

My head snapped to her so quickly, distracting me from the car in front of me, I nearly caused a collision. "Why would you see him? You already see a therapist every week."

"He said it would do me some good to have extra counseling," she shrugged.

"Cara, you can't see him." I tried hiding the panic I was feeling, but I could tell in her big brown eyes that I wasn't succeeding.

"Do you know him?" she asked me, nervously chewing on her lip.

I shook my head as I pulled up to Dane's shop. "Just forget I said anything. Okay, brat?"

Her eyes still big and fearful, she nodded, and I hated that I had scared her. But she was much older than I was when I met the son of a bitch. Like me, she'd also lost her mom and even a bit of herself. The thought of him anywhere near her... It wasn't going to happen.

She climbed out of the car, grabbed her backpack, and waited for me for a second. "I'm not coming in, brat. Tell your brother I'll see him later."

"Are you okay, Madsy?" she asked, and I wanted to kick my own ass for making her ask that.

I forced a smile as I nodded. "I'm good, darlin'. Go inside to your brother."

I had another class that afternoon, but I didn't go. I went home and began researching the man that made most of my teen years hell. It was something I should've done long before, but I wanted so desperately to forget.

I would never forget, but I had it put away until it was something I refused to think about, even if I couldn't stop the dreams.

And seeing him brought out urges, strong urges that I'd been fighting for over three years. It also made the noise in my head get louder. So loud, it was hard to focus on the computer screen, but I managed somehow. I searched the web for several hours, making my way through every legal and illegal database I could until I finally found what I was looking for.

I leaned back in my seat, my eyes tired and blurry from the endless scrolling and reading, with a sick satisfaction. I had the bastard's address. I didn't know what I would do right then, but I knew where to start.

Pounding at my door broke the satisfied silence in my apartment. I looked at my watch, noting the late hour, wondering who it could be.

Even though I already knew the answer to that question. Especially when the door flew open and Ryder stormed in, looking frenzied and pissed. "Why the hell haven't you answered your phone?" he barked, his face red with frustration.

"On silent," I answered as I stood up from the computer.

"Dane called me. Said you freaked Cara out over her new school psychologist, then we couldn't get you for hours. What happened?"

"Nothing," I waved him off. "Just had a lot of work to do and lost track of time."

"Bull fucking shit, mate. Try again. I know her new psychologist is O'Dell. Wanna try that again?"

My jaw clenched for a second before I forced the tension away, determined to be cool. "I overreacted."

"Same thing you told me four years ago. Care to enlighten me why you keep overreacting to the same man?"

Smile still firmly in place, I shook my head. I forced myself to remain calm and breathe normally. I didn't want him to see the anger that was building. Not at him. At myself for lying to him. But I couldn't tell him the truth. "It's nothing," I repeated. "What are you doing out so late? Or here anyway?"

"When my best friend doesn't answer his phone for nearly twelve hours, I find it necessary to make sure he's okay," he snapped again.

195

Of course, I felt guilty. Ryder had been through a lot in the last couple of years. And I knew why he was worried about me. He'd watched me like a hawk—or best he could—since the night I found out Jewel was my mom. It wasn't fair of me to make him worry more.

"Come on," I jerked my head towards the couch. "I'll get us something to drink, and we can watch a movie or something until you calm down."

"Maddox, why don't you tell me what's going on? You're always hiding stuff. You know I'll love you no matter what, right?"

I walked over to him, gripping him by his neck, and pressed my forehead to his. "I know, Ry. It's something I just can't tell anyone, but you know everything that matters. You know me," I promised as I pressed my lips to his. What had started as a way to relieve stress all those years ago progressed over the years into something else. We weren't in love, but we did love each other. And we found our own sort of comfort in each other.

Needless to say, we didn't watch movies that night. For a little while, O'Dell didn't matter.

But when the sun came up. I had a plan.

Over the next few days, I watched the apartment complex where O'Dell lived. It wasn't far from my apartment, and that in itself didn't sit well with me, but it did make watching him a lot easier. I used the excuse of coffee and a different place to study, as I sat for hours inside the café across the street from him. I made mental notes of his routine. Noticed every time he left and came home. If he was alone or had someone with him. I followed him, always maintaining a safe distance, appearing to be part of the crowd as I stalked his every move. I even hacked into his emails and social media pages to monitor his plans for the weekend. It was something that I should've spent weeks on, but I didn't have weeks. I had to do this before Cara saw him the following week because I'd fucking die before I let him hurt her.

Ryder and Dane were both suspicious. They questioned every denial to hang out when I told them I had to study. Of course, they both knew I didn't study, but it was the best excuse I could come up with. When I called in sick to Lucky's, the bar where I worked, Ryder appeared at my apartment again. An argument almost broke out when I turned down a gig that Saturday.

Dane instantly questioned if I was drinking or getting high. He'd been playing big brother since I met him, but he actually started feeling like my brother in that time. Ryder was beside himself, not understanding what was going on with me. I hated lying to them, but it had to be done because Saturday was the day.

Of course, nothing ever really went according to plan for me. There was always something to get in the way. Like when Bastian called to say he was in town, and I'd been dodging Bryan for days. He kept popping up everywhere. I didn't even know when he got into town. I just knew I really didn't feel like dealing with him.

But I knew better than to ignore Bastian. He was not a man to be ignored. So it shouldn't have surprised me when the six-two muscle-bound asshole sat next to me. "Keep ignoring me, and I might get a complex," he deadpanned.

"I've told you before, Bastian. I'm just not that into you. You'll have to find someone else to break your ass in."

"Fucking little shit," he chuckled under his breath.

"Why are you stalking me anyway?"

"Who said anything about stalking? I just happened to walk in, and here you were."

"Sure, that's what happened," I smirked, "because you love restaurants where you have to actually eat food instead of women."

He shrugged, not bothering to deny that he prefers strip clubs over restaurants any day. He gestured to the bartender for a drink, then looked over at mine. "Need a refill?" he raised an eyebrow. It was his not-so-subtle way of asking me if I was drinking.

"Not drinking, Bastian. Just soda. I haven't touched a thing, I swear."

"Says every addict everywhere."

"Trust me, if I go back to it, everyone will know," I told him honestly. "No sense in more secrets," I muttered under my breath.

"So, are we watching the man or the woman?" He nodded toward O'Dell and his date. "You the jealous lover or something?"

I scoffed in disgust, then silently cursed myself for my slip when he gave me a curious look. "I'm not a jealous anything. I don't even know them.

197

They just caught my attention, is all," I lied and prayed like fucking hell that it was believable because Bastian wasn't the type to just let it go.

"Looking to join then," he grinned widely, and I exhaled a breath that he seemed to buy my story.

"Maybe," I replied.

He stood from his seat with a shake of his head. He tossed a couple of bills onto the bar with a laugh. "When you get done with whatever weird shit this is, come find me. I'll be here for a few days."

I nodded with a wave of a finger as he left.

I continued to sit there, waiting and watching. The longer I saw O'Dell and whoever this unsuspecting woman was enjoying their night, the more anxious and irritated I became. The woman had no idea she was in the company of a vile predator. And O'Dell turned on the charm. He wasn't an attractive man, but he had a certain charismatic way about him. It was always a trap to make you feel comfortable before he struck like the snake he was.

I turned in my seat when they got up to leave, not wanting to be spotted. When they stepped out the door, I got up to follow, only to run into Bryan. He stood in front of me with his usual sardonic grin, wanting to be acknowledged, but I didn't have time for his games, so I sidestepped him and went out the door.

Of course, the asshole never knew when to take a hint. I got it. I'd been giving him the brush off for days, but I had more important things to do. I started to follow O'Dell from a safe distance, hoping he was taking his date home, when Bryan grabbed my arm, distracting me from my target.

"I'm starting to get the feeling you don't want me around," he half-joked.

"I'm just busy right now." I tried to keep walking, but he wasn't letting up.

"Why don't we go up the street to the club and have some fun," he waggles his brows with a jerk of his head.

"I said I'm busy." I watched as O'Dell seemed to get further away. I started walking faster, Bryan lagging behind, trying to catch up.

"Come on, man. We haven't hung out in months, and I want to get laid."

198

"Son of a bitch," I yelled out as O'Dell and the woman got into a cab. "I fucking lost him. Are you satisfied?"

"Lost who? The child rapist? Is that who you're after?"

I dragged my hand down my face, exasperated that he just said it so loudly. "Maybe a little quieter next time."

"Why don't we just go wait at his apartment?" he suggested with a devious grin. "If you're gonna finally off the bastard, may as well scare him a bit before you do it. Tie him up in a chair, maybe. Better yet, hang him from the ceiling. Carve him up, then show him what it's like to have something shoved up his ass."

Nausea filled my stomach with every word he uttered. I didn't want to do any of that. I couldn't stand the thought of being in a room with him that long. I just wanted to end him. But it did make more sense to wait him out at his own apartment rather than spend another day tracking his every move.

I turned around and made my way back toward his apartment. Once I got there, I waited for someone to go in or leave so that I could slip through the main door, then made my way upstairs to his apartment. The fifteen flights did little to lessen my nervousness, and the gun I had tucked in the waist of my pants seemed to get heavier with each step. I knew what I had to do, but that didn't make it any easier.

When I reached his apartment, I was thankful the hallway was empty. I didn't have anything to pick the locks, so I could only pray my credit card worked like it had in the past. The more upscale a place was, the harder it was to get such rudimentary methods to work.

I got lucky.

I pushed the door open, slipping into the shadows of the space. I didn't turn on any lights, wanting my presence to be completely unknown when the asshole walked in. Bryan had other thoughts, walking through the space, touching everything in sight.

"When they pick you up for this, don't come crying to me," I hissed, hoping it would get him to stop.

"No one will ever know I was here," he promised.

We waited for what felt like days, but it was only an hour when the doorknob began to turn. Bryan slunk into the shadow behind where I sat. When the light flicked on, O'Dell jumped, realizing he wasn't alone.

"How did you get in here?" he demanded as he tossed his keys into a bowl on his counter, seemingly unfazed by my presence.

"You should have them replace your locks," I told him. "Kind of flimsy considering how much this place costs. Seems like my dad's money has served you well."

"That it did," he smirked. "I'm living quite comfortably."

"That why you're working at Cara's school? Did you go there because you know she's important to me?"

"I had no idea. Didn't even know who she was, but I can't say I was disappointed when she walked into my office. Pretty little thing. You been teaching her how I taught you?"

I leaped from the chair, moving quickly to stand in front of the asshole but careful not to touch him. I was afraid if I touched him, I'd lose it completely. "I could never be a sick fuck like you," I reached behind my back, pulling out the gun, aiming it right at his forehead. "And I'm not letting you anywhere near that little girl."

"Ah, Maddox," he tuts. "Always trying so hard to be the hero when we both know you're not. You enjoyed our time together. Why do you always deny it?"

"You should ditch the gun and show him exactly what he thinks you loved so much," Bryan growled from across the room.

"Shut up," I hissed at both of them. "I'm not a damn hero, but I'll never let you hurt anyone I care about."

"You did try so hard to protect Ryder. You never realized all your efforts were in vain, and I must say, if the rumors were true, the two of you learned quite a lot from each other."

It felt like the room was spinning. He didn't touch Ryder. He would've told me. I would've known. I shook my head in denial, knowing he was baiting me, but...

What if he did? What if he got to Ryder after all? I have never told Ryder any of this. Maybe he is choosing not to tell me too.

"Show him, Maddox. Show him the monster you are. Carve it in his flesh for everyone to know." Bryan taunted me. "Don't be chicken shit."

"Ryder enjoyed our time together, probably more than you did. He was such a good boy for me."

I gripped at my hair, trying desperately to stop the noise that was so loud. The roaring in my ears and head wouldn't stop. They continued to taunt me until I thought my head would explode.

In my distressed distraction, O'Dell lunged for me. Catching me off guard, he took me to the ground, knocking the gun out of my hand. I looked to where it slid under his coffee table, just out of reach, when he managed to get another cheap shot in on me. Ignoring the sting, I reached for the gun, wanting to end this, but it was just too far.

Then my eyes landed on an object sitting on his coffee table. The solid brass, bass cleft paperweight I'd given him before I realized he wasn't my friend sat there like a trophy. I remembered all the times I would focus on it as he kept my face pushed down on his desk. The times I would imagine it coming to life and forming notes that I could escape to.

Something inside me snapped as I realized the position we were in at that moment was all too familiar.

Except, I wasn't a little boy anymore. I was a six-foot-three grown man, who'd lived through the abuse and the shame, and was determined it would never fucking happen again.

In one quick move, I flipped us over, grabbed the paperweight, and slammed it into his face. His eyes widened in pure fear as he began begging for his life, but I heard none of it when I brought the object down onto his face again. And again. And again.

I continued to bludgeon him until we were both covered in blood. My hands shook as the brass weight fell from my grasp. I crawled away from his lifeless form as quickly as I could, wiping the blood from my hands frantically on anything I could touch.

It wasn't supposed to be like this. It was supposed to be quick. Not this blood bath.

Bryan lurked in the corner, laughing maniacally while I tried to get to my feet. I couldn't leave like this, so I went to the bathroom to try to clean some of it off. I scrubbed and scratched, but I couldn't get it all.

"If you don't leave soon, you're going to have more than a little blood to worry about," Bryan told me as he leaned in the doorway.

"Why didn't you stop me?" I yelled hysterically. "You should've stopped me."

"Why? That fucker got everything he deserved."

I shook my head. I didn't think I agreed, but I didn't even know anymore.

I fell into a deep depression after that night with O'Dell. I guess that's what you could call it. Maybe it was extreme paranoia. But the guilt was eating me alive.

Ryder and Dane's worry grew exponentially when I didn't leave my apartment for days. They kept stopping by to check on me and calling throughout the day. I lied and told them I had the flu. It wasn't a far stretch. I know my entire body ached, my head was foggy, and all I wanted to do was sleep.

I laid in my bed day after day and night after night with the images of O'Dell's disfigured face haunting me. I couldn't look at my hands without seeing blood. The sounds of his bones crunching filled my ears.

I couldn't get it to stop. No matter how much I slept, it haunted my dreams. No matter how much I tried to stay awake, the memories wouldn't ease up.

It hurt. So much. My head throbbed incessantly. My eyes felt like they'd been raked over with hot coals. I tried to pull myself from the bed, but the effort was exhausting. Even going to the bathroom was a struggle.

I couldn't take it anymore. It was too much. I just wanted it all to stop.

I went to the bathroom and pulled out my prescription of antidepressants from rehab. I stopped taking them years ago because they made me feel—well, off. I could never explain it, but it just felt like I wasn't quite me. The voices and noises got louder. I was forgetful, and for someone that remembered everything, it was discombobulating. Sometimes I felt disembodied, but not in a fun way.

But for some reason, I kept them.

I filled my mouth with water from the faucet and poured the bottle into my mouth, and swallowed without hesitation. I didn't care if I lived or died as long as I stopped seeing and hearing everything.

I woke up three days later with Ryder next to my bed and tubes in my mouth. Though I could tell I was in the hospital, I still panicked. I pulled the IV out of my arm and began working on the tube in my throat when Ryder jumped from his chair.

"Whoa. What the fuck? Stop, mate, before your hurt yourself." He ran to the door and began yelling for a nurse.

In seconds, several were in there holding me down. "Mr. Masters, we need you to calm down. I'm going to take this tube out, okay? On three, I need you to blow."

I did as they instructed. When the tube was out, I began coughing and fighting them again. "Let go of me. I'm leaving."

"You can't leave, Mr. Masters."

"Watch me," I shouted loudly.

The next thing I remembered was a needle and falling to sleep about thirty seconds later.

I woke up later, mad as fucking hell, and strapped to the bed. Ryder was asleep in the chair next to me, and I wondered who he had to pay to be allowed to stay. "Wake up, asshole," I barked with a scratchy, gruff voice.

"If it weren't for me, you'd be fucking dead. Not the right one to call asshole, don't you think?" He said it like a joke, but he was pissed. He was pissed at me. I couldn't blame him, but at that moment, I didn't care. I didn't want to breathe, much less be there. I knew what was coming next. Days at minimum in the psych ward for suicide watch. Weeks were possible as well.

"Why didn't you just leave me there? How did you even get to me?"

"I come over to check on you. Something told me the flu bullshit was just that. And why the fuck would I have left you? You really have lost your mind if you thought I would do that."

"You should have. Usually, when someone tries to kill themself, it's because they want to fucking die. Why won't you just let me die? Are you really that selfish that you'd make me suffer too, so you don't have to be alone?"

It was out of line. I knew it was. Ryder wasn't the selfish one. I was. I knew that, but I didn't give a fuck at that moment. I just wanted to stop seeing O'Dell's face.

"Right. I'm the selfish one. Sorry, I didn't want you to die, your highness. I forgot that Maddox Masters and what he wants is the most important thing in the universe."

I'd be lying if I said that didn't sting. It hurt like a bitch, but I deserved it for everything I kept from him. For all the things I had no intention of ever telling him.

I didn't acknowledge anything he said. When he walked out the door later that day, I figured he was done with me. I spent the next thirty days in the hospital. I only gave them generic answers. I was told I had a God complex. That was probably one of the most accurate things I'd ever been told.

Therapy didn't help. Therapy doesn't help if you're not honest, but I didn't trust therapists or doctors in general. But time seemed to help. The dreams seemed to lessen, and eventually, I became numb.

I'd put him through hell, but when I walked out of the hospital on that last day, Ryder was right there. He drove me back to my apartment in dead silence. When we walked through my apartment door, he nailed me right in the face. I didn't blame him. If the situation was reversed, I would've done the same.

Then he grabbed me, pulled me into his arms, and sobbed. "Don't fucking do that to me again, you son of a bitch."

I gripped the back of his head and held him tight until he finally pulled away. "Swear to me," he demanded. "Swear you won't try to check out on me again." He looked me in the face and had me make a promise that I've kept all this time, no matter how much I wanted to break it.

Until now.

CHAPTER TWENTY-THREE

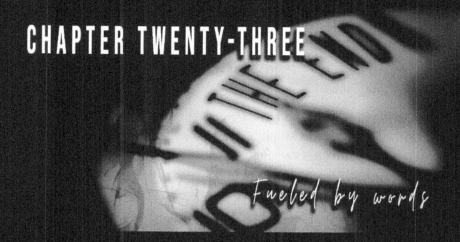

Fueled by words

Present

"Looks like you're finally closing in on the finish line," Bryan remarks as he looks over my shoulder.

I look back at him with a hard glare. The memories of that day have never left me. He was right. The man did deserve to die for what he did to me, and only God knows how many other kids, but it never sat right with me. But it did make the next time easier.

"Hurry up and get this shit done so we can get the fuck out of here."

"Why are you in such a hurry?" I ask curiously because he's been rushing since we got here.

"Because I'm over this shit. I'm just ready to go and be done with all of it. You backing out on me?"

"No," I shake my head. "I have nothing left to give any of them. Or anyone for that matter."

"Good. I was worried a certain blond might be making you have second thoughts."

Bryan is right. I'm almost finished with my great mea culpa.

"You gonna tell them the rest?" Bryan asks.

"Not about Alton. Zoey thinks he's alive. Let her keep believing. She doesn't need that guilt."

A few years after O'Dell and after some digging by my private investigator, I went to South America, found Zoey's rapist, and pulled the trigger without hesitation. Even enjoyed the terrified look on his face. He thought he'd gotten away alive, if not intact, when Rory and Bastian let him go upon Zoey's request that he suffer but live. Zoey didn't make me promise shit, and after finding her in that alley and then again bleeding out on my bathroom floor, there was no way that bastard was going to keep breathing. The same went for Rossi. He might have gotten away that day in Chicago after trying to sell Tori and Cara, but he wasn't going to keep breathing. The entire River City mafia has been looking for him since, but I found him first.

Call it vigilante justice if you must, but it was something I had to do. A compulsion, I guess. Each time added more weight on my shoulders, but I would always look after the people who were important to me.

"You two are a fucking pair. Always feeling guilty for other people's shit."

"It's called having a fucking conscience. You might do well to find yours."

"I have you for that, even though I've tried like hell to get you to let it go."

I shake my head again as the noise starts again. I look over to my stash sitting on the table. I've been high and drunk for days with only a few moments between for writing. But it's necessary. Without all of it, I'm not sure I could've written this much. Confessed my deepest darkest secrets.

But the walls are closing in on me. Puddles of blood are all over the floor. The wallpaper is starting to crumble with every minute that passes. The noise is grating, and it's been a while now since it was quiet despite the fact that I just did a hit twenty minutes ago.

I walk to the bed and pick up the guitar. I don't have a lot more to add to the journal, but I have a few more songs to finish. I begin picking at the chords until I finally settle on the ones that sound right.

This road has been long and winding

And I'm too tired to go on

Pain and sorrow have haunted me

Guilt and regret fill my mind

I can't go on. I can't keep fighting

This is my goodbye but it's only for a little while

You were the one who kept me afloat

For you have I tried to keep breathing

But these ghosts haunt my soul and mind

This may be my last note

But from you. I'll never be far

This is goodbye but it's only for a little while

It won't be long now but don't shed a tear

Don't cry for me or mourn my name

Cause I will always be with you

Even after I'm gone

My last song is goodbye but it's only for a little while

I hum the words as my fingers move across the strings. I close my eyes and finally let tears I've held back far too long fall. I feel the song inside me.

Each note is like the beat of my heart. My soul is poured into that song for my family. The only people that have made me feel loved and accepted.

I open my eyes. The room still feels too small, but at least everything seems normal again. I decide it's as good a time as any to move on to the next story in my tale. At least until the next episode hits.

I don't know what's going on with me. It's never been like this. Like I'm swimming through muck and mire and it's trying to drag me down. Where I can't distinguish reality from fiction.

I walk back to the table with my notebook and pen, just noticing that Bryan has left. I don't know where he went this time, but I guess it's only fair. I can't expect him to stay with me every second. In fact, this is the most time we've spent together at once since we met.

Even after that night with O'Dell, we left and went our separate ways.

Journal entry #7

May 2014

Life resumed after O'Dell. I pushed forward even when all I wanted to do was drown in a bottle or in white powder, but somehow I managed to stay away from it. Eventually, graduation day came, and it felt like any other day. If not for my dad's insistence, I would've skipped the whole thing. Ryder agreed with me, but his grandfather also insisted.

I stood up on the stage and gave the Valedictorian speech, and looked out among the crowd to see my friends and family beaming with pride that I didn't understand.

I guess it was an accomplishment for someone that couldn't focus on the work. Very few assignments were ever turned in. I worked it out, though. Some I convinced to just let me prove to them without extensive papers that I knew the material. A couple of the other professors were more than obliged to accept sexual favors in exchange for a good grade. I didn't mind. They were hot, and I was horny.

There was one professor that gave me hell. He hated the fact that a bullshit test said I was smarter than him. He was determined to prove otherwise. When he failed me, I appealed the grade. When I won, he was pissed. That started a new policy where professors were obligated to provide other means of proving a student knew the material. The professors knew I knew the material, but even after all that time, the work wasn't something I managed well. Neither was my time. But I personally thought the policy was bullshit. I also thought my appeal win was bullshit. It didn't seem fair that I got a free pass because I could explain it to them instead of doing the work. Contradictory, I know. But if no other word describes me, it's that one.

I spouted off the bullshit speech about new chapters, moving forward, and preparing for the future and didn't bother to hide my eye roll when I received a standing ovation. My hat was off, gown undone, and tie loosened before I finished walking across the stage. I wanted to get out of there and fast. I was in no way mentally ready to deal with my dad.

But Dad was nothing if not smart and cunning. He already knew what I would do and was waiting in the wings before I got there. "I'm proud of you, son," he told me with a smile.

I ignored his comment and grabbed Callie in a swinging hug. Spending time with Callie over the years hadn't been easy. I tried hard when I was in River City to make time for her. I didn't want our relationship to become strained like Chris's and mine did, even before my massive fuck up. And my relationship with my newest sister was non-existent since Jamie left Dad. Not that it would've been much of one given the nearly sixteen year age difference and thousand mile distance between us.

"God, you get more and more beautiful every time I see you," I said as I kissed her cheek. "Not a little girl anymore, are you?"

I set her on her feet, and she beamed proudly while shoving me. "Is that your way of apologizing for forgetting my birthday?" she teased. Except, I knew her well enough to know it wasn't entirely teasing.

"I didn't forget. I called," I reminded her. I would never forget her birthday. Much less her sixteenth birthday. But she was miffed I didn't send her a present like I had every year.

"You did. You called, said happy birthday, I love you, and then promptly said you had to go. The most important birthday in my life, and I barely got thirty seconds out of you." She set a hand to her hip and cocked her little blond brow.

"Can't do much more from a thousand miles away, Cal." I bobbed her nose, earning a scowl. "I know you're fishing for a present. I promise I got you something, but you have to wait until later to get it."

She leaped into my arms with a squeal. "You're forgiven, Madsy," she said loudly, then dropped her voice to a whisper. "Please tell me it's not old lady jewelry like Daddy got me."

I squeezed my eyes shut, knowing Callie didn't understand that the *old lady jewelry* was Mom's. Dad had been giving her a piece for her birthday every year since she died. He told her he would explain why they were all so special one day. I didn't know why he hadn't already told her. "Not jewelry, Cal. Not sure I'd be very good at picking that out, but I guarantee you will love it, and Dad will hate it."

"Don't fight again, Madsy," she pleaded with another whisper.

"You know it's not me that starts it, Cal."

"All right," Dad interrupted us. "I've got us a reservation for eight. Christopher and Ryder will be joining us."

"Sure," I nod. "I need to go shower and change. Tell me where and I'll meet you there."

He gave me the name of the place that I wasn't the greatest fan of. It was a suit and tie kind of place, and I wasn't feeling it after spending all day in one for graduation.

I went home, showered, ran some product through my hair, then threw on a pale gray suit. I returned to the bathroom to put my jewelry back in place, knowing how much Dad hated it all. Nose, eyebrow, lip, and ears were fully adorned and on display for all to see. I also threw on the ring that my gran gave me years ago that belonged to my pawpaw.

An hour later, I walked into the restaurant, already feeling claustrophobic from the amount of snobbery in the place. When I reach the table, a wide grin spreads on my lips at the sight of Ryder. He ditched the jewelry, but the leather jacket and jeans were still firmly in place. We were the bane of the society pages. Just like we liked.

I shook the hands of the men around the table and gave Callie a kiss on the cheek before I took my seat. We ordered our meals, and the small talk began.

210

I hated small talk. Especially business talk. I didn't give a crap about the stock exchange, the prices of oil or gold. I couldn't have cared less about the current real estate market. Oh, I understood it perfectly, I just didn't give a shit.

But I also knew this wasn't dinner for celebration or congratulation. It was a setup in a public place with friends and strangers. My dad thought he could spring whatever it was on me there, and I would just go along.

So when he started, I was ready.

"Maddox, now would be a good time to discuss when you're coming home," he said as he shoved his plate away. "Your position and office are already waiting. All you have to do is show up."

Mr. Rosenthal's brows shot up. I'd had plenty of discussions with him over the years. He knew my plans did not include sitting in an office discussing acquisitions and the latest drilling techniques. Masters Inc was not where my future lay.

Callie's entire body went rigid. She knew the reason I hadn't been home a lot lately was because of Dad's incessant yammering about me working for the company after graduation. No matter how often I insisted I didn't want to, he'd just wave me off. It was unfathomable to him that I would want to do anything else.

"I'm not coming back to River City, Dad," I told him as I wiped my mouth on the napkin. "I've told you before, I'm not working for the company. I'm staying here, and I'm going to play my music."

"Maddox, why would you throw everything away for a hobby that won't lead to anything? You are too brilliant to waste yourself like that."

My fist clenched under the table as I worked to contain myself. "It's not a hobby for me, Dad. It's been my life for years. You know that."

"It was only meant to be something to settle you down. Not a career, Maddox. Music is not a stable career. It's a fantasy for dreamers. You cannot support yourself on something so inconsistent and unstable."

"Good thing I was born into money then, right?" I snap. "I mean, technically, I don't have to ever work a day in my life."

"That's not a damn life, Maddox. I didn't raise you to sit on your ass." He was right about that. My dad was all about work. He never had time for anything else.

"Working on my music is not sitting on my ass. And I also work at Lucky's practically every night."

"And that's another thing. You're a goddamn drug addict and alcoholic. You have no business anywhere near a bar or the music industry."

My jaw clenched tight. I turned my head to the side, closing my eyes tightly to stop the tirade that wanted to escape. "And I became those things long before I set foot in a bar or played on a stage," I said through my gritted teeth.

"You're coming home, Maddox. I'm not going to watch you throw your life away on a pipedream."

I stood from my chair quickly, rattling the table. "I know I'm nothing but a goddamn disappointment to you. I've been a burden since the day I was born. But would it fucking kill you to support me?"

"Not when you insist on living your life without a plan. If you don't come home, I'll cut you off."

I leaned over the table with a snarl. Anger poured from me so thickly I was sure the others could taste it. "Then fucking cut me off. I don't want or need your fucking money. Remember, *Dad*, I got my trust when I turned twenty-one. Between you, Mom, and Pawpaw, I'm set. You already have Chris. You don't need me too."

"Chris can't take over the company," he yelled loudly.

I jerked back, confused with what the hell he was talking about. "Of course, he can. He's already your right-hand man."

"Chris can't take over the company because he's not a Masters by blood," Dad snapped. The look on his face showed instant regret. I imagined the look on mine matched Callie's.

"What did you say?"

"Perhaps it would be best if you took this conversation somewhere else," Mr. Rosenthal said calmly.

"Fuck that. I want him to explain." I didn't mean to be so disrespectful to Ryder's grandfather. He was an amazing man and had treated me like his own grandson for years, but I needed answers.

"Chris was three months old when I met your mother, Maddox. He's not my biological child."

Callie gasped at the revelation, but I only felt outraged at another lie. "Is Callie even yours?" I snapped. "You're already oh-for-two. Why not make it a strikeout?"

"Watch your mouth, Maddox. You are not too old or too big for me to remind you who your father is."

"Well, it sure as fuck isn't you. All this time, I thought you took me out of a sense of obligation to family and because you felt sorry for me. I've always felt like I was a damn burden to you. Now I know you just needed an heir to your fucking throne. Well, guess what, *Trey*, it ain't gonna be me."

I turned and stormed out of the restaurant. Later that evening, my dad showed up at my apartment, banging on the door, demanding I let him in. I didn't.

I didn't answer his calls or texts. I didn't answer his emails. For months, I refused to speak to him. When I finally started again, it was for Callie, but it was only a word or two.

That continued for years.

CHAPTER TWENTY-FOUR

Standing here alone

Present day

The warmth in my veins is a high all in itself. The feeling of it flowing, coursing through me, soothes long before it takes effect. Maybe it's just in the knowing. Knowing that feeling of release and euphoria. Knowing that relief is coming.

I need it right now. My irritation is reaching astronomical levels as well as my inability to sit still. My mind is racing ten thousand miles an hour as I think about my dad. So many secrets all my life. So much left unresolved. That will never be resolved.

He wanted to protect me. He wanted me to be happy. He wanted what was best for me. He loved me.

All of these things he told me dozens of times over the last few weeks. I just don't understand why he couldn't say them to me when I was a kid. When I needed to hear them. When it might have made a difference.

So much time wasted. So much time we can never get back.

Five weeks ago

After spending most of the day just driving around, I walk into Bastian's house. It's all I've done for days. I've been avoiding all of them. I'm just not in the mood to talk about what went down at his dad's over a week ago.

Usually, at this time of day, no one is around. Bastian is doing whatever nefarious shit it is he does and calls business. I suppose it probably is since he and Rory worked hard to make most of their business legal, but it's still hard to imagine it.

Verity is never home at this time. She teaches at a school for special needs kids and never gets home before four. It is always enough time for me to disappear again or hide in my room until they go to bed. It's when I try to sleep since it's been basically nonexistent since the latest bombshells in my life.

Since the revelation that Pawpaw and Jewel both heard voices, I've been struggling. It's been fucking with my head, especially after learning Pawpaw didn't fall.

I've wondered what they heard. Did they hear the same unexplainable white noise I do? Did they see things they knew weren't there? Did they obsess as I do?

Like I have been doing. To the point that I want to pull my hair out and scream at anyone that comes near me.

So when I walk into the door to find my dad sitting at the table, deep in conversation, I get pissed all over again because I know an ambush when I see one.

I yank the earbuds out of my ears that I've have been blasting practically nonstop because they quiet the noise a bit with frustration. "What are you doing here?" I bark out while glaring at Bastian.

Again, I notice how old my dad looks. He's only about sixty, but he was always in such great shape. I'm still thrown off by how much he's changed since I saw him at Jewel's funeral. He's a good thirty pounds lighter at least. His coloring isn't great.

I get a sick feeling in my stomach, but I brush it off. If I let it, I'll be the one apologizing for being his greatest disappointment, or he'll have me buying into his sudden concern. Concern that he hasn't shown in years.

He stands up from the table. My stomach flips when I notice how slowly he gets up. I look at Bastian for a second, sending out my silent question, but he gives me nothing. Just fucking blank eyes.

"I didn't come to upset you, Maddox. I just wanted to talk. Will you let me talk?"

I roll my head a few times to relieve the tension building in my neck. "Fine," I snap. "Talk."

"I'll just let you two—" Bastian begins but I cut him off.

"Nah. You can stay. I'm sure it will be a short conversation."

"Maddox." My dad's head hung with a sigh. Just like the other day, I can see so much regret in his eyes.

I drop mine from him. I don't want to see the regret. I don't even want this conversation. Because I want to stay angry with him, but I can't stand to see him in pain.

I sit on the sofa, and gesture for them to sit. Bastian grunts and grumbles something about being invited to sit on his own couch as he sits on the other end from me with a scowl. My dad takes the chair across from me.

Nothing is said for several seconds, prompting me to move the conversation along. "Whatever you want to say, just say it," I grate. "I'm not going to sit here all day."

Dad nods, while tugging at his tie, his discomfort showing. "First, I wanted to bring you this. I was hoping you'd come to the house, but I realized after the other night that probably won't happen." He reaches inside his jacket, pulls out a small leather journal, then hands it to me. "It was Jewel's. We found it shortly after she passed. I started to read it, but realized it wasn't for me."

"It's her journal," I say impassively as I jerk the book from his grasp. "Of course, it wasn't for you."

"It's for you, Maddox. I can't say for certain, but it seemed like it was all for you."

216

I look at the book in my hands with surprise then back to him. Jewel and I were trying to rebuild our relationship, but it wasn't easy. I was always on the road. We were both junkies and that didn't lead to anything good. We bonded over shit we shouldn't have.

When she died, I should've reevaluated my life. In a way I did. I realized just how fucked I was and went even deeper down the rabbit hole.

I set the book to the side and wait on him to continue. "Maddox, I've been a terrible father to you. I know that. It was never your fault that you reminded me that my sister was a mess, and my best friend fucked me over. I love you, son. I have loved you since the day you came into this world, but I didn't show it. I've been too hard on you. Demanded too much. Tried to force you to fit the mold of what I thought you should be. Just like I did with Jewel. I was never able to make things right with her. I need to do that with you, Maddox."

I shake my head. A mirthless laugh escapes me. "My entire life, all I wanted was your damn approval. I wanted to make you proud. I hated myself—still fucking hate myself—for every time I was a burden. For every damn time I let you down. You decide *now* to let me know it wasn't my fault?"

"It wasn't, Maddox. You were perfect. Flaws and all, you are perfect."

"Is that why you bought my record label behind my back? Is that why you enlisted this asshole," I jerk my head toward Bastian, "to help you? To make amends?"

"We bought it for you, Maddox," he tells me. "When I found out it was for sale, I knew I'd never get the shareholders to approve buying through the company. I didn't have the liquidity to buy it myself, so I sought out Bastian. I knew he would help because it's for you. To make sure you didn't lose your contract."

"Because, of course, I couldn't keep the contract on talent and merit alone, right?" I said sarcastically.

"Shut up, Maddox," Bastian snaps. "I've already told you it had nothing to do with that."

"Right. The other interested party wanted to turn it into a pop label. That's what you said, right? Except guess what? I could've bought it. And I didn't need to go through shareholders to do it because despite what you've

217

always believed, I *did* make it. On my fucking own. I didn't spend one fucking cent to get the deal. We got it because we are good."

"I know you're good," Dad argues. "You're the most talented musician I've ever heard. We just wanted to help. Why is that so hard for you to accept?"

"Because you did it to control me," I yell. "Everything in my life has been about pushing me away while pulling all the strings."

"It's. For. You," Bastian growls again. "I don't want a goddamn record label. Your dad doesn't want a damn record label."

"Too fucking bad I don't want shit from either of you." I stand up and start to walk away.

"Maddox, don't go. Please." Dad begs me. Again. And something about it sends a chill down my spine.

"Why?" I ask, trying to hide the uneasy feeling in my gut. "Why now?"

"Because I'm dying, son."

Four words. Four words I wasn't prepared for. Four words I never thought I would hear. Because William Masters III was immortal.

"What do you mean dying?" My voice shakes. Hell, my entire body starts shaking.

"I have a tumor. It's spread to my lymph nodes. It's inoperable, and treatments have been ineffective."

I look over at Bastian, and for the first time since I've known him, he cannot make eye contact with me. "You knew," I accuse.

"He wanted to tell you himself."

"How long?" I whisper.

"It doesn't matter, Maddox. All I want is to spend what time I have left proving to *my son* that he has never been a disappointment and that I am so very sorry for the part I've played in how hard his life has been."

"How fucking long," I hiss again, this time fighting back the tears.

"A few months, hopefully. More likely a few weeks."

"Weeks," I croak as tears sting the back of my eyes. "Weeks! You come to me with all of this. Telling me you want to make amends. And you only have weeks!"

"I know I have a lot of making up to do, Maddox. I know it's not much time, but please let me try."

"Did you know when you bought my label? Were you sick then?"

"Yes. I've known for a few months now. I didn't tell you kids because I didn't want you to worry."

"Callie and Chris know?"

"No. I haven't told them yet. I needed to tell you first. You're the one that I have so much to make up for."

I shake my head. The tears I'm trying desperately to hold back begin to fill my eyes, but I won't let them see. "I can't do this," I tell them as I grab Bastian's keys. "I... No." I'm out the door before they can stop me, needing to be anywhere but there.

I hauled ass on the bike with no plan at all but to ride. To escape. As hard as I tried, I couldn't put what Dad told me out of my head.

Which is how I find myself on the Island. It's been years since I was out here. Since the night I met Zoey, in fact. I just haven't had the time.

I pass a few tourists, but it's mostly locals fishing for whatever is in season as I walk out onto the long pier that stretches into the gulf with my hood up, glasses on, and head down. Around here, that's not the best thing to do. It gets more stares than walking out with a fruit bowl on your head, but I need to stay as unrecognizable as possible.

I reach the end of the nine-hundred-foot pier, squeezing between two fishermen to lean against the railing. I look out over the water and exhale heavily as I remember this place being one of the few places Dad came with us before Mom died. It was one of the few places where we felt like an actual family, and I wasn't a nuisance.

We'd spend hours here every Sunday walking the beach or fishing. Dad complained the entire time that he had boats for this sort of thing, but we all knew he loved the simplicity of it. It was the only simple thing in his life. The only simple thing he allowed himself.

I don't know what to do with what he told me. I can't fathom him not being around. I also can't fathom us getting past our differences. It feels like a crossroads where every path is the wrong choice.

I reach into my hoodie pocket and pull out the bottle of whiskey. It's not what I really want right now. Just like I know that neither will really help. But the need to be numb is too strong.

I take the first burning swig and sigh with relief. I relish the sweet flavor with its smokey undertone as it warms my insides. Feels like regret, but it's so good going down.

I sip straight out of the bottle and enjoy the sounds of the waves crashing and the pelicans calling out. It's the same type of noise that fills my head sometimes, but when it's actually there, it's almost soothing.

The pier begins to clear, more and more calling it a day from whatever they were doing, leaving me mostly alone in solitude. Not something I wanted as badly as I thought, I realize when the two on either side of me leave.

I grab my pocket, pulling out the phone I take with me for emergencies but haven't turned on since I got here. I need to talk to someone. Not about me or Dad or anything else but just talk.

My finger lingers over Ryder's name. He's the voice I want to hear. I've missed him so fucking much, but he's still in rehab for a few more days. Besides, he doesn't need my shit. Not now or ever. He needs to focus on getting better for Heaven and Tyler.

So I tap another number. One I know that will be as deep or as casual as I want the conversation to be.

"Well, if it isn't my favorite tattooed sex pot. What did I do to deserve a call from the great Maddox Masters?" he quips after the third ring. Hayes has always been such a smart ass.

He, Ryder, and I just clicked from the moment we met. I'd be forever indebted to him for protecting Callie and saving me from killing an asshole. Three guys with shit childhoods, a myriad of baggage, and more pain and anger than one should carry. We were all perfect examples of money doesn't buy happiness, but it sure as hell bought fast cars on our highway to hell.

Even though our lives were so different on the daily, after that first meeting, we'd always made time to see each other every few months and to call as often as time allowed. Although, with Ryder's and my schedule, that meant Hayes came to us more than we went to him. And we would live up the nights with booze and debauchery.

"Hello to you too, asshole, So, how does she look after all these years?" I chuckle as I sit on the pier with my back against the corner beam.

"Breathtaking and contemptuous. Same as always. So, tell me, what the hell you've been up to? I was beginning to think the Internet lied, and you really did die."

"No. I'm invincible. Didn't you know only the good die young? The rest of us motherfuckers have to live in this shithole."

"Aww, Maddox, there you go waxing poetic. You know how much that turns me on. I'm getting in the car right now to come and see you. Seriously, though, how the fuck are you? Media is telling a story that's half bullshit and half concerning because I know you."

I focus my eyes where the sun is beginning to sink into the water. Like that's the very edge of the world if you could just follow it. "Been better, but I don't want to talk about me. I want to talk about anything but me."

"And you called because you know my favorite topic is me, right?"

"Something like that," I chuckle. "So, tell me, how have you been?"

"I wake up and remember I'm Hayes motherfucking Davenport," he laughs. "Nah, you know how it goes... Nothing in life ever really changes, does it?"

"I take it that means you still haven't gotten the girl?"

"Which girl are you referring to? The sassy toddler I catch glimpses of or her spiteful creator? I don't know, man. She's always been and will always be mine. Ya know? She just refuses to cooperate."

"Does she know that you know?" I ask, keeping it vague because—well I don't know why I'm being secretive. No one around me would have a clue what I was talking about.

"Man, I don't know. I think she suspects but doesn't want to say anything in case I don't. You know, southern women are fiercely protective of their children and intuitive as fuck. If they perceive a threat, they'll shut it down, and I assume until she no longer sees me as one to her or Elliot, she'll remain silent. That's life, right?"

"Seems to be," I mutter.

We talk for several more minutes, and he does exactly what I need. He takes my mind off of my shit for a while. The sun has fully set when we end the call, and I know I need to go.

I toss the empty bottle of Johnny into the trash as I head back for Bastian's bike. I climb on, speeding out, leaving only dust and sand behind.

CHAPTER TWENTY-FIVE

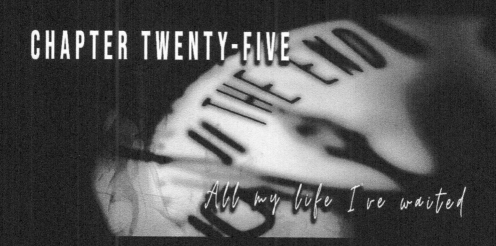

All my life I've waited

Five weeks ago

I walk back into Bastian's loft shortly before midnight. I toss his keys back into the bowl and head to the fridge for something to eat when I hear movement. I turn on the cabinet lighting and turn to find a little canary asleep on the sofa.

Deciding food can wait, I walk over to check on her. I've avoided her since that night at Bastian's dad's. She doesn't need my bullshit. If she were smart, after hearing everything she did, she should be running as fast and as far away from me as possible. Though that's difficult when we're both staying with Bastian temporarily. Which gets me thinking it may be time to move on.

I grab a throw off the back of the sofa, spreading it over her. I know I need to stay away from her, but I can't resist brushing the fallen hair away from her face. Her lashes begin to flutter right along with my damn heart. I start to pull my hand away when she grabs it, placing a kiss against my palm.

The gesture is so intimate it throws me off. I know how I feel about her, but she can't feel the same. It has to be just an act of kindness.

even divorced yet. I'm just a rebound for her. She's never hinted at anything else.

Or has she?

No. No, she hasn't. I would've noticed. Wouldn't I?

Because the way she's looking at me right now makes me question everything I've thought. "What are you doing, *cher*?" I ask her the loaded question.

She sits up, those wild curls flying around her face like a yellow bird's nest, then stands in front of me. She lifts a tiny hand to cup my cheek, sadness filling her eyes. "Verity told me about your dad. I wanted to make sure you were okay."

"I'm always okay, *cher*." I lie easily as I lean away from her touch. But those fucking eyes of hers. Swear to all that is holy, they see right through me.

"You've been drinking," she whispers.

"You gonna run and tell big brother, *cher*?" I ask, intentionally being a dick. "I mean since everyone has decided they know what's best for me and everything."

"They just care about you, Maddox. Is that so wrong?"

My eyes squeeze shut, hating the way she is looking at me. Full of sympathy and understanding when she should be pissed. Not when I left her there with my two dads and the war that I'm sure nearly ensued. Especially not when I was the only reason she was there.

"Why would you worry about me? Any of it. Especially after I ditched you the other night, and I've made a point to avoid you. Why do you care?"

She reaches for my hand, pulling me to sit beside her. When she crawls into my lap, I know I should make her move, but instead, I grip her tighter. Her tiny hands reach up to cup each side of my face as she presses her forehead to mine. "I know when someone is trying to push me away. I did it for too long not to recognize the signs. You say things, do things, whatever it takes to make the people who are trying so hard to love you throw their hands up and walk away. You shut down, close yourself off so they can't see how much you're hurting, and so you don't have to talk about it. I've done all those things, so I know that's what you're trying to do. But I won't let you. I care about you, and I can see you're hurting. More than you want anyone to know. I can give you space, but there's nothing you can do that will make me toss you aside."

"Where the fuck did you come from, Canary?" I breathe out more to myself than her.

"I see you, Maddox. I know what pain looks like. Pain that is in here," she presses her hand to my chest and then to my head, "and in here. I also see that goodness – the reason that Bastian is determined to help you. That your friends call day after day even when you refuse to take their phone calls."

"You don't know me, Quinn," I say as I shake my head against hers as I close my eyes. "You don't know anything about me."

"I know I'm falling for you," she whispers and my eyes snap open.

"Don't say that," I plead with her. "Just – just don't. Don't fall for me, Quinn. You'll get hurt."

She stares straight into my eyes with a fierceness that takes my breath away. "Since I was seventeen, I was with my ex-husband. I loved him with everything I had, and he completely ripped me to shreds. I know what it feels like to be hurt, Maddox. It sucks. But I would rather suffer the pain than never experience the beauty. And oh, Maddox Masters, I've never seen anything more beautiful than you. You have the power to demolish me, and it terrifies me. But I'm more terrified of never experiencing it."

I want to tell her that I'm not falling because I've already fallen. When it happened, it wasn't a gradual thing. I went from lust to love in a single beat of the heart, with a single note hummed when I felt like the world was crashing down on me.

But I don't. If she knows how I feel, it will make the inevitable crash that much harder. But god fucking dammit, I can't stop myself from having her.

I grip the back of her head, pulling her mouth to mine. I kiss her with everything in me. I may not say I love you, but I know she feels it in this kiss. I tell her as I devour her mouth like it's my last meal. My hands slide up her legs, caressing the soft flesh as she moans against my mouth.

225

I grip her hips and wrap an arm around her waist as I stand. Her legs wrap around me as I carry her to my bed. Our lips never break contact. I'm a starving man in the desert, and she is my oasis.

I lay her on the bed, hovering over her delicate body as my mouth devours every inch of her sweet flesh. My hand caresses her body, relishing the feel of her soft skin as I trail my way down her ribcage, the dip in her waist, and that delicious flare of her hips.

I hook my thumbs into the waist of her shorts, pulling them down to her ankles. My eyes never leave hers as I kiss my way up one leg then the next, stopping at the juncture of her thigh. Sliding my way back up her body, I take her thin tank top, tugging it over her ahead. I lean back, admiring the work of art before me because she's nothing short of a masterpiece.

She sits up and slides her hands under my shirt. Her nails scrape gently over my abs, causing the building fire in my belly to burn hotter. I let her remove my shirt, her mouth leaving an electric current as she kisses every inch of my chest.

I stand up to rid myself of my boots and jeans then return to her. She takes my hand, tugging me into the center of the bed. "Let me love you, Maddox. You've never felt it before. Not like this. Let me show you how it feels to be loved, cherished, and adored."

I kiss her lips softly. Then her nose and eyes and forehead before pressing mine to hers. "I don't think you ever really felt it either, have you?" I ask as I grip her neck.

Those soulful eyes meet mine, and I see the truth in them. She has been burned, bruised, and beaten, but she has a fierce, quiet strength that keeps her moving forward. She holds everything close to her chest as I do, but she wants to let go.

"Love me, *cher*. Show me that you mean it."

I dip my head, taking her mouth again, and she shows me everything. I allow her to push me until I'm lying on my back. She hovers her tiny little body over mine, kissing me in places I didn't know I liked. I never did until now. She nips gently at my neck as she presses herself against me. Just as I did to her moments ago, she makes her way down my body slowly. Too damn slow, but I let her have her way.

When she takes me in her mouth, my head falls back on a groan. She swirls her tongue around the head, stroking it in the most insanely intense way I've ever felt in my life. Inch by agonizing inch, she bobs that pretty little head around my decorated shaft, driving me to the brink of madness. I resist the urge to thrust into her throat, to force her to take all of me.

Sure, I did it the other day, but that was different. That was an angry, pissed-off man looking to find some type of relief. And she took my punishment so well.

The anger hasn't subsided. The hurt and the pain still linger. But at this moment, something else builds inside of me also. Need. Not sexual need. Not the urgings of physical release. But the need for a connection, and not one built on rage and fury and misery like Ryder and me. Or the bond founded on our adolescence like Zoey and me.

I need her love. I need this strange faith she has in me despite the short time we've known each other. I need to see myself through her eyes.

I am a selfish, self-absorbed bastard, but the thought of hurting her crushes my soul. The weight—the burden of knowing the pain I will cause her cuts deeper than any double-edged sword. When the bough breaks, all that will remain will be the devastation I'll no doubt leave behind.

But refusing her right now? Impossible.

Unable to take another second of the delicious deviance she delivers—and it is devious, dangerous, and downright sinful the way her sexy-as-hell mouth works me over—I grab her, dragging her up my body for a taste of the sweetness she offers. When her hot sensuality hovers over my mouth, I devour her, again, for purely selfish reasons. The taste of her arousal melting on my tongue and the sounds of her little moans are more powerful than any other pleasure I've ever experienced. She's the best drug.

I just wish it were enough to eradicate the inexorable demons that plague me.

"Maddox," she cries out, and the sound of my name on her lips is everything. "I'm going to—" she whimpers in desperate pleasure.

"Come, *cher*," I command as I latch on to her pulsing bundle of nerves.

I drown in her sweet nectar as I continue my unyielding ministrations. I won't stop until she's a puddle of euphoria and satisfaction.

Or until she begs. Because as sweet as her moans of pleasure are, the sounds of her begging light a fire in me. An urge to be the master of her body and the owner of her pleasure.

And I do just that. With her juices flowing into my mouth and down my chin, knees weak and shaking, she pleads for my mercy.

In one swift move, I have her on her back. Her wild curls cling to her sweat-soaked face. The magnificent flush of her cheeks and haze in her eyes are the most beautiful things I've ever seen.

Reaching over to the nightstand, I grab the foil package, ripping it with my teeth. She watches me with hooded eyes as I roll on the latex. I drag my length through her over-sensitized folds, relishing the way she squirms beneath me, then slowly sheath myself in her tight, wet depths.

Her eyes flutter closed as I begin to move inside of her. Her walls grip my hard length, dragging me deeper with each stroke. Dragging me into her spirit and soul.

Her head falls back with pleasure as she meets me thrust for thrust. Tiny mewls of pleasure fall from her lips.

I grip her legs, wrapping them around me. "Keep them there," I command. I place my arms on either side of her head as her arms wrap around my neck, bringing me closer. Angling my hips, I pull back slowly before thrusting back into her welcoming body with a hard, vicious stroke. I tip my pelvis upward, reaching the most sensitive spot in her depths, earning me a gasp of pleasure.

I repeat the motion over and over. Harder and faster with every thrust of my hips as she clings to my body for dear life. My spine begins to tingle. Electricity and fire flood my body. Her mouth falls open with silent screams of ecstasy, and her pussy strangles my cock, milking my release for every drop.

Our breaths come hard and heavy. Hearts pound in unison.

She looks up at me, her eyes glassy as I kiss her forehead. A single tear falls from the corner of her eye as she cups my face, gently caressing my cheek. I catch the stray tears with my finger, tasting the salt of her emotions.

Words aren't spoken. They don't need to be. What just happened between us was cosmic. Our hearts and spirits are intricately tied together.

And I begin to think maybe she's right. The pain of the crash is worth the beauty of the fall.

Wrapped tightly in my arms, I stroke the soft skin of her hip as her fingers trace the ridges of my abs. A question burns on the tip of my tongue. One that has plagued me since I laid eyes on her.

"What happened with your husband?" I whisper into her hair. It's not my business, but I cannot fathom how the hell anyone could just toss her away for another.

The day will come when I walk away too. When I break her heart into a million pieces. It will be for her own good. She doesn't need my demons tearing her down. If I were stronger, I wouldn't have let things go this far. I would've pined from a distance like I did with Zoey for so damn long.

But she is not Zoey. Resisting her is like resisting the need for oxygen. One day I won't need to breathe. Until then, I have to have her.

"That's a very long story," she sighs sadly. I keep my muttered curse silent. I hate that I just reminded her of her heartbreak. I also hate that she ever felt it. Hate that anyone ever made her do anything but smile.

I open my mouth to tell her she doesn't have to tell me when she begins to speak. "I was painfully shy when I was little, and it lingered throughout my early teen years. It didn't help that my mom was overprotective to the point of helicopter parenting. She had me afraid of my own shadow at times. Afraid I'd get sick or hurt or in trouble. I cried once when I got sent to the principal's office for passing a note. It wasn't even mine. I was the middleman, I guess, and I got caught because I didn't know how to be sneaky. When high school started, I changed. I was still quiet and timid, but I was more willing to try. Mom didn't like it, but she conceded I was growing up. My senior year, I met Scott at a party I was *not* supposed to be at." She pauses for a minute. Her breath flutters across my skin as she releases a tiny chuckle.

"What's so funny?" I ask with a grin.

"I just thought about how tame I was. Sneaking out to a college party seemed like a huge deal to me at the time, but looking back, I was so naïve. My friends were at those kinds of parties all the time, but I thought I was so badass."

"That's actually kind of adorable," I laugh. "I was strung out and in rehab at seventeen," I say in an attempt to make light of the situation.

"That's not funny," she whispers softly as she looks at me. "I hate that you went through that."

"It was self-inflicted, darlin'. No one to blame but myself, so don't feel bad for me." She opens her mouth, another argument on the tip of her tongue that I quickly swipe away with my own. "Now, finish your story."

She shakes her head with a sad smile, knowing I'm deflecting. "Fine. So at this party, I met this guy. He was older, a senior in college, and he seemed into me. We spent the night talking and making out. When I left, he asked for my number. Over the next couple of weeks, we talked on the phone and texted, just getting to know each other a bit. He finally asked me out, but the rules with my parents were they had to meet the guy first. I just knew they would say no. I mean I was seventeen and in high school He was twenty-two, nearly twenty-three, finishing his final semester of a five-year degree."

"But they didn't say no."

"Nope. They wanted to. I could tell they did, but they said they wouldn't stop me since I had enough respect for them to ask permission. Fast forward eight months later, the day after my graduation, I'm standing in the middle of his apartment with a positive pregnancy test in my hand."

I inhale sharply. I have no idea what I expected, but that wasn't anywhere near my thoughts. Even though I have never wanted kids, my heart aches for where I know the story is going. For her loss.

"Scott was great. He didn't panic or freak out at all. Not like I did. 'We'll get married,' he said. I loved him, and panicked or not, I knew I would keep my baby. So that's what we did. Two weeks later, in front of the Justice of the Peace, we said 'I do'. I was scared as hell, but I was also happy. I fell into my role as a wife very easily. Looking back now, it's kind of scary how easily I took to it. What the hell kind of teenage girl just falls into wedded bliss like that?"

"A girl that wants simple things," I tell her. "You don't have to dominate the world to be a strong woman, Quinn. There's nothing wrong with a woman that wants to rule fortune five-hundred companies while being supermom. My mom was like that. But there's also nothing wrong with choosing to stay home and take care of your husband or children. My mom did that too. She did that for me."

She inhales deeply then exhales with a stuttered breath. I feel a tear land on my chest as she sniffles softly. "I was twenty-two weeks when I was awoken from a dead sleep with so much pain, I thought my insides were ripping apart. I couldn't breathe; it hurt so badly. Scott sat up beside me, asking me what was wrong, but I couldn't answer. He cursed when he pulled the sheets back. The bed was covered in blood."

I squeeze her tighter, trying to comfort her while she relives the horrible memory, but I stay quiet, letting her work through it at her own pace.

She wipes her face and tries to pull away from me. I don't let her. I keep her close, letting her know she's not alone.

"Anyway, I went into a deep depression after that. For months all I did was cry. I was unbearable to live with. I realize that now. I realized it then, but I didn't care. Scott and I barely made it through that time. Honestly, we should've called it quits then, but I couldn't stand to lose him too. Then one day I decided that another baby was what I needed. I needed to fill the void inside me. Scott didn't think it was the best timing, but he went along with it. We tried and tried for over a year and nothing, so we went to a specialist. Turns out I have a septate uterus which makes me more likely to miscarry or deliver prematurely, and in my case, also nearly impossible to get pregnant. My particular abnormality is one of the more severe cases. Less than two percent of women are affected. Getting pregnant the first time was basically a fluke. All of this triggered another depression. I was angry—so damn angry that my baby was gone, and my hope of having another went up in flames with a few words from the doctor. I became a raving bitch. No one could stand to be around me. Once the anger subsided, I just wanted to be left alone in my misery. Finally, one day, my mom and dad showed up. Said if Scott wasn't going to do anything, they were. A few hours later, I was sitting in the middle of a therapist's office, refusing to speak."

I don't mean to, but when therapist leaves her mouth, I flinch. If she notices, she doesn't say anything. "Did it help?" I ask a little gruffly, trying hard to cover up my slip. "Therapy."

"Not at first, but eventually. Eventually, I realized I'd been pushing everyone away because I didn't think they could possibly understand my pain. Because I didn't want their pity. The truth was that was when I needed them most. It was an instant fix. It took months, but I did get there, and I was determined to take back my marriage." She lets out a mirthless chuckle. "I felt horribly guilty for everything I put Scott through. I knew he was probably hurting too, but I didn't care at the time. I worked hard to repair our relationship. I honestly thought it was worth saving. What I didn't know was the entire time he was with me, he had another girlfriend. I don't mean during the time I was pushing him away. I mean from the very first hello. I want to say he was living a double life, but the other girl knew about me from the beginning. I guess he was content to have his cake and eat it too. Until she got pregnant. That's when he decided he had to *do the right thing*. I came home from work to find my bags packed and waiting by the front door. He and his new, old girlfriend were waiting with the news that I was out and she was in. His parents had bought him everything before we were married, so there was no property to divide. He had me sign a prenup before we got married, and according to it, I wasn't entitled to anything except half of the shared accounts."

"I think he's got to be the biggest idiot on the planet," I say as I kiss the top of her head. "He had everything and tossed it away."

"He's not the biggest idiot," she says as she shakes her head. "I was. I was so caught up in him, then scared to be a teen mom, and then consumed by grief, that he made a fool out of me. That makes me the biggest idiot."

I flip her over to her back, hovering over her. "You have a good heart. You're trusting and kind and gentle. That doesn't make you an idiot. That makes you a good person."

"Tell me something about you. Something no one else knows."

"The world knows everything about me," I tell her with a grin. It falls quickly to match the frown on her face.

"The world knows what you let them know. I've read the papers, and I've met the man. The two don't line up. You're not the rockstar bad boy you portray yourself to be."

"Oh, Canary, you have no idea how bad I really am," I half tease. Then I drop my forehead to hers in surrender. "What do you want to know?"

232

"Something real, Maddox. Not deflection or fluff. I want you."

"The last time I saw Jewel before she died, I told her I hated her," I whisper softly. "I'd been on a bender with Bryan, who'd come to New York after our tour ended, when she showed up at my apartment. She knew I was wasted. If anyone could tell it was her. I could hide it from the world but never her. She'd been clean for over a year. She wanted me to go to rehab. She begged and pleaded with me. Bryan laughed and asked her why she thought she could convince anyone they should get sober. She ignored him and continued to beg. Told me I was ruining my life, and she didn't want me to be like her with a life full of regret. I told her it was too late. That she made sure my life was nothing but regret the day I was born. I told her I hated her for not aborting me in the first place. Then I kicked her out. A week later, she OD'd. I broke her. Because of all this hurt and anger I've had for so long, I crushed her spirit. She's dead because of me."

"Why do you do it?" she asks, and I am thankful that she doesn't try to convince me it's not my fault.

"Why do I do what?"

"The drugs," she says softly but clearly. "Why do you do them?"

"Don't you mean why *did* I do them?"

"I can see you still struggle with it. Just like the drinking tonight."

"Drinking was never as much of a crutch as the drugs, but I won't deny it's a problem too," I tell her honestly. "I use a lot of things I shouldn't, sex included, to shut out this." I tap two fingers against my temple. "It's loud and noisy in here. The drugs help with that. Or they did for a while. Now they're just part of me. You're right, *cher*, it's a struggle." I lean back from her as I reveal the next truth. "They're one of many reasons you should stay away from me."

"But you're trying to get better."

"I'm not, darlin'. I'm going through the motions to make everyone happy for now, but in the end, the addiction will win. And make no mistake, Quinn, I am an addict. I crave the drugs as much as I crave you."

"You can do it, Maddox. I know you don't think so, but you're strong too. I can see it in your eyes, that you've got so much you carry, but you're a good man, Maddox."

233

I start to move off her bed, unable to hear this again. Especially after what I just told her. "I'm not. The sooner you see that, the better off you'll be."

She grabs my hand, and though I want to pull away, I can't. "Your friends call every single day even though you won't answer their calls. Sebastian and Verity have you in their home no matter how many times you lash out at him. Your father came here, pleading for forgiveness and understanding, knowing the chances you would grant him either were slim. People don't try that hard, fight that hard for someone who isn't worth it."

"Goddammit, Quinn," I mutter. "I'm going to rip you apart."

"The funny thing is, I know if you do, it will be because you're trying to save me. It's just who you are. You want to save everyone. Even if it's from yourself. I also know it will rip you apart to do it, but guess what? I'll still be here waiting, and I'll put us both back together."

"I'm not worth it, Quinn."

"Or maybe you are worth everything."

CHAPTER TWENTY-SIX

All you leave behind

Five weeks ago

I stand at the kitchen island, shoveling food in my mouth like I haven't eaten in days. Over the past twenty-four hours, I wonder how it went from hell to heaven. Moreover, how I ended up breaking my own fucking rule.

Quinn stayed with me all night.

I should've made her leave. Or, at the very least, I should've gotten up. I didn't really sleep anyway. I listened to her peaceful breathing and wondered at the way she clung to me. She really amazed me. After what she went through with her asshole ex, I'm surprised she doesn't hate all men, especially ones with my reputation. She doesn't even seem jaded.

Or that's what she says. And maybe she really believes the beauty is worth the pain, but I can see the heartbreak still lingers. I saw in her eyes as she told me her story just how much she still hurts. I want so badly to take it away. To show her how beautiful and amazing she is. How much I treasure her. When I am the cause of the pain, I hope she still thinks it was worth it.

When she woke next to me, the smile on her face could've lit up the entire east coast. My heart leaped at the sight, knowing I put it there. I even asked her to take the day off. She said no, of course. She only left a few minutes ago for work.

Work is what I need to be doing. I need to get back to New York soon. We need to lay tracks soon.

Except I have nothing. I haven't written one motherfucking song since the one I wrote for Jewel after she died. If Ryder and Angel don't have ten tracks between them, then we don't have an album. And though music has always been my escape, it's eluded me for a while. My only relief came from getting high. That was the one constant, but the effects weren't lasting as long.

I am shoveling the last remnants of eggs into my mouth, considering going downtown to buy a guitar because I'm not ready to go to my dad's where my other guitar has been kept for years, when the elevator comes alive. For half a second, I think Quinn has forgotten something, but the minute the doors slide open, I know it's not her.

I drop my head onto the back of my hand and curse. "I've got to get Bastian to delete everyone's codes until I leave," I tell them.

"Well, hello to you too. Long time no see."

"Why is it so difficult for everyone to understand that if I'm not answering calls or texts, I probably don't want to see them?"

"I got the message loud and clear. I mean, you made your point pretty apparent on Jax's face."

I turn around to face her. Those icy orbs reflect sadness and hurt and a whole lot of pissed. "That why you here, Zoey? To ream me out over your husband's face? Don't you think he had it coming after all these years?"

"Don't you think you had it coming after what you said?" she spits. She is so angry she's practically vibrating. The problem is, coming from her barely five-foot frame with her tiny voice, it's about as intimidating as a fight with Lyra.

"Sorry I spilled the beans that I was the one who touched you first," I say with dripping sarcasm.

"It was never a secret, Maddox. I've never told Jax because I didn't want him coming after everyone I was with before him." She sets her fist on her hip and narrows her eyes. She really makes it difficult not to laugh. She is trying so hard to look tough.

"Darlin', it wasn't the fact that I touched you that pissed him off. It was the fact that while you were riding my cock, Ryder was fucking your ass that set him off."

Her eyes widen at my vulgarity and crassness. I've never talked like this to her before. Not once. I'm not sure anyone has. Zoey has always been treated with kid gloves, much to her chagrin. But the fact is, she is delicate and fragile. And I'll be in for another fight if she tells her husband what I just said.

Her eyes close, and her head falls back as she takes a deep breath. When her gaze finds mine once again, all that's left there is resolve. "Why, Maddox? Why are you working so hard to push me away?"

"It's not just you, Zoey. I don't want anyone around. If you'd come down from your throne once in a while, you'd know everything isn't about you."

Her mouth falls open, tears fill her eyes, and my resolve to chase her right back out the door wavers. "I've never thought everything was about me. I know what you're doing, Madsy. I've done it too, remember? I know what it looks like to be in hell. I also know what it looks like when you're trying to push everyone away because you don't want to drag them down with you." She walks to me and grips each side of my face as those tears fall down her cheeks. "We want to be there for you. Let us be there for you."

"Zoey, I don't want any of you to see me like this." I fight the need to wipe her tears.

"See you like what, Maddox? All I see is the same beautiful person I've always seen."

I shake my head with a huff of laughter. That's the thing. I've always seen Zoey. Know every inch of her heart, but she's only ever seen Jax. "Look harder, Zoey. I've been a train wreck since the day we met. I don't want anyone to see just how fucking helpless I feel. How much pain I am in."

"Is it withdrawals?" she asks, her brows furrowed into a deep V between her eyes. "You were doing so good for so long. Why did you start using again?"

I grip her hands, removing them from my face with another humorless chuckle. "That right there, darlin'? Zoey, it's not a recent occurrence. Your brother and husband know that."

Shock mars her delicate features as she takes a step back. "What do you mean?"

"Exactly what I said, Zoey. I haven't been sober for nearly five years. I just made sure I was never high around you."

"Five ye... Maddox, when did you... I mean—"

I can see her doing the math in her head. She's trying to figure out when without me telling her. Because I won't tell her. I won't tell her that I started drinking again when she lived with me. When I was watching her waste away a little more every day. And I won't tell her that I did that first line of coke after I cleaned her blood off my bathroom floor. That she left enough behind on the counters for me to get the relief I needed.

She can't handle it. She's come a long way from that broken girl that had so much stolen from her. Her fire is back, even if she still has moments where she looks like she could crawl out of her skin. Her eyes are full of life and love again. I'm not going to take that away from her.

"When doesn't matter, Zoey. The point is that this didn't happen recently. It wasn't a slip-up."

"Why?"

"That doesn't matter either. My point remains the same. I don't want you or anyone else around me right now. Is that so fucking hard to understand?"

"But I just want to help you," she begins to sob. "I love you, Maddox. I don't want to lose you."

Unable to stand the tears, I pull her into my arms, holding her close. "You won't lose me, Zoey. I'll always be with you."

"Why do you say that like you're going to—"

"I love you, too, Zoey," I cut her off with a kiss to her forehead.

I linger there for a minute, not realizing the elevator had begun to move again when my eyes are met with wide eyes the color of whiskey.

They are filled with embarrassment and hurt as her cheeks flare bright red. "I—uh—I forgot my—my outfit for tonight," she stammers as she darts quickly to her room.

I pull away from Zoey as my eyes follow the tiny blond that just took off like a hurricane across the room. "You need to go, Zoey," I tell her while my eyes linger on the path just taken by the little canary.

She turns her head in the direction of Quinn's trail then looks back to me with wide, knowing eyes. "You like her," she announces. I open my mouth to deny it, but the words don't come out. Zoey's eyes get impossibly wider as she slaps a hand across her mouth. "Oh my God, Maddox. You're in love with her."

My jaw clenches. I can't allow an admission, but denial is firmly stuck in my throat. "It's complicated," I finally relent.

"Go get her, Maddox." Her tone holds no room for argument as she steps away from me, pointing down the hallway. "Go get her now. I don't know what you've told her—"

"Everything that matters," I confirm.

"You mean everything to chase her away." She shakes her head quickly, her hair flying around her face. "Go tell her how you feel, Maddox."

"Not that simple, Zoey. She doesn't need me or my complication."

"Looks like it's too late for that if her face was any indication. Now, go!"

She starts to back away from me some more, her eyes lingering where Quinn just disappeared. Just before she reaches the elevator, her eyes find mine once again. "You deserve to be happy, Maddox. Don't let your need to save everyone keep you from that."

When the elevator has descended, Quinn comes out of the room with a small bag draped over her shoulder. She doesn't look at me, but I can tell she's looking for Zoey.

"She's not here," I tell her in a weak attempt to alleviate her insecurities.

"Oh," she exclaims, pretending to be oblivious. "I wasn't looking—"

I move to her, crossing the space between us in three long strides. Gripping her by the waist, I pull her into my chest. "Don't lie to me, *cher*," I warn her. "I saw your face when you walked in."

Her eyes drop to the floor, avoiding my stare. I grip her chin, forcing her to look at me. My eyes dart between hers, and I see her anxiety, embarrassment, and insecurity. "I was just surprised," she tells me as she begins to nibble on her lip. "I swear that's it. I know we're not—"

"We're not what?" I ask with a jerk of her head when her eyes leave mine. "We're not what, *cher*? Tell me."

"We're not, you know, together."

"Hmm." I see it. I see everything in those words, in her eyes. The sweet girl whose confidence was trashed by an asshole, trying so desperately to cling to hope. She may believe the beauty is worth the pain, but she's still terrified of the agony.

And fuck if I don't see the love there too. I need to end this now. It would be easy to just pack up and return to New York, but I can't let go just yet.

She tries to pull away from me as redness once again creeps up her neck. My silence has embarrassed her further. I tighten my grip, holding her in place, and drop my lips to hers. "We may or may not be *together*," I emphasize the word, "but whatever you thought you just walked in on, you're wrong."

"But you love her," she whispers, reminding me of my confession a few weeks ago.

And it hits me like a ton of bricks. I do love Zoey. She and I have a strange bond that I can't explain. But just like with Ryder, I'm not *in love* with Zoey. I never have been. I was only in love with the idea of her.

An idea that was shattered the minute a set of whiskey eyes replaced the icy ones in my dreams. The second I heard that sexy voice singing of heatwaves and southern boy smiles, my desire morphed from wanting to feel a connection with someone special to knowing it was right in front of me.

This is a train on a broken track traveling at high speed. There is no stopping it. Not for either of us. I guess my only choice is to enjoy the ride before it goes up in a blaze of fury.

"I do love, Zoey, *cher*. I love Ryder too. I cannot fathom a life without them in my life. They're both connected to me in ways that not many would understand. Especially Ryder. We're connected by our souls. But with you, I've found something else. Something I didn't know existed until you walked into my life."

Her eyes glisten with unshed tears. "I feel it too," she whispers.

"I hope you meant it when you said it's worth the pain." I swipe my thumbs under her eyes, wiping away those unshed tears. "Because, darlin', this will be one hell of a crash."

CHAPTER TWENTY-SEVEN

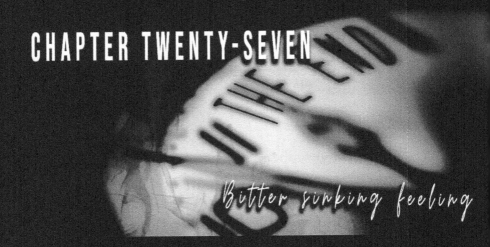

Bitter sinking feeling

Present

The walls are closing in again. I've decided to embrace it though. I've spent years trying to fight off the inevitable, and it has been for nothing. These demons that haunt me were always going to win, but there's not anything left for me to fight for.

Time and time again, I've hidden away the part of me that would cause concern. I've hidden it all for so long that I didn't notice I'd been slipping. I missed the lingering looks from Ryder when I would comment on something that I thought was there. Or the worry in Dane's eyes when I answered a question no one else heard.

I know how dramatic I sound. I'm like a teenage girl commiserating over her first broken heart. Except, I broke my heart. I broke it to save hers.

I broke it because the noise has become voices whispering to me in the dark. The hallucinations started to control me. The thoughts of desperation began to consume me.

I tried so hard to latch on to her. I wished and commanded and prayed and pleaded for her to be the antidote to this poison that flows through me.

Two weeks ago

"What time do you get off of work tonight?" I ask her as I pinned her against the shower wall with my body, my lips tracing a hot path down her neck.

"What makes you think I don't have to work at the club tonight?" she murmurs as her breathing picks up.

"Because I've got your schedule memorized, Canary. I told you two weeks ago if you're going to take your clothes off for an audience, I'm gonna be sitting front and center."

I slide my hand down her back, dragging a finger between her cheeks as I nudge that tight hole she hasn't let me have. Yet.

"Maddox," she breathes as I tease her.

"What time, *cher*?" I ask again as my mouth trails to her peaked nipples.

"I—uh—four-thirty, I think." Her hands tangle in my hair as she presses herself into my mouth.

"Good. Gives us plenty of time."

"For what?"

"Don't worry about that, darlin'. You just plan on a good time. *Laissez les bon temp rouler, cher.*"

When my fingers dip lower, finding her slick and wanting, she begins to beg and try desperately to push my head lower. "Maddox, please."

I chuckle at her pleas, loving the sounds she makes. She's so fucking insatiable, and I love it. "Please, what?"

"Please make me feel good."

I would never deny a woman begging. Not this one anyway. When she comes all over my face, I look up with a wide grin. "*Ça c'est bon.*" I slant my mouth over hers with vigor.

243

"You know," she giggles when I pull away. "Your accent was barely noticeable when you first got here. Now—"

"I sound like I was born on the bayou," I huff out a laugh. "It tends to happen the longer I'm down here. Takes me months to shake it when I get back to New York."

"Mmm." The change in her tone, look in her eyes, is immediate, and happens every time I mention New York.

She has no idea that when I go back, I plan on taking her with me, and I'm not above kidnapping.

But I won't say it. I won't even bring it up because I don't know that I won't fuck all this up today.

I kiss her quickly as I turn off the water. "Stop thinking so much," I order. "I do enough of that for everyone."

She releases a sigh with a small grin. She shakes her head as she walks out of the oversized shower. I slap her ass hard, earning a coy smile. "One day, Bastian and Verity are going to kick us out for making so much noise."

"Nah. These rooms are all soundproofed," I inform her as I grab a towel from the hook.

"How do you know that?" Her eyes are wide at the revelation, and I'm reminded how little she knows. Even about her own family. It makes my stomach clench, but at the same time, there's no reason for her to know.

"First, I'm a musician, so I recognize it. Second, I know Bastian. He and Verity probably did it for everyone else's benefit more than their own." I waggle my brows at her suggestively.

"Ooh," she responds, turning bright red.

"Damn, you're so fucking cute."

"I'm not an innocent, naïve little girl," she huffs.

"No. You're definitely not," I say as my eyes rove her wet, naked body. "But it's cute how hard you blush at the mention of sex after the things I've done to you."

The flush spreads across her cheek up to her hairline, and I laugh.

An hour later, she is out the door, and I am in search of something to do. Anything to kill time while I wait for the next several hours to pass.

I find myself staring at the solid oak door I haven't entered in years. It mocks and taunts me, daring me to push it open, to take those first steps inside.

I'm just about to turn around, still not ready to face the other side when it swings open. I take in my beautiful little sister that I haven't seen since the last time the band played in River City.

"Maddox," she squeals as she launches herself into my arms.

I set her to her feet, brushing the dark blond locks from her face. Gripping each side of her face, I kiss her forehead with a smile. "What are you doing here?" She's supposed to be in North Carolina finishing out her masters' degree.

Her smile drops, bright blue eyes fill with tears, and I know Dad told her. "I couldn't stay away, Madsy. He hasn't always been the greatest dad, but he tried."

"It's okay, Cal. You don't have to explain. Is he here?"

She nods as she wipes away the tears. "He's in his office," she chuckles. "Wouldn't expect him to be anywhere else, would we? He's been hoping you'd come."

"I don't think it's a great idea, Cal. I—I just don't see—" I shake my head, no idea how to finish the sentence.

"I know, Maddox, but he's trying to make amends."

I don't argue with her. I let her drag me into the house that feels more like a mausoleum than home. "Daddy," she calls out, "you have a visitor. Please, Maddox, just try."

I nod as I turn down the hallway that leads to his office. I knock twice and immediately hear his deep voice call out.

I step into the room that was always off-limits to us as kids. He looks up, and the relief in his eyes radiates throughout the room. But I find no relief in his dark depths. Not when I see how much worse he looks since the last time I saw him. It's only been a couple of weeks, and he already looks so much more fragile and frail.

245

I swallow hard against nausea and fight my urge to turn around and run. I don't want anything to happen to him. I don't want to feel the weight I've felt over Jewel. And I know this weight would be so much heavier.

"Maddox," he exclaims as he stands from his massive chair that sits behind the ornate desk that my mom picked out for him years ago. He moves slowly with the help of a cane that makes my breathing stutter.

This is what it looks like when larger than life is nearing the end. The sight and the thought fill my heart with dread. My fists clench at my sides as I take in the man that once stood tall and proud, towering over everyone. I close my eyes with a deep but silent inhale of air as I try to keep the tears at bay.

"You're a Masters. We cannot afford to show weakness."

The words echo in my mind as I fight against the compulsion to curl into a ball and sob. I'm here to make amends, but how do you repair twenty-nine years of damage when you're in a race against time?

"How are ya, Dad?"

"So much better now that you're here." He takes a seat in the chair next to the window and gestures for me to do the same. "Thank you for coming, Maddox. I wanted... Well, I wanted to call you again, but Callie and Sebastian said I needed to give you time."

I lean forward, my elbows on my knees, and drop my head. "I need a lot more time than we have, Dad," I tell him honestly.

He places a hand on my back. The dam I'm fighting threatens to burst. I try to focus on my breathing, but goddammit, why?

"It's okay, Maddox. I know I can't possibly make up for all I've done. I placed unrealistic expectations on you. Tried to impose what I wanted for your future on you. When I got Bastian to help me buy your record label, it was never with the intention of controlling you."

"You shouldn't have done that. No matter the reason, you shouldn't have done it. I don't need saving, Dad."

"Oh my boy, you needed saving long ago. I was just too blind to see and in too much denial."

246

I narrow my eyes at him. I didn't come for him to lay more guilty on me. To make me feel like an inadequate disappointment all over again. I can do enough of that without any extra help.

"Let me finish before you blow up," he says, causing my jaw to clench. He better make it good and fast before I walk. "What Paul said the other day about your grandfather and Jewel. He was right. There were things—" he looks at his hands, taking a deep breath. "I always thought Jewel's issues were the drugs. My father, on the other hand, we all thought he was eccentric. We knew he suffered from severe bouts of depression, but it wasn't until we found his journals years later that we realized something else was going on there. I don't know what it was, but it was something. But you, son, you were always so brilliant."

"Sure, I was," I taunt. "That's why you were so surprised about the test results when I was a kid."

"I wasn't surprised. Not really. I just didn't realize how brilliant you were until then. But you were always too smart. Too perceptive. Your mother treated you with kid gloves because she recognized something in you. Something that needed to be nurtured. While I... I thought for you to reach your full potential, I needed to make you strong. I wanted you to take over the company, not because you were the only one unless it went to Callie, but because I thought you were born for it."

"I wasn't born for anything, Dad. Only thing I've ever been good at is letting everyone down."

"Dammit, Maddox." He lowers his head in shame. When he looks up at me, my heart stops. My father who demanded that tears held no place in our lives, face was streaked as they cascaded down. "You never disappointed me. The moment Jewel brought you to me, I was in love. But every time I looked at you I felt so much pain, knowing one day you'd find out everything and hate me for it. Every time I saw you, I saw everything my sister was missing because she couldn't put you first. But disappointed, son? I have never been more proud of anyone in my life."

And the dam breaks. I can't stop them. Everything I've wanted to hear for as long as I can remember from the only person I ever wanted to hear it from.

Hayes was right when he said life's not fair. He may not have said it that way, but it's what he meant. Because how damn fair is it that I finally feel love and acceptance from my dad, and he's living on borrowed time.

With my face buried in my hands, I sob like a child. I'm angry with him, but more than anything, I'm more grief-stricken knowing that so much time has been wasted. Time we can never get back, and we will never be able to make up for it because fate is cruel and destiny is a joke.

I suppose Dad can't take it anymore because he stands, grabs me by the arms, and drags me into his arms, embracing me tightly for the first time since I was a teenager. "Keep fighting, Maddox," he whispers in my ear. "I know you have demons, but I need you to keep fighting for me. I need you to win."

Another sob escapes me because it's a promise I can't make.

I leave there wishing I could say I feel lighter, but I can't. The weight on my shoulders feels infinitely heavier, and I know the worst is yet to come.

Quinn walks out of her room with Verity, looking dressed to kill. I've been waiting for her to get ready for over an hour. Bastian has tried to talk to me, but my mind has remained back with my dad. I can't stop thinking about it. I just hope that I can focus on her tonight as I planned.

I also hope my plan doesn't epically backfire.

"Ready?" I ask as I take her by the hand.

She gives me an excited nod, making me smile.

"Sure you don't want to come?" I ask Bastian jokingly.

"Fuck you," he grunts, causing Verity to chastise him and Quinn's brows to jump to her hairline.

Driving down the busy streets in Bastian's Lamborghini, I lace my fingers through hers as I shift gears. Fast has always felt free, and I push the limits. She squeezes my fingers for dear life as I race through the streets, knowing that Bastian's plates that say *Babau*, another damn word for boogeyman (he has gone a little overboard in his embracement of the damn nickname) will stop me from getting pulled over.

"Oh my God, you're gonna get us killed," Quinn screams as she grips the door.

I laugh at her reaction. It shouldn't be funny, but I can't stop laughing. Finally, I slow down as we get closer to the busier part of town, and I bring her hand to my lips. "I may not have promised I won't break your heart, but I'll never let anything happen to that beautiful body."

She throws her head back with a peel of laughter. "Of course, you're more concerned with my body than my heart."

I smile. I don't tell her I'm concerned with both but can only prevent one.

We pull up to the place I'm bringing her and hand the keys off to the valet.

"What is this place?" she asks as we walk into the smokey club. But my lips are sealed until I know I have her blocked in a booth with no escape.

We slide into the booth, and she turns to me with questions in her eyes.

"What?" I chuckle.

"How are you able to just walk around without getting mauled?"

A boisterous laugh explodes from my chest as I shake my head in amusement. "Really? You're just now asking that?"

Even in the dark club, I can see the flush that spreads across her cheeks. "I just thought of it."

"This is home," I tell her with a smile. "No matter how long I'm away, it will always be home. Usually, if I'm in town for a concert, I have to lay low, but when I'm just *home*, people don't get crazy. Tourists get more excited than locals. You have to remember, I've been playing concerts for locals since I was ten years old."

"Wait? What?" she chokes on her coke the waitress brought her. "You mean recitals, right? Like normal ones all kids play in."

"No," I chuckle. "I mean charity balls, benefit concerts, and with the River City Orchestra once or twice."

249

"Holy crap," she breathes. "I was freaking out about singing in a school musical when I was ten."

"What happened?"

"I forgot the words, my voice screeched, and I started crying. God, it was humiliating."

"You had stage fright." It's a statement, not a question. "I've had it before. Not performing. If I wasn't born for anything else, I was born for music. But the interviews and photoshoots. Those suck. I've lost my lunch more than a few times. I eventually figured out that I shouldn't eat first."

"It was stage fright. I was the joke of the class for a few days but nothing too awful. I tried again a couple more times, but eventually, I quit being able to hum a note in front of anyone. Until you."

I blow out a breath, knowing full well she's about to lose her shit when I tell her why I'm really here. It's a dirty, despicable plan that I came up with a few nights ago in hopes of helping her break out of her shell.

"*Bienvenue*, and thank you for coming out to our weekly karaoke night."

Quinn's eyes meet mine, filled with terror. I squeeze her thigh in a weak attempt of reassurance. "What did you do?" she rasps out.

"Our list for the evening is full of people ready to show their talents and one very special performance that I know you all will love."

"So, I signed us up."

Her whole body begins to shake, and I get the feeling I have seriously underestimated her fear. "I can't, Maddox. I can't go up there."

I pull her close to me, kissing her head. "You won't be alone. I'll be right there with you. And not to brag or anything, but it's me, so no one will be looking at you."

She giggles quietly into my chest then sighs. "Maddox, I can't."

"If you get scared or nervous, just look at me, okay? Sing for me like you do every night. I'll sing for you." Since that first time she hummed for me, she has slowly given me more. Every night as her fingers weave through my hair, she gives me more of that sultry voice that's as sweet as a lullaby.

"Why is this so important to you?"

"Because you're crazy talented, baby. I'm not sure I've ever heard anyone as good as you. It needs to be shared. Step one to breaking you out of your shell, you did on your own. You sing for me. Now we need to get you to sing for an audience. But this doesn't really count. Look," I gesture to the tables around the bar, "there are less than fifty people here, and you're singing with me. We can even do it with the track if you want."

"How am I supposed to say no to those blue eyes?" she asks as she gently strokes my cheek.

I drop my forehead to hers with a sigh as my eyes close, remembering the first woman who said those words to me. "Easy. You don't."

The next few weeks flew by in a blur. I spent more time at my dad's place, even bringing Quinn with me when I could. It wasn't easy. It seemed every visit he was worse. But we talked more in the last few weeks than we did for most of my life.

I stand out on Bastian's balcony, smoking a cigarette and waiting on Quinn to get home. The river is choppy today. A storm is blowing in, and an uneasy feeling settles in my chest. My mind has been a wreck today for no reason. This sense of foreboding has felt like a heavy blanket over my soul.

I grab my phone, looking through the missed calls and texts because I'm still avoiding everyone, but I've kept it on for my dad and Callie.

My gut twists every time I see the missed calls. Especially Ryder. He got out of rehab a couple of weeks ago, and I've dodged most of his calls. I knew I had to talk to him soon after he told Bastian he'd be here in a month if he didn't hear from me. Honestly, if I don't go home soon, he'll be here anyway.

I may not want to be a burden on Ryder, but I know he misses me. I miss him too. Not seeing him has been hard. I've tried to hang onto my resolve, but he's been my best friend for nearly two decades. Quitting him is nearly as hard as quitting heroin.

I also feel guilty about the calls I've dodged from Dane. The guy has been more of a brother to me than my own. Not that it's their fault, but still, Dane's and my relationship is stronger, built on a foundation of trust and loyalty.

A few missed calls from Liam. I know he's worried too, not just as our manager, but as my friend. Jake and Angel have also called.

I start to put my phone back in my pocket when it starts ringing. My stomach clenches before I even see the name. It roils like the storm brewing over the city when Callie's name flashes across the screen.

That sense of foreboding has turned to utterly indescribable dread. My hands shake as I tap the icon and bring the phone to my ear. My heart shatters before she says the first word. Her sobs say everything.

"He's gone, Madsy. I went in to take him his supper and—"

"Shh," I say to her, trying to control my emotions while consoling her. "It's going to be okay. He was ready." My voice breaks on the last words as I fight back the tears.

"But I wasn't, Madsy. It felt like I finally had a dad, and now he's gone."

I understood well. I knew exactly how she felt. Maybe more so because while Dad wasn't the most attentive with any of us, Callie was his princess.

"I know, Callie. I know. I'll be over as soon as Quinn gets here."

"Okay, Madsy."

I hang up the phone, trying hard to control the raging emotions burning through me. My mind feels like it's moving in a million different directions, splintering and shattering right along with my heart.

The balcony door opens, and I feel her behind me. She wraps her arms around me from behind, laying her head against my back. "What did the doctor say?" I ask, not ready to divulge my heartbreak just yet.

After spending the last couple of days not feeling well and spending nearly every waking minute in the bathroom, with Verity's help, I managed to convince her to go to the doctor.

"He said I'm pregnant," she whispers in a dreamy tone.

And the bough breaks.

CHAPTER TWENTY-EIGHT

I know that you tried

Present

"Go ahead, Maddox," Bryan tells me as I press the plunger of the needle, "just a little more, and we can go."

"Yeah," I tell him as my lids flutter. "We can go. There's nothing left to tell. I just want to write them each a letter really quick."

He throws his hands in the air in exasperation. "Isn't that what you've been doing for days?"

"It's not the same," I mumble. "That's for all of them. I need to tell Ryder and Dane goodbye. And Bastian and Quinn."

"Damn, how things can change in such a short time. Zoey didn't even make the list."

"Fuck you," I breathe out as the calm, relaxing feeling takes over. As my racing mind begins to slow into nothingness.

"God, you're so fucking high, you can't even talk," he jokes. "Looks like you got enough for one more hit. Why don't you go ahead and do it?"

"I plan to," I tell him. "Just as soon as I write these letters."

I pick up the pen and stare at the fuzzy lines that won't stay in focus. He's right. I am so high; Heaven is just a sin away. Too bad Heaven won't let me in, and the devil won't let me go.

Dane,

Letting people in may seem easy for me at times, but you know it's not. But the bond I felt with you was almost instant. I always admired the way you were unwaveringly loyal to those you cared about. Even when you drove me crazy with your pushiness, I knew it came from a place of concern and worry. I never wanted to make you worry. It was my job to take care of you since this crazy ass journey of ours was my idea. But I know about the many nights you'd tag along to the clubs and bars and whatever else between just to make sure Ryder and I were okay. I hope one day, you'll look back and remember me for the good things instead of the constant worry I caused. I'm sorry for all the pain and disappointment I've caused. Remember to love hard but to know sometimes you have to pull back. You can't be everyone's protector. Sometimes you just need to do what's best for you. You are my brother in every sense of the word, and I'm a better man for having known you.

Bastian,

I've given you hell over the last few weeks. I've raged and roared like a petulant child, throwing a tantrum. But I've seen the lengths you'll go to for me. I don't deserve it, and you damn sure should have had better than to get stuck with me. You can't choose your family, right? Except you did. Blood or not, you didn't have to watch out for me like you did. You didn't have to accept me at all. I'm glad for the years of friendship you've given. I'm thankful for every time I call, how you dropped everything to be there. I wish we'd had more time together, but life doesn't always go as it should. Take care of Verity. That girl is too good for you, and you fucking know it. And take care of my little nephew she has baking. Maybe one day, tell him about the good things I did instead of all the ways I fucked up. And in case you didn't know, I do love you.

Ryder,

What a fucking ride, huh? Who would've thought that two snot-nose kids would end up on the road we have. The highs have been great, but it's the lows I kept from you. You didn't need any more of my shit than you already saw. You had enough of your own going on.

My point is that I know you're going to blame yourself. Question what you could've done differently. I swear, Ryder, you couldn't have done a damn thing differently. I fought hard. I fought for you. You're the only reason I've made it this damn long.

Remember a while back when we both said we were tired? Well, I still am Ryder. I am more and more exhausted every damn day. The darkness in my head has taken over. The heaviness in my heart is unbearable.

Please forgive me for breaking my promise. I have kept it for a long time. You have no idea how many times I've wanted to give up. But this road has been hard, and I'm too tired to carry on.

Always remember that I love you. You are my mirror. My other half. Nothing and no one will ever change that. And no matter where life takes you, I will always be with you. I'll live forever in your spirit and in your mind. Our memories are written in our scars and hearts, and there, I will always remain.

My beautiful canary,

I told you I'd break your heart, cher. It was destiny. But I need you to know that I have never loved anyone the way I love you. I couldn't tell you before because I thought if I didn't say it, it would hurt you less. I was a fool. Just like I'm a selfish bastard for telling you now. Like this. But I can't leave this world without letting you know that you were the air in my lungs, the sun in my sky, and the stars that lit up the night. You were in my blood and marrow.

I wanted to be enough for you. I prayed you could keep my demons away. I tried to drown myself in everything that was you.

But I told you these demons would win. No matter how hard I tried. I just couldn't fight them anymore.

I'm sorry for what I said. I know how much you wanted a baby but didn't think it would happen. I'm sorry I snatched that joy from you. In a different life, I would've loved to have all that with you. But to burden a child with whatever this is inside of me is cruel. Cruel to the child and cruel to you. No one should have to suffer as I have, questioning their sanity a little more every day.

Please forgive me. Forgive me for breaking your heart and mine. Forgive me for being a coward and a quitter.

I hope you find love. A love you deserve, though I'm not convinced there is anyone who could deserve you. I hope you find happiness and peace. I hope you have that family you always dreamed of.

Most of all, I hope you think of me and know that I loved you the best I could. I loved you with every molecule and cell. I loved you with every breath I took. There was never anyone else. I'd waited my whole life for you, and the moment my eyes met yours, I was done. It was only ever you. It could only ever be you.

My heart is forever yours.

I set the pen down with a sigh.

"Ready to go?" Bryan asks me.

All I do is nod. There's nothing left to say; the story's been told. I close my eyes and welcome the darkness.

CHAPTER TWENTY-NINE

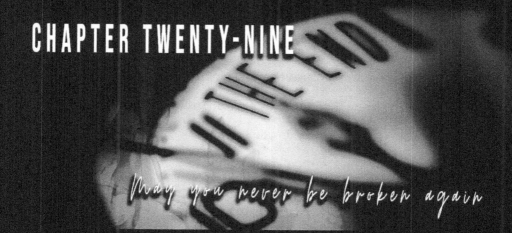

May you never be broken again

Quinn

I've been lying in bed for nearly eight hours in tears. My heart feels like it has been ripped out of my chest. The sobs won't stop.

I know him. I know him inside and out. He has tried to keep himself from me, tried so hard to keep his darkness away, but I see him. I see his fight and his struggle. I know his fear.

He's terrified, saying things he doesn't mean because of his skewed view of himself. Because he thinks he's not good enough to be a parent.

He was trying to hurt me. I know his comments about Zoey and other women aren't true in my heart. I know he loves me. I can feel it in his touch, see it in his eyes.

But I don't know what to do if he pushes me away. He has the means to vanish, and I can't follow him.

Another round of nausea swims in my belly. I lay still, hoping it will go away. After a few minutes, it still hasn't subsided, so I decide to go after some crackers and ginger ale I know Verity has kept on hand.

When I open the door, I realize Maddox was right about soundproof rooms because the yelling and shouting couldn't have been missed otherwise.

"Where is he?" a deep raspy voice demands.

"How in the fuck do you even know he's missing?"

"So he *is* missing?" another voice questions.

"Yes, but I reiterate, how do you know?"

I step quietly into the room, not wanting to eavesdrop or interrupt but desperately needing the crackers and ginger ale. I keep my head down, like that will make me less visible or something, as I move across the room.

"You," a gruff voice calls out. "Who are you?"

I freeze in my track as heat crawls up my face, embarrassed to be called out as I have. I turn slowly and meet the eyes of a very pissed off Ryder Jamison. Dane Pierce and some other guy I don't recognize stand behind him with concern etched on their faces.

"Leave her alone, Ryder. She doesn't know anything," Bastian warns him as he drags his hands down his face.

Ryder ignores him, coming to where I still haven't moved. "You're her, aren't you?"

"Excuse me?" I ask, not knowing what he's talking about while also knowing this has something to do with Maddox. Worry fills every inch of my body as I realize something is wrong. Something is very wrong.

"You're the girl he was telling me about," Ryder says again. "The one he said he hurt."

Bastian's eyes fly to mine in question. "What happened, Quinn?"

"I don't understand what's going on," I tell them.

"Maddox has vanished. Right out from under your fucking nose," Ryder growls, getting in Bastian's face. "I ask you to help him, and now you're telling me you don't have a goddamn clue where the fuck he's at."

"Ryder, it would be in your best interest to chill, man," the guy I don't know warns with a hand on his shoulder.

"Yes, Ryder, it would be in your best fucking interest," Bastian spits.

"Fuck, you Bastian. Your reputation precedes you, but you don't know shit about me. I trusted you."

"He was here last night, Ryder. When I came home, the Ducati was gone, and he'd beaten the crap out of Christian and Drew. I've called Zoey. She said she hasn't seen him since she was here a few weeks ago. I called Delaney, and she hasn't been him either but I've got people looking."

"Why would he do that?" Dane asks. "Maddox doesn't just beat people up like someone else we know." He turns a pointed glare to Ryder and the other guy.

"Fuck you, Dane. I'm working on it."

"Yeah. Working on it," the other guy agrees.

"Look, it hasn't been that long. He can't have gone far," Bastian says. "Are you sure you don't know, Quinn?"

I shake my head as tears begin to spill over.

"You are her," Ryder tells me. "What happened with you two?"

More tears fall like a river down my face. "I told him I was pregnant."

Ryder's head snaps back with shock. "Come again?"

"I'm pregnant."

"Fuck," Ryder hisses.

"He got his girl pregnant, *and* his dad just died. That's what set him off all right."

"Stating the obvious, are you now, Hayes?" Bastian snaps.

The guy, Hayes, looks him over with a grin that seems anything but friendly.

But it's what he said that has my attention. "Mr. Masters died? When?"

"According to Callie's social media, it was around six last night."

My hands fly to my mouth. That would've been right before I told him. He was in shock from his father's death, and I dropped another bomb on him.

263

"We have to figure out where he went," Dane says calmly, trying to keep the situation under control.

"I've already called all his favorite haunts," Bastian tells them.

"There has to be somewhere else we're not thinking of," Ryder suggests.

"Maybe you should call Bryan," I tell them, as desperation fills me. He has to be okay. He has to be.

They all look at me like I've lost my mind. "He doesn't have a friend named Bryan," Ryder tells me with worry filling his voice.

My brows fall between my eyes. "Of course he does. He's told me about him. Bryan Michaels"

"Look, love, I've known Mads since I was twelve. I know *all* his friends. There is no Bryan."

"Isn't that the name he gives when he wants to check into restaurants or hotels incognito?" Hayes asks.

"Yeah. He uses it because it's his middle name. Maddox Bryan Michael Masters." Dane answers.

"Oh fuck," Bastian hisses. "Fuck. Fuck. Fuck."

"What?" Ryder asks, now fully panicking.

"I think I know where he is. Son of bitch, the motherfucker lied to me."

"What's wrong, Bastian?" I ask as my stomach flips with worry, nausea growing by the second.

"Quinn, Jewel named Maddox after her father and brother. His grandfather.. The same grandfather that killed himself. The same one that heard voices. William Bryan Michael Masters II and III. I just didn't..." He shakes his head with disbelief. "There is no Bryan.""

"Are you trying to say Maddox hears voices?" Hayes asks with furrowed brows.

Bastian lifts a finger as he pulls out his phone. "Chris, we can't find Maddox. Is he there? No, I need you to check your grandparents' place. He'll have my bike. Yeah, that's the one. Yeah. Okay. We're coming."

He hangs up the phone; his eyes radiate fear and concern like I've never seen in Bastian.

"We need to go," he tells Ryder.

"Bastian, is he okay?" I ask, my voice wavering with emotion.

"No, sweetheart, he's far from okay. Hopefully, Chris gets to him before he hurts himself."

"What's going on, Bastian?" Ryder asks.

Bastian's eyes flit to mine, then back to Ryder. He doesn't want to say it in front of me. "Please just say it, Bastian."

"When Chris looked at the security feed, Maddox was fighting with someone, except no one was there."

I gasp, throwing my hand over my mouth to contain the sob. Bastian walks to me, pulling me into his arms. Promising me that everything will be okay. I watch helplessly as they rush to the elevator, on their way to find the man that I love and the father of my child.

Please, God, don't let them be too late.

ACKNOWLEDGMENTS

This is always the hardest part for me. There are so many wonderful people who deserve recognition as they continue to support me in this process.

To my husband (who will never see this), who tolerates me when I'm in the zone, unable to accomplish the simplest task like buying groceries because I'm so consumed. I love you more than you will ever know. Thank you for encouraging me to follow my dream and thinking I'm a rock star even though I won't let you read my book. Thank you for working so hard so that I can stay home and do this thing I call work. Thank you for loving me because I know it's not always easy.

My beautiful geniosity club members, Sionna, Devin, and Anita, you guys kept me laughing through this book, which has been one of the most emotionally and mentally draining stories I've ever written. I love our chats, or when I'm not chatty, "lurking," as Devin calls it, to see the insanity and hilarity going on at any given time.

Daria, my fellow insomniac, when there was no one else awake to hold my hand, you encourage me to keep going, even offering a few great ideas to help me figure out my path. I owe you a tremendous amount of thanks for keeping me going when all I wanted to do was sit in a corner and hide.

Crystal, you are the beta reader we all need. Your thoughts and opinions are candid and genuine, and you're not afraid to tell me when something doesn't work. You look at each book as just a reader who enjoys a good story. You fill in the blanks and tell me when something doesn't work. I really appreciate every second you offer me.

My street team that is also half of my ARC team, you guys are fabulous. I want to name you all, but I know I will forget someone, so I will let this encompass all of you. Your encouragement, banter, and support mean everything. Thank you all so much.

266

SNEAK PEEK

BREATHE AGAIN

We pull up to the house, and panic rushes into me at the sight of the ambulance lights. My heart thrashes in my chest, and my lungs seize with every inch we travel through the gated property, up the driveway that leads to the house directly behind Maddox's fathers. Bile rises in my throat as we watch EMTs running to get inside.

The entire ride here, I've suffered the glares and outbursts. I've tolerated the accusations thrown at me. In part because I know they're angry and worried and scared. The other reason is that I know I should've done more.

How did I not know? How is it possible that I missed this? I try to think if there were signs I missed. I knew he had problems with depression. Fuck knows, he had a right. The shit he's gone through was more than anyone should have to handle. The weight he carried, trying to be strong for everyone, to hide his demons, was insurmountable. I knew he'd tried to hurt himself in the past. Shouldn't I have seen this coming?

We jump out of the SUV, running to the house. Police sirens sound in the distance, no doubt coming this way, and I'm already dreading the media circus. They don't care about our feelings. They only want their story.

When we step into the house, my knees nearly give out. Paper litter every surface of the large, dusty living room that was once the home of Maddox's grandparents. Furniture has been broken. Glass is shattered across the space. The walls look like they've had a hammer taken to them.

"Give us room to work," one of the paramedics says as he waves his arms to keep us away. Their orders don't mean shit to me.

I keep walking until I'm standing right over them—one of the few times in my life, the sight of blood curls my stomach.

"Twenty-nine-year-old male. Gunshot wound to the chest," the paramedic answers the questions of the cops who just entered the scene. My eyes jump to Chris who's standing in the far corner, trying not to be seen. His behavior seems off.

But it's a small gasp sounding behind me that has my attention. My eyes close, knowing exactly what I will find when I turn around.

267

Quinn stands there with tears in her eyes that make me weak because they remind me so much of my wife's. *She* reminds me of my wife. They're so similar yet so different.

She begins to sway on her feet. I start for her, but Ryder gets there first. "Hold on, sweetheart," he tells her as he wraps an arm around her. "Don't give up on him," I hear him whisper to her.

I grip the back of my neck as I watch them load him onto a gurney and rush out of the house. "I'm going with them," Ryder tells them.

"Me too," I hear Quinn reply.

"I'm sorry," the paramedic tells them. "We need the room to work. You'll have to follow us."

"No one is leaving until we ask a few questions," one of the officer's commands. "And I'm going to need you to put that down." He nods to Dane and Hayes, who are standing there with confusion and pain in their eyes as they hold several sheets of paper.

I look over to the officer. He must be new because I don't recognize him. I turn my attention to his partner. "You don't have any questions to ask because nothing happened here, right?"

Officer Jackson swallows hard with a nod. "Yes, sir, Mr. Delrie. Nothing to report."

"But—" his partner starts.

"*Nothing* to report," he repeats with a warning. Better his than mine.

The man nods, clearly confused, but seems to get the message. "What do they say?" I ask as I nod to the sheets in their hands.

"Mostly nothing," Hayes says with a crack. "Just a bunch of gibberish. Except these."

I take the papers from him. My black heart bleeds at the words written on the papers, and I wonder how I missed the signs for the second time. I should've been more vigilant. Kept a closer watch on him. This is my fault.

"He was saying goodbye," Dane whispers as he holds the broken neck of an antique guitar in his hands. "I don't understand. I knew he dealt with some dark emotions, but why?"

"There's a lot you don't know," I tell him.

"And you do?" he challenges.

I expected this reaction from Ryder, not Dane. But as I look him over, I realize Ryder knows more than he's told them. Or, at the very least, he suspects.

"Not everything," I finally admit. "Or this wouldn't have happened."

"Then tell us what you do know."

It's Maddox's story to tell. It should be his decision to share it. But he lost that right. Now it's on me to fill in the blanks.

I toss Ryder the keys to my Suburban with a jerk of my head. "You guys take the truck and follow. I'll follow on my bike. I'll tell you what I know when we get there."

They look at me reluctantly but nod in agreement. They follow when the ambulance leaves, and I prepare to tell them the story of Maddox Masters.

ALSO BY NOLA MARIE

ABOUT THE AUTHOR

Louisiana-born and raised, Nola Marie loves crawfish, music, and high drama. She is a true southern mom with the attitude and mouth to prove it. Evil to the bone, she rejuvenates her life forces with the blood of her characters and the tears of her readers.

Made in the USA
Coppell, TX
30 March 2022

75751660R00155